# RISE OF THE
# LOTUS

VIOLET HIRMAN

PUBLISHED BY

MINNETONKA, MN 55305
WWW.SIGMASBOOKSHELF.COM

# Dedication

*For my parents*
Who always read to me no matter how tired.


*For my Nana*
For the countless trips to little libraries,
big libraries, and home libraries.


*For my Papa*
And all the quiet hours we sat
drinking hot chocolate with books in our hands.


*And for Ana*
My friend, my home, and my twin flame.
Thank you for never letting me stop.

*Chapter 1*

# Corinne

A hand twists in the hem of my jacket, hauling me back behind the cluster of trees. Just in time, too. The Nighter turns his head at the small commotion, but we stay still, holding our breath until he moves on.

"Corinne!" hisses my sister from next to me, the sound of my name drawing my attention. "Watch it."

When the Nighter disappears into the inscrutable darkness, we move. I practically bounce with excitement over to the fence, keeping the citizens of Kleka—my hometown— where they are.

After months of frustration, scrapping and reworking our plan countless times, we're finally going to climb the fence. It buzzes with electricity as we near it, pushing deeper into the underbrush of the Shifting Woods.

I clutch the roll of twine tightly as it unwinds behind me, and we step carefully to avoid making any loud noises. The string is just an extra bit of security, in case we need to ditch the plan and get back to Kleka. Selena takes shallow breaths next to me, probably just as impatient as I am to finally achieve what we've always dreamed of doing.

When I glance back, the trees aren't where they were before, and I nod to myself, glad we brought the twine after all.

The Shifting Woods are named the way they are for two reasons. The trees are constantly moving and the paths are always changing. You never see them move, but they do. Many have gotten lost, never to be seen again. The second reason is because these woods are infested with unpredictable shape-shifters: Mutations–or Mutes for short–with the ability to transform into one specific animal.

Up close, the fence almost seems to glow. My sister and I pull out the thick rubber gloves from our packs, using duct tape to secure them around our wrists so they don't slip off. I guide the lotus coin pendant out from under my shirt at the last minute, kiss it for luck, and slowly reach out my covered hand. When my hand grazes the wire, a small shock of adrenaline travels up my arm. I release a captured breath before letting my hand drop.

"It's safe!" I whisper excitedly, barely able to contain my joy. I wedge the rubber sole of my boot into the small wire holes that make up the fence and haul myself up. My skin tingles with electricity or more adrenaline—I'm not sure which—and I continue to scale the metal links with Selena right below me. The fence rattles, but I keep going; no one comes after us. At the top, I maneuver my hand to the side pocket of my backpack and free the wire cutters. Taking great care to keep my bare skin away from the charged barrier, I carefully begin to snip at the barbed wire coiled thickly around the top.

A sheen of sweat develops on my forehead during the few minutes that pass in tense silence before I create a space at the top big enough to fit through. I shift my weight and swing myself over, crashing into the fence on the other side, barely avoiding direct contact with my bare skin. We both freeze and listen intently for any sign of approaching Nighters. I exhale when I hear nothing, but then a voice rings out from Selena's side of the barrier, more shouts answering moments after. Without skipping a beat Selena races up the fence and flips herself over. We practically fly down the other side and land running, abandoning all pretense of stealth as we dash through the underbrush.

The cool, early-autumn air parts around me, and the voices grow louder, causing me to pump my legs faster to hopefully put some distance between us; a huge mistake. A root, invisible in the near-perfect blackness, slithers out of nowhere. Before I can break the fall, I slam hard into the ground. The taste of blood fills my mouth. Selena grabs my sleeve and yanks me to my feet, pushing me forward again while I gasp for breath, each inhale sending icy stabs of pain through my chest.

Both of us realize too late that the trees are moving as Selena smashes into one. She stumbles in a daze before speeding up back into a run, also panting. The din of voices recedes behind us, and I'm so grateful for the string if we need to find our way back—the string. Shit, I must have dropped it when I had fallen a moment before. It's too late to turn back, so I grit my teeth and keep running.

At last, we break through the tree line into a clearing. It's rumored that the Shifting Woods are so thick that it's almost impossible to find one—a clearing that is—but we found one. The leaves of the trees are so densely grouped that they entirely block the light of the full moon, which washes over me now, and I'm momentarily stunned as memories flood my senses: sitting in a dirt shelter years ago and ogling up at the moon with a lynx cub laying beside me with her head in my lap.

But the sight that greets us, in reality, is rather an eyesore. It's about forty yards in diameter and a perfect circle. At the far end of the open space, there are about twenty small, black tents and fascinating campfires that emit no smoke.

Selena and I immediately melt into the tree line again and turn to each other to converse in hushed tones.

"Who do you think they are?" she asks, visibly worried.

"Dunno. Should we go over there and ask maybe?" I respond, forcing as much sarcasm as I can into the question. She rolls her eyes.

"Well, what should we do then? We got over the fence, and we need to get to Westol. How do you want to do that?"

"Honestly, all I want right now is to get far away. Let's make camp somewhere for the night and plan out the rest tomorrow morning. Sound good?"

She nods as we stand up, brushing dirt off our clothes. I wipe my nose with my sleeve, watching the fabric stain a deep scarlet. I ignore it as we begin to creep around the clearing, being sure to stay out of view. Three sharp, practiced whistles sound to our left. The Nighters.

"How the hell did they find us?" I whisper fiercely. Selena shrugs helplessly and we keep moving. Much to my growing dread, the camp's inhabitants have been alerted by the signal and are emerging from their tents. Men in all black blend in seamlessly with the surroundings, appearing only to be floating heads in the dark. I curse again.

"Let's go back the way we came. If we find the Nighters, the worst that'll happen is a week on janitor duty and maybe a lecture or two. And if we don't, we'll just head off in a different direction. I don't like the look of those guys," Selena mutters.

I gaze longingly at the other side of the glade before nodding. All we've worked for these past months, waiting for an opening, tracking the Nighters' schedules, everything down the drain because of a split-second decision.

We run blindly back the way we came, little branches pulling at my clothes as I run past. The Shifting Woods is the last place you want to be faultlessly lost in.

One long ear-splitting whistle rings on our right side, and Selena shouts, "Run! They're catching up!" Her voice is raw with anxiety and fear, and we barrel full speed ahead.

A faint buzz makes its way into my ears, gaining volume every second, but I don't let up. There's only one thing that could make that noise. I silently curse myself just as my sister and I slam full speed into the electric fence.

*Chapter 2*

# Corinne

Reluctantly, I crack an eye open to my classmates and a few complete strangers surrounding me. Behind them is a clock that reads 9:12 a.m. The hands are ticking hypnotically. When they notice that I'm awake, they all start talking at once, stumbling over one another to ask their questions.

"What happened?"

"What were you thinking?"

"Are you feeling better?"

"Did it hurt?"

"Why'd you come back?"

"How'd you do it?"

I push myself into a sitting position, waving their questions away and taking a quick, instinctive inventory. We're in the hospital. The scent of fake lemon and cleaning supplies assaults my nose as I take a deep breath. My entire body aches from the electricity channeled into it, and I have a firm bandage over the bridge of my nose. It's probably broken, but it doesn't hurt too bad. I have a few minor cuts and scrapes on my arms and legs, but otherwise am unharmed. But when I try to move, my shoulder stings in protest. I glance down to see it wrapped with a white bandage. I'll most likely have some burns, too.

With a start, my hands go to my throat, not feeling the

6

chain at first. But then the pendant's smooth metal slides along my skin, and I feel myself able to breathe again.

A nurse walks over, shooing the people out of the way and out of the room, reminding them they need to sign in at the front desk, and that only two people can be in the room at a time if they're not family.

"Eat this, dear, it's to help with the pain," she says once everyone is out. She places a small green gummy in my hand and waits. I put it in my mouth and force myself to chew, ignoring the sour taste. Once she's sure I've eaten it, she sets another one next to Selena's bed and bustles back out the door. We're left in silence, listening to the buzz of people outside.

That is until Ella and her parents push through the door and rush to our sides. Ella's family is our adopted family; they took us in when we were little. She's my and Selena's best friend.

"You're all over the news! Have you seen the footage yet?" gasps Ella. Her blond hair hangs loosely around her shoulders, the ends dyed purple. She has bags under her eyes, too; I wonder if she's been worried about me. Her parents, Sean and Lincoln, look a mixture of concerned and wary, as if they fear we might jump up and make a run for it again. They're not terrible parents, or terrible people for that matter, far from it. But they've accepted that Selena and I have our own agenda and don't get too involved. This time might be different, though. We've never pulled a stunt this big before.

My partner in crime lies in a bed on my left, just coming out of her sleep.

"What's all this about?" she asks through a yawn, struggling to sit up. She sees the gummy the nurse left on her bedside table and picks it up.

"Apparently we're famous. All over the news," I say coolly.

She pales a bit, but recovers quickly, popping the vitamin in her mouth and grimacing.

"Can we see the footage?" she requests, the question directed at Ella. Her parents leave the room while she rummages through her bag for her phone. Linc pats my head and Sean gives me a quick hug on the way out.

Guilt clings to my skin when the door swings shut.

Ella arrives at the local news website and a clip of fuzzy security footage comes to life. The footage shows us scaling the fence, our faces blurred by the long-distance feed. We seem calm at first, but then scramble over the wires. Most likely when we had heard the Nighters shouting.

It fast-forwards a couple of minutes then returns to a normal speed, and zooms in on two small silhouettes moving quickly to the fence again. My sister and I burst from the trees and I cringe as we collide with the metal. Our forms drop like stones, tendrils of electricity arcing over our bodies as we convulse on the ground. My own limbs ache in sympathy.

I'm reminded of the men in black we saw last night, or at least I think it was last night, but I'm not sure who to ask about them.

Matthew, the newscaster, appears on the screen with a grave expression. His lips move, but the phone is muted, making the situation seem only slightly less serious.

I'm about to comment on the video when the doors to our room silently swing open again. Two boys walk in, one with honey brown hair and one with chestnut hair so dark it appears almost black. I bite back a startled noise and struggle with my blanket, which is tangled around my legs. They seem both tense and at ease as they near us.

Rowan and River, Mayor Andrew Moore's two boys. The boys glance around like they own the place; which, technically they do. I force myself to get out of bed and stand up as tall as I can. They're probably here to chew us out on behalf of their dad. I look down at my pale blue hospital gown and smile humorlessly. What a first impression this is.

They saunter over and the gold-brown-haired boy, Rowan, stops only a few inches away. He towers over me, probably over half a foot taller. I keep my gaze anchored on his right shoulder, not daring to meet his eyes. How much trouble have we gotten into? A sharp resentment grows in my chest at the thought. Who said I have to feel threatened by them?

He waits for me to lock eyes with him, and when I can't stand it anymore, I look up, unwilling to be intimidated by him. I'm startled by their color—a pale green, like the color of corn husks. I have no idea what he's going to say and my body stills in anticipation, waiting for some sort of reprimand, but I wish he would just get it over with already. The suspense is killing me faster than the electricity from the fence last night.

"If you are feeling alright, would you and your sister care to join us for dinner once you've been discharged from the hospital?" he asks. I freeze, waiting for the punchline, but he's serious. This is the last thing I expected. I try to answer, but I only make a small, undignified squeak. Selena is dead still behind me. They've never really spoken to anyone, and hearing from them now of all times is definitely an unexpected turn.

"May I interpret that as a yes?" he inquires, quirking an eyebrow. I don't know how to answer, but Ella steps in, always the savior of my awkward moments.

"Yes, she would love to! Wouldn't you, Rinny?" she presses, using my least favorite nickname for me and looping her arm through mine. I nod, dazed, and she continues, "She can get a bit tongue-tied when talking to—shall we say, dashing young men." Ella smiles maliciously at me, jumping at any opportunity to set me up with people. Words die in my throat, but Rowan merely laughs, his brother smirking behind him. His laugh sounds real, tangible.

Ella is the definition of boy-crazy, always trying to "get me back out into society", as she calls it. Personally, I think she wants to be the reason I find someone.

"Well then, tomorrow at six? We'll pick you up," he states with a bemused gaze focused back on me. Ella nods vigorously, giving him an innocent smile. So, I steel my gaze and try to make my face one of smooth indifference. With that, the boys depart, leaving me swaying on my feet with out-of-control nerves. And not necessarily in a nice way.

I slump back onto the uncomfortably firm mattress, Selena impersonating a dramatically deflating balloon next to me. When it's just the three of us again, Ella squeals with delight, bouncing up and down like a frantic rabbit.

"My best friends are going on a date!" she titters, fanning herself and sighing. "And with the Moore boys of all people!" She bounds over and takes my hand. "You'll let me help you get ready, won't you?" Her eyes glisten on the verge of tears at the thought of not being able to help me get ready. I wave her away, assuring her that she'll be in charge. She beams at me, promising to return tomorrow when I'm let go from the hospital.

Selena starts to ask something but exhaustion weighs on me like a suffocating blanket and I hold up a hand to quiet her. On top of that, anxiety and frustration are churning up my thoughts relentlessly thanks to the Moore brothers. I don't yet trust their intentions.

***

The next day, as it turns out, is very eventful. Ella is sitting in the waiting room, her leg bouncing distractedly while she chews on her nails. Selena and I have dressed in our clothes from yesterday again, and my friend jumps to her feet when she sees us.

"Just wait until you see what I've picked out for the both of you," she bubbles, taking me by the arm and steering me outside into the bright sunlight of mid-August. I blink into the sky, taking Selena's hand so she doesn't fall behind Ella's excited pace.

She drives us back to our house—she's been driving us everywhere since she finally received her license at 18 a few weeks ago—where Linc and Sean are prepping for lunch. Up in our room, I feel at home in the small but orderly space with the loft bed, bunk, painted dresser, and book-shelves sagging with the weight of our two hundred and thirty-six books. We once got so bored over summer we counted them all.

Ella sprawls out on the floor and beckons us down with her.

"So what do you think they want?" asks Selena tiredly.

"They want to go on a date, obviously," scolds Ella. Her voice softens when she addresses me. "And, Corinne, I know what happened with Eli might deter you from wanting a relationship again, but maybe this could help you if it works out."

I take a deep breath. "I don't think a single date is going to help me forget that, but thanks for the enthusiasm." I smile sadly, masking my chills by standing up again and pacing. "So, you said you had outfits picked out?"

Ella grins and bounces over to her closet, pulling two outfits from its depths on blue plastic hangers.

One is a modest yellow sundress with a ruffled neckline and a circle skirt. The other is sleek and a deep green, the color of shade-darkened leaves in a jungle, with a gracefully, loose bodice and a layered skirt ending at the knees. The sleeves on this one hang loosely around the shoulders, while the yellow dress has cinched tank-top styled straps that will keep the dress up better. But as soon as I take a step forward, Selena is already clinging to the yellow dress, looking very much like a feral cat.

"There is no way you're putting me into that one," she shivers, eyeing the green one with a mixture of fear and contempt. I mutter to myself and Ella claps, handing me the green dress, so dark it's almost black. It's a nice color at least, like the depths of the woods.

The dress is loose enough that I can pull it over my hips, but the unique design of the sleeves makes it tedious. I have to use the mirror to make sure I adjust it right, and I catch sight of my back in the reflection.

The wine-red birthmark spans my upper back, the edges licking my shoulders like tongues of fire. It looks like a set of broken, misshapen wings. I grimace and make sure the dress covers the entire thing.

Selena got lucky. Hers is on her lower back, always out of sight as long as she stays away from cropped shirts.

I come out of the bathroom and see Selena spinning in circles in the open space, the skirt fanning out around her. Ella gasps when she sees me, taking me by the hand and twirling me around. I feel self-conscious and exposed in my ridiculous attire.

"Ella, are you sure we need to be this dressed up on a trip to a café?" I waver, measuring the mental cost of wearing this all night against Ella's sadness if I ask to change.

"Obviously, silly!" she giggles. "It's the Moore boys, after all, you should make a good impression." I curse under my breath. Who cares about the Moore boys? Selena and I didn't get out. This city is too constricting, cameras on every street corner, restrictions and signs everywhere reminding us to report any unnatural occurrences we might be witness to. Of course, it's clear they're keeping a lookout for on-the-run

Mutes, ones they can turn over to bounty hunters, who then turn them into the governments for absurdly large sums of money.

Ella pulls me back to reality with an arm looped through mine.

"Time to go!" she sings, as happy as ever as she takes us back outside, passing her parents on the way out and assuring them she'll be back in a minute. I smile at them and they nod their heads in return.

It's six o'clock on the dot when Rowan and River show up, wearing casual, clean jeans and t-shirts with pretentiously ironed zip-up hoodies layered over. I have to beat myself into submission inside, pushing down the urge to turn tail and go change out of my ridiculous outfit. Rowan smiles when he sees us, sees **me** more specifically.

"Is a café suitable for you?" he asks, tucking his smile behind the corner of his mouth. I stick my nose in the air and cross my arms in indignation despite the redness crawling along my skin.

"I picked the outfits," claims Ella proudly.

"I figured," says Rowan, flashing Ella a smile that sends her into a fit of giggles behind her hand. He sure is a charmer, that one. Ella gives Selena and me a little push forward and blows us a kiss before skipping back inside. I want so badly to follow her but the boys bring my attention back to them.

"Let's get going," says Rowan warmly. River stands emotionless next to him, the faintest of smiles etched onto his face. We walk rather quietly down the streets, and I try to rub away the goosebumps coming to life on my arms despite the heat. People whisper, but the boys saunter down the street like they don't hear them. Maybe they don't. Selena doesn't seem to notice either. Not looking where I'm going, I stumble into Rowan who's walking only a foot away. He grabs my arms, steadying me, and my breath sticks in my throat. I mumble a thank you and quickly step away again. The fabric feels too tight despite the loose design, inhibiting my ability to even walk in a straight line.

I hear the whispers passed between the few groups of people, ranging anywhere from, "Aren't those the girls who tried to run away?" to, "Are the Moore boys going out?" I avert my eyes and Rowan, who had been staring silently out at the Marley Canal, brushes my arm with his fingers.

"What's wrong?" he asks, eyes full of concern. I stiffen, unfamiliar with this kind of situation.

"Why are you taking so much interest in us all of a sudden?" It comes out a bit sharper than I intended, and I bite my lip. "Sorry."

"Don't be. And what? The Mayor's sons can't treat two girls to dinner after they were just electrocuted by a ten thousand volt fence? You look terrible." He scrutinizes me, frowning. The corners of his mouth turn down and his eyebrows draw together when he does that. "Also, we wanted to get to know you. You two seem like down to earth people."

I look away at that and clasp my hands to keep them from doing something dumb, like hitting him. For a minute he looks blond and emerald-eyed.

*Get a grip, Corinne. Don't think about him now.*

But Eli's hair and glittering green eyes are now etched into the backs of my eyelids.

*Chapter 3*

# Corinne

Now it's Rowan's turn to look away as he says, "The main reason is that our dad asked us to interrogate you ourselves, so as not to make a huge production." I look back up, understanding throwing itself at me like a truck on a freeway, and he rushes on, oblivious to my sudden disengagement. "He just wants to know why you were trying to leave." Rowan clears his throat as his words fizzle out under his brother's withering stare. "Anyway, we've told him that we would, but that it would be very rude to just show up at the hospital and start pushing for answers. Hence the café." His voice is determined and sure, so I ponder his words.

"Makes sense," I say, forcing a smile. "Although I doubt there will be anything like what you're thinking." He nods gratefully, mirroring my smile before returning to a frown.

"You look cold, here." He slides his hoodie off and throws it around my shoulders, which catches me by surprise. "It might smell like smoke, though. We had a bonfire last night and I didn't have time to wash it."

It does. But not in a bad way, like spiced tea, maybe chai, laced through. I mumble another resentful 'thank you' then turn to my sister, who looks too innocent not to have been eavesdropping. I give her a knowing look and she sighs, exasperated. We stray a few steps behind the brothers, making sure to stay out of earshot.

"Yeah, I was listening or whatever. I'm going to be frank and just say that I don't know how much I'm willing to help them. What do they want to hear, that we know some enthralling, classified information and were trying to smuggle it out? Personally, I just wanted to get out of this place," she bemoans. I roll my eyes as we arrive at Bubble's Café, the blue and white awning so familiar to me. The owner's name is Baldwin, but really no one knows the significance of the name of the café.

On our way in, I see Tarissa, a close friend from my martial arts class, finishing up some studying on the patio. I watch her down the last dregs of her coffee and begin piling books and papers back into her messenger bag. She catches sight of us and waves enthusiastically, holding open the door for us on her way in to pay.

"Corinne! Selena! You both look stunning! I'm in a rush, but I'll see you for practice on Wednesday, yeah?" She beams, giving us each quick embrace before cantering back outside. I call out a farewell, watching her black curls bounce around her head. A little ways down the street, a group of people dressed in black disappear into an alley.

"Get home safe, Tarissa!" I add last minute. She throws a thumbs up over her shoulder and then is gone. With that, I return to the dilemma at hand.

Baldwin is a big man with a sweet personality. We're familiar enough that he lets Selena and I call him by his nickname: Winny. I easily identify his bright red crew cut in the colorful interior, and he waves at us as we walk in. Much to my surprise, the café is virtually empty except for a group of black-clad men in the corner booth. They disturbingly remind me of the men from last night again, and I decide to ask Winny about them, seeing as he probably hears lots of interesting bits of gossip working in a café. I don't plan on mentioning them to the Moore brothers.

We slide into our own booth near the front window, Selena on my right, Rowan on my left, and River on his left. Baldwin strides over to us with a huge grin on his face as he stops in front of our booth.

"Late night study group orrrrr, something else?" he says, wiggling his eyebrows at me.

"Winny!" I scold, giving the boys a sidelong glance; they're absorbed in the menus. He chuckles and slips his notepad out of his back pocket.

"Alright, alright. What can I get for you youngins?" he asks, a smile still spread out to reveal his perfectly white, yet slightly crooked teeth. I order a green tea, whatever Winny has on hand at the moment. Selena requests water, and both the boys order hot chocolates. We decide to share one of the chicken wing combos. Baldwin writes down our orders and is then about to leave, but I grab his sleeve.

"Winny, who are those guys over there?" I ask, lowering my voice and nodding at the men in the back. His face darkens and he brings his voice to a whisper.

"They've been here since this morning. Haven't ordered a single thing and been completely silent the whole time. And they've been eyeing you four since you got here, too."

River, who hasn't said a single word the entire time, leans forwards and says, "Just ignore them for now. Don't do anything to draw attention to ourselves." Winny nods then goes behind the counter to make our drinks. I glance once more at one of the men. There's a deathly pale one sporting a buzz cut and sunken eyes that bore into me. Our gazes meet.

I look away quickly to find Selena grasping my hand under the table, earning her a grateful look as we both glance at the boys.

"What's she doing?" asks Rowan, clearly puzzled.

Selena sighs. "Drawing attention to us."

"I made eye contact," I breathe, eyes glued to my plate. River glances at the group, Rowan patting my shoulder awkwardly. "They aren't here for coffee, or dinner for that matter and I vote that we get out of here as soon as possible. Maybe your questions should wait for another time?" I suggest.

Baldwin returns, a tray of drinks in one hand and a tray of food in the other. River stands to help him unload. He passes out our drinks first, and I blow on my tea to cool it down.

Everyone consumes their orders as quickly as possible, all of us casting nervous glances at the shady group in the back corner. Now, instead of throwing the occasional looks our way, all seven of them just stare at us. I can't help but shift in my seat, uncomfortable with their full shameless attention. The other three seem to be experiencing the same feeling because they're all glancing around and rearranging themselves on the booth seat.

Baldwin returns to collect our dishes, so I pull out a wad of cash from my purse. But he simply shakes his head with a smile. "This one's on me. I don't have a daughter of my own, so I have to spoil someone." I stand up to give him a hug, filled with gratitude. We don't deserve him. Winny goes behind the counter to close up for the night, and nods to the door, signaling we should go.

We begin moving to the door when the other group rises, fanning out in front of the exit before we can get to it. Our only way out is now entirely blocked.

"'Scuse us," says River, trying to edge around them. One of them, the one I made eye contact with earlier, holds up a hand, stopping the boy's words.

"Sorry, can't do that. You four will need to come with us please." His voice is a deep rumble, reminding me of an earthquake. The boys seem to instinctively step in front of us, acting as some sort of shield as possible scenarios ricochet off the inside of my skull.

"On whose authority?" No response. So River continues, "Well then, no thanks. My parents expect us home in about," River checks his watch, "thirteen minutes. We all really need to get home and get these lovely ladies back to their home. You wouldn't want to cause a stir up, would you?" He tries to forcefully push past them this time by driving his hands between the arms of two men in front of him. However, another man with a dark green Mohawk shoves him back.

"Now, wait just a minute here gentlemen!" interrupts Baldwin, emerging from the back to take in the situation. "Let these kids go home, otherwise I'll have to kick ya out myself. This shop closes at seven o'clock on Sundays, so I have to ask y'all to kindly leave them alone."

"Shut it old man," growls Mohawk, grabbing Selena's arm and wrenching her forwards. She cries out and stumbles, which allows him to pin her arms behind her. Moving so swiftly, he gave none of us any time to react. I shake my head ever so slightly in her direction, telling her not to start anything just yet. Master Jeen's words ring in my head, warning me to wait for the right moment to strike.

"Let that girl go at once!" Baldwin roars. "Now you've done it!" He charges towards us with fury blazing in his eyes when Buzz Cut whips something sleek and metal from his jacket.

A gun.

I'd seen guns in movies before, but they always looked like just that, a movie, a matter of fiction. But in real life, it's much colder, all the smooth metal pieces linked together to create a deadly machine.

I scream as a bang goes off, watching Baldwin crumple. Hot blood starts pooling on the checkered floor. My eyes unwillingly seek out the entrance hole of the bullet set about an inch above his heart. His pale eyes stare at the ceiling, devoid of life; a doll's eyes.

A sob escapes my throat and I yell, "Now!" Selena kicks her leg back, hitting Mohawk's kneecap and eliciting several curse words from him. Using his moment of confusion to her advantage, she bends at the waist, keeping her knees locked, and uses her captor's grip on her arms to roll him over her shoulder. He lands hard on his back, awake, but dazed. We all drop to the ground as another bang goes off.

*I have to get that gun away from him,* my mind screams.

Gritting my teeth, I silently plead for Ella's forgiveness and tear the skirt down the sides, finding solace in the leggings I convinced her to let me wear underneath. With my range of motion back to almost normal, I sink low, swinging my foot outwards across the floor to sweep Buzz Cut off his feet. He goes down, firing another shot into the front window, which shatters, spraying me with glass. I fight back the pain spreading from various minuscule cuts on my collarbone and hands. The repetition of the injury makes me nauseous, and I sway on my feet for an instant before forcing the bile down.

Before he can get back up, I straddle Buzz Cut's legs and Selena manages to yank the gun from his grip. He bucks and thrashes, but she brings the handle of his own weapon down hard on the back of his head, knocking him unconscious.

Breathing hard, I stand back up to face the remaining five. Rowan and River have taken out two, their bodies still on the floor, and are fending off the last two. Which means one of them is missing—

Rough hands wrap around my neck from behind. I don't waste a second. I twist so that I face my attacker, and find that he can't be but a few years older than me, with brown eyes that reveal just how frightened he really is. I feel a pang of pity, but bring my fist up to connect with his jaw. His eyes roll back in his head as the pressure on my trachea lets up. I cough violently and brush the tender skin on my neck assaulted by both glass and now this. Unable to hold it anymore, I run to the garbage can near the door, vomiting up my dinner and feeling utterly drained. Another glimpse of Winny's corpse sends a fresh wave of sickness through me, arms shaking and knees weak.

The café is deathly quiet behind me, and I struggle to get to my feet, slipping on loose glass and blood. My eyes lock with Rowan's, and he pants, "So glad you two take martial arts."

I try for a smile, but I can't bring myself to. Instead, I respond, "So glad you two don't back down from a fight." to which he grimaces. I turn back towards Winny's body. He was smiling his crooked smile at us just a few minutes ago. Another sob builds in my throat, but I swallow it, turning away and retrieving my phone from my bag.

I dial 9-1-1 and press the phone to my ear, fingers trembling and breathing shallow. No one answers, frustration blossoming into panic in my gut as I tuck the device away after the final dial tone sounds and the automated message starts up.

"Tarissa's dad is an officer, so our best bet is to go report this directly to the police station."

***

The station in question is deserted upon arrival. I look around in confusion at the upturned desks, broken lamps, and scattered papers fluttering weakly in the wind coming through the broken window.

"What happened here?" Rowan breathes.

"Why don't we ask them?" his brother suggests. I pick up

on the slightest waver in his voice and look up from the papers I had found. When I follow his gaze to the open door of the back room, my heart stops in my chest.

At first, it appears as if all the police who were on duty were playing a game of silent ball in a circle in the other room. But their postures tell me otherwise. They're all passed out, not dead, their chests rising and falling in a synchronized rhythm, each in their own chair. Their eyes are open and glossy, almost like they're in a trance. I recognize Tarissa's dad as one of the unconscious, and I notice her bag slung over a chair in the lobby. The sight shocks me and raises goosebumps on my arms as we creep closer simultaneously. Then something catches my eye.

In the center of their circle, is a familiar face. Tarissa is rocking back and forth, her arms wrapped tightly around her knees. She's muttering something about starving souls, and I edge towards her like she's a wild animal.

"Tarissa? What happened? Why are you here?" I ask cautiously, kneeling next to her. She raises her terrified blue eyes to mine, clamping her arms around my forearm like a vise.

"They're coming, Corinne, they're coming!" she says insistently, eyes wide. "They're coming, you have to listen to me, they're coming!" Fear is a tangible thing, crawling across my skin like dozens of spiders, or sitting in my gut like an immovable rock. Tarissa's manicured, periwinkle nails sink into my arm, making me wince as she wages a battle with something I can't see. Her excited demeanor from earlier has been evaporated by terror, and replaced with insanity.

"Okay, okay they're coming, yes." This seems to pacify her, and she begins muttering to herself again, easing her grip slightly and the shivering subsiding the slightest amount. "Can you tell me who *they* are?" She shakes her head violently and stares at the floor. "Then do you know why they're here?"

She squeezes my arm again, this time drawing blood. The girl's got an iron grip in and out of class. She glances around before speaking as if she's afraid someone's listening. Then she whispers, shiny eyes as big as quarters, "They're here for you, Corinne."

*Chapter 4*

# Selena

Corinne pales, and the boys go still beside me. "Excuse me?" she whispers. "They're here for me?"

Tarissa nods exaggeratedly. "Oh yes, you're invaluable to them. They need you to complete the process and only you have the ability that will satisfy the experiment—" she rambles on, spouting nonsense about monsters in the dark that take your soul and others that invade your mind and so on. They need *Corinne?* And what ability? Only Mutes have—

I shiver. "Tarissa, don't be silly. Only Mutes have abilities." I plead silently to be mistaken, that I misheard her or that she really is just crazy. She nods quickly again, then gets a dreamy look in her cloudy blue eyes.

"You should really run. Run away, run away run awayyyyy!" she sings, giggling like she's just told us a funny joke. "Run run r-r-runnn awayyyyyyy!" She stops mid-laugh and goes whiter than a sheet, clutching her stomach and moaning. Corinne helps her lie down, and I hear her exhale.

She doesn't breathe in again.

"Is she dead?" murmurs Rowan, River looking grim beside him.

Corinne looks like she's about to hurl. "Tarissa? Tarissa! Wake up!" she whispers, the urgency in her voice palpable. Tarissa doesn't move, only stares at the ceiling with a faint smile on her lips. My sister presses her trembling fingers against the girl's neck, checking for a pulse while tears run down her face. I can see by the hopelessness in her eyes that she's searching in vain. "She told me we'd see her on Wednesday," Corinne whispers haltingly, eyes glassy and body rigid.

Two people we know. Both dead in the same hour. I feel like throwing up, and there's a potted plant conveniently placed by the door.

"We have to go. We have to get out of Kleka *now*," says my sister, still pale and shuddering, her eyes flitting from me to the boys. I can tell she's seeking a glimpse of anything but our friend's body, laid out like an abandoned marionette. "Selena, we need to get our stuff from home. Then we might have a chance at getting out of here." I nod, understanding starting to dawn on me. We cover Tarissa's body with a tablecloth from the break room before we leave, Corinne gnawing on her knuckles to keep from sobbing. I feel my own shock starting to fade as I look one last time into Tarissa's celestial eyes, then pull the sheet over hurriedly.

All four of us race back through the dark streets, which are now in complete chaos. I nearly lose the others in the melee, people racing back and forth while buildings catch fire or implode. For a second we all just stand there gaping as the Mayor's house blows apart, debris flying into the street and crushing several dozen people under their weight. I recognize men from the camp from the other night, the ones dressed in black, the ones now shoving people into lines and cuffing them together.

I bite back a gasp at my next thought in line: the Mayor would be inside the house, wouldn't he? Rowan and River's dad. I look to them, slack jawed, awaiting any sort of reaction.

"I'm very glad Dad is on a business trip right now," says

Rowan in a small voice. I nearly trip with relief despite the fact that he had requested we be interrogated by his children. We dodge a metal strut flying through the air, watching it crash through the window of the station; this spurs us back into motion. Corinne urges us to keep moving, nearly at her breaking point. I can see her fraying at the edges as we weave in and out of the havoc. I try not to imagine the police, sedated but still very much alive, all still in there. Not to mention Tarissa's body, which will probably never get to receive a proper funeral. God, she was only sixteen.

We reach Ella's house just as a siren goes off, the ebbing and flowing of its wailing voice signaling that everyone should try to find shelter indoors. How ironic, that the siren telling us to get inside still works while every other building is being blown to bits.

I frantically ring the doorbell, and on the second press Ella opens the door, eyes wide and worried.

"Thank God you're all okay!" she whimpers, pulling all four of us in.

"Ella, where's our stuff?" asks my sister, getting straight to the point. "We've gotta get out of here. We're the reason this place is getting blown to bits, although we don't know any more than that." Ella pales a bit, but hurries upstairs nonetheless, returning moments later with our bags. Her parents are nowhere to be seen.

"Good luck, Corinne," she whispers, giving my sister a tight hug, and then me. "Return safely, okay? Please?" Corinne nods confidently and gives Ella one last embrace before she leads the boys out the door. I give our sister and friend a wavering smile before following the other three back outside.

I immediately recognize the route we're taking as the one Corinne and I formed for our escape, the missing pieces of her intentions clicking into place to fill the gaps, making me smile internally. It's a good idea, however risky it may be.

When we reach the outskirts of the city, Corinne holds up a hand to give herself time to scan the forest. When she deems it to be clear, she sprints into it, quickly disappearing into the foliage.

"But she—she just—what—" stutters Rowan, mouth open. River simply raises his eyebrows. Jeez, talks a bunch doesn't he? I roll my eyes and grab Rowan's arm, pulling him along.

"Just go with it," I warn him. "She knows what she's doing." He clamps his mouth shut after that, and I let go of his arm. We dash after Corinne, who's waiting for us on the other side of the tree line. When she spots us, she beckons for us to follow, and I speed up to walk next to her.

"We'll only be able to last a few days with how many supplies we have, you know that don't you?" I ask, straining my eyes to see through the predominating darkness. She ignores me and forges ahead.

We reach the fence and walk along the perimeter until we find the spot where she cut the barbed wire at the top on the night of our escape. Corinne and I dig in our packs for the thick rubber cleaning gloves. I still have mine, but Corinne frowns, coming up empty handed.

"We'll have to take turns tossing them back over. Selena, you first," she says, not letting her concern show through. "But first," she levels a stare at the boys, studying them, "why are you going with us? You really only just met us over a dinner that was supposed to reprimand us for doing this exact thing. Now you're about to climb over the only thing protecting your cushioned lives," my sister warns.

Rowan sucks in a breath, but River steps in for him without skipping a beat.

"We're kind of in this mess, too now," he reasons. "Plus,

those guys that just attacked us? The people in the city? They've been lurking about here for quite some time, and our father needed our help to follow their movements as best we could for the past week to try and sort out their intentions. However, it looks like we were too late. The only reason I'm telling you this brings me right back to where I started: we're now all in this mess. So maybe we're going because we all have incentive, or maybe we're going because we all want out."

I'm shocked, having expected nothing like the speech he just gave. Corinne, though, appears assuaged, nodding, before signaling to me to get going. I sigh in resignation, clamping down on the argument straining against my lips from the inside.

I tug on the gloves and start scaling the fence. I feel nothing, the rubber completely blocking the electricity. The only shiver running through my veins right now is adrenaline.

Once at the top, I swing over to the other side, and climb back down. Peeling the gloves off, I toss them back over, narrowly missing the wire at the top. Rowan catches them.

He's a bit slower getting over, but surprisingly graceful. Once on the ground, he throws the gloves to his brother, and they arc high over the fence; River catches them without difficulty. Once at the top, instead of climbing down the other side he jumps, rolling off the momentum as soon as he hits the ground before popping back up on his feet unscathed.

"Show off," Rowan mutters.

I laugh nervously. "You'll have to teach me that sometime," I say. His smile sends a thrill through my body as he throws the gloves over. One snags on the coiled wire, the other dropping to the ground on the other side. Corinne picks up the single glove, and frantically searches her backpack again in search of anything to use as a substitute. Coming up empty handed, she grimaces, and pulls on the lone glove.

I watch her painstakingly climb the fence, having to let go of the wire and then quickly grab on again a little higher, since she can only use one of her hands. She keeps the other one firmly tucked behind her back to make sure she doesn't hit the charged metal by accident. Every time she lets go, my heart skips a beat. Visibly sweating from the effort, she finally reaches the top and balances precariously on the bar, really only able to hold on with one hand. She then reaches for the second glove, about three feet down the line. Her fingertips brush the yellow rubber and I hold my breath.

It topples off the wire, landing on the ground on the side none of us are on.

She makes a frustrated noise and sits back up carefully.

"I can't climb down," she pants. "Too difficult. I'll fall for sure."

"Try what River did," I suggest. "Can you instruct her what to do?" I ask him. He nods, stepping forward.

"Okay, just pull your arms in like this, yeah." He demonstrates with his own body, hugging his arms to his chest. "And then jump. When you're close to the ground, curl up tight, and just roll it off. Try to move as soon as you hit the ground." He sounds calm, but Corinne's eyes are wild with terror poorly veiled. It's a fifteen foot drop at best, and she's never been too good with heights.

I see her swallow, then she jumps. She curls her body tight and a small scream escapes me as she plummets towards the ground. As soon as she makes contact, she rolls forward, and ends up sprawled on the dirt, clutching her wrist. I instinctively run to her as she sits up.

"You okay?" I ask. She nods, but her eyes are tight with pain, wincing as she flexes her wrist. "C'mon, let's get a move on." I help her up, and the boys join us.

"You did pretty good, considering it was your first try," he notes.

"Thanks," she says through gritted teeth. He smiles faintly and Rowan grins. They must both be running on nervous adrenaline, just like I am.

We wind our way through the Shifting Woods, and I try to keep my mind off the strangers in black from two nights ago. Were they the same people who attacked our city? The forest is literally the only way out, as the next supply train isn't coming for another week.

We forge ahead as quickly as the moving trees will allow, and before long find ourselves back at the edge of the clearing from last night. The tents are gone, along with any trace of a camp. A puzzled frown pulls at my mouth. We walk out into the moonlight, but no sooner do we come into full view, a haunting shriek peals through the woods. My skin crawls, as more moans answer. They sound like a band of dying feral cats.

I focus my attention on movement near the base of the trees on the other side of the glade, and two figures emerge. I can't make out any distinguishing features from where I stand, but apparently Corinne can.

"Mohawk and Buzz Cut," she whispers. I remember the two men at the café as my captor, and the one who shoved River. How fitting.

The animal noises sound again, this time closer, and I have to cover my ears to prevent my eardrums from bursting. The boys follow suit, but Corinne can't with her wrist. Only able to protect one ear, she sways on her feet.

The stench of blood and rotting corpses permeates the air, and I gag, trying to breathe through my mouth. The smell gets stronger as more movement draws my attention to the trees again. Tall humanoid creatures push their way into the open, forming a loose ring around us and screeching at the tops of their lungs. But my mouth goes dry when I see that they *have* no lungs. Just an emaciated rib cage and painfully thin, stretched out limbs. Their arms are so long that they nearly brush the ground, each and every one of them carrying a butchering knife as long as I am tall in both hands. They drag them along, leaving deep trenches in their wake. The scent becomes stronger, and Corinne falls, unable to cover her ears from their next scream. I nudge her with my foot, but she's out cold. They shriek one last time, and this time it seeps between my fingers to rattle my eardrums.

My scream is lost within their noise, and I collapse next to my sister, letting the darkness overtake me.

## Chapter 5

# Corinne

I try to sit upright as my consciousness returns, but my head is heavy and my vision is blurry. A throbbing headache numbs my skull.

"Hello?" I ask no one in particular. My eyesight clears up a bit, and with it my memories, all that happened coming back to me, flooding my system and drowning me in fear. I swallow the bile trying to make its way up my throat, searching for the monsters in a panic.

But rather than the dewy grass in the clearing, I'm sitting on a padded medical chair with a frigid light pointed directly at my eyes. It's so bright that even if I turn my head, I can't see any of my surroundings.

My wrists are bound to the chair by metal cuffs, and I feel my heart rate speed up with the sudden deprivation of movement. Time moves too slowly.

Some immeasurable amount of time later, footsteps sound from close by, growing closer and stopping near my head. Silence. Something clicks and whirrs. The light goes dark, and I'm left seeing afterimages blooming across my eyelids. Blinking several times to clear my vision, the silhouette of another person starts to form in my peripheral. I turn my head to get a better look.

A tall, skinny man stands next to me, hands behind his

back. Greasy black hair tumbles over his shoulders, framing his softly smiling face. He stares at me with wide, pitch black eyes. A sort of serenity lives there, but only as a memory of something once lost.

"Welcome, darling," he murmurs. "I apologize for the rather disorienting position you're in, but I needed a moment to prepare."

His voice is slick and oily, sliding over my skin and worming its way into my head.

"Who are you? And where the hell am I?" I demand. My mouth feels dry and full of cotton.

"Forgive me, I have not introduced myself. I am Pierre, head of the Phantom Order. And you, my dear, are the one whose help I am begging for. Let's get you to a more comfortable place and then we can discuss, alright?"

A slight pressure on my wrist draws my attention and then the cuffs are gone. I sit up, keeping an eye on my captor—if not that then what else—who just watches me with those big, black eyes.

"Follow me," he murmurs, turning around and walking soundlessly out of the room. I scan the room once before pursuing: I was right, I was in some medical facility, the smell of bleach suffocating the air and clean, steel counters on three sides. Above one of them is a window, blinds shut tight. I reach out for them, just to get an idea of where I am.

"Dearest," sings Pierre from the other room. I flinch away from the window and hurriedly move towards the door.

Outside is a simple hallway, lined with doors just like the one I walked through. At the end, the corridor opens into an office, or a waiting room of some sorts.

Pierre sits in one of the plush, old-fashioned chairs, resting his smooth, pale hands on the armrests, legs crossed, and smile inviting. "Sit with me, let's chat a bit."

I tentatively lower myself into a chair across from him,

sinking into the upholstery much farther than I had thought possible.

"Tea?" he asks, snapping his fingers.

"No, I—"

Before I can get even a sentence out, a man appears from nowhere and places a small folding table between us. A tray of tea and delicate looking cookies is quick to follow. The man hands me a tiny cup and saucer, already filled with steaming liquid.

"Thanks," I mutter, watching the man disappear through a nearly invisible side door.

"Now," begins Pierre. He lifts a second cup to his lips and takes a small sip before continuing. "Let's see here. I want to apologize again for the ways in which you came to be in this place, but it was the most efficient manner. As I've mentioned, I'm in dire need of your assistance." He pauses for dramatic effect, frowning slightly and taking another sip of tea.

"You, my dear, have something that I need. This might come as a bit of a shock, but you are in fact one of the Changed."

He lets me absorb this information. My face is numb and I distantly feel my teacup slipping from my hands. One of the Changed? That can't be right. Mutes start showing signs of their mutations around age six. I'm eighteen.

"I'm—I'm sorry," I mumble, reaching with shaking fingers for my shattered cup on the floor. My tea spilled everywhere, soaking into my pants and the carpet.

"Don't stress darling, it's quite difficult news," he says sympathetically. Another snap of his fingers and the same man from before is at my side, soaking up the mess with a rag. I try to help pick up the shards of porcelain, but one slices my finger and spots the carpet with blood. The man grabs my hand and meets my gaze harshly, pushing me back into my seat.

Pierre clicks his tongue.

"It's quite perfect timing, if you think about it." He leans down from his chair, picking up the porcelain shard that cut me. "You see, your blood is what I need. Not all of it, don't worry. Your blood has some unique properties that trace back to some important people, the people who sent off the last bombs of the third World War. The people with the most powerful mutations. One of the same mutations that runs in your genes as well."

My blood turns to ice, slush moving slowly through my veins. Pierre brings the porcelain to his mouth, licking the blood from its flawless surface. His tongue starts to bleed, the crimson settling into the crevices between his teeth. He doesn't seem to notice. If he does, he doesn't care.

"Your hometown, Kleka, has been a hotspot for Mutes seeking shelter within the last few decades. They hide among you all, watching, waiting. They terrorize the Unchanged, normal people who hold nothing but contempt for them. The individual governments started experimenting with different drugs and preventatives. They have not yet discovered a cure for the mutations. They are impossible to terminate without extensive gene therapy.

"However, they *have* developed a way of temporarily shutting off the mutated genes. You can think of it like flipping a light switch. Kleka has been the guinea pig in all of this. For the last thirty years or so, they have been distributing these treatments in the form of vitamin gummies. Like yearly vaccines, they are taken once a year or so, more often if a child begins to act abnormally. The goal is to start the new generations off from birth. And they work. Look at you, twelve years past your due date and as ordinary as an Unchanged."

My mind reels with a hurricane of questions and confusion. But my mouth is zipped tight, forcing my breath through my nose, shallow and quick.

"Why?" is all I can manage, and my voice cracks on that single word.

"Why did they do it? Why do I need you? There are twice as many questions as answers, and none that are satisfactory." Pierre smiles understandingly, taking my hand in his ice-cold grip. The inner area of his lips are stained a striking scarlet.

"As I mentioned, you have a more potent series of mutations. Your sister was skipped over, given quite common, generic alterations. The abilities you possess—yes, you have more than one—could aid in creating a cure more potent than any we've developed thus far. Not to mention you would be cured of your mutation, as we would be removing the infected gene sequences. Based on your medical records, I've already confirmed that you are compatible and the process will be virtually painless. In return, I am offering you a permanent place within my closest circle of trusted individuals, and protection from all sources. Not to mention you would be paid handsomely and granted immunity from bounty hunters."

"I don't even know what ability—what abilities I have," I croak, still unable to process his words. It's too much to remember.

"I have my suspicions, but we would of course have to help you develop them safely. It can be dangerous when you're on your own."

"What about my sister? Where is she?"

"Safe, I assure you. Although I have to admit, the boys were an unexpected addition."

He took all three of them? My heartbeat thunders in my ears, blood pounding. Suddenly my body doesn't feel connected to my head. Bile scorches my throat and the world spins.

## Chapter 6

# Selena

My ears are still ringing from the screaming of the creatures in the woods.

I smack the side of my head to try and get it to stop while I scan the room for the hundredth time. A spotless, bleached room. Small, but not too small. Two doors, one leading to a tiny bathroom with a toilet, shower stall, and sink, and the other presumably leading out of here. A small cot with the sheets pulled tight and crisply ironed. I've hardly wanted to touch anything because I'm afraid of screwing it up.

When I woke up there had been a neatly folded set of sweats on the bed, but I haven't touched those yet, either.

I peek out the tiny square of glass set into the second door, but still all I can see is a blank, white hallway.

I sigh in frustration, pacing around the room to burn off some energy. Questions spin and bounce in my head, leaving me dizzy and overwhelmed. Where am I? Where's Corinne? How much longer do I have to be here? What happened to Kleka?

With any answers coming up blank, I snatch the clothes off the bed and march the few feet to the bathroom, deciding that maybe a quick rinse will clear my mind.

The water only has one setting, and that's cold. Like, really cold. Cold enough that when I turned it on I shrieked and fell out of the stall. Muttering obscenities and massaging my hip, I shower as quickly as possible, gritting my teeth against the stinging water.

I towel dry and redress in the sweats, leaving the tattered yellow sundress in a heap in the corner. It's like a sore thumb sticking out against the clean environment. I gaze at it for a moment longer, a strange longing for the closed-in life we had tugging at my memories.

*Chapter 7*

# Corinne

Everything is clean, too clean.

The bare walls, the tile floor, the pressed sheets. Even the gauze secured around my finger. It's not devoid of color, oh no. There are rich, gold curtains and a crimson canopy; a thick comforter; and decorative pillows. But it's all so *perfect.* A south facing window bathes the room in a buttery light.

I woke up a few hours ago and hardly even looked around before dashing to the attached bathroom and emptying my insides into the porcelain toilet. I sat there for a while, just zoning out at the floor. Then came the inevitable drag to the shower. By the time I got out and went in search of new clothes, the bed had been remade, every fold sharp and clean.

A note had been propped up against a slender vase of flowers on the nightstand, sealed with a scarlet spill of wax.

*Dearest Corinne,*

    *I hope that once you've had some rest and time to yourself you'll be willing to discuss arrangements in further detail. I am deeply sorry for overwhelming you last evening. It pained me to see you in such a disoriented state. Once you feel settled, please pull the rope near the door*

*and someone will bring you to me. I will happily
answer any questions you may have.*

*Deepest sincerities,*
*Pierre Dolion*


And that's where I am as of now. Sitting carefully on the edge of the bed, Pierre's note clutched in my trembling hands. I look down and realize I've crumpled it.

I suppose waiting is pointless; I've got nothing to do and sitting still will only turn my brain to slush.

But Selena.

I practically sprint to the red and gold tassel hanging by the door and haul it down, grunting with the unexpected weight of it. Within a few heartbeats, the door opens and Pierre is peering in. I blink.

"I thought someone was going to take me to you," I stutter. This throws a wrench in things.

"I happened to just be passing by. You received my note?" He smiles serenely, but his eyes still unnerve me.

"I did." I take a deep breath to steady my rattling nerves. "But, I want to see my sister."

Pierre stares, mouth still curved. But I notice the momentary confusion cross his face.

"I told you she's safe," he begins. I cut him off, hardening my voice.

"I am aware. Nevertheless, I want to see her in person to make sure she's okay."

He stands straight up, sighing through his nose and says, "Alright, if that's what you want. I'll call Jax to take you down." And then he's gone. As silent as a breath of air.

I wait on the edge of my bed for Jax, swinging my feet in circles.

Someone knocks twice on the door and peeks around.

I had been expecting another stern, silent worker, but he can't be more than a few years older than me. He has shiny black hair and a glinting grin. He slips in and I stand up to meet him.

"You must be Corinne," he states, extending his hand. "I hope the room has been up to your standards."

"Yeah, it's uh, it's great." Silence. He's still gripping my hand. "You're here to take me to my sister?"

"Come this way."

Before he turns away I notice his unusual eyes. One is a pale, glittering silver, and the other is unmistakably gold. How odd.

I glance again at the vase of flowers, and, at the last moment, select a bright sunflower out of the bunch.

We follow a curving hallway to where it tees. Jax pushes a heavy metal door on the opposite wall with a grunt, revealing several flights of stairs.

"Where are we?" I ask, racing to keep up with his ridiculously long strides. He doesn't answer, only sticks his hands in his pockets. I blow a strand of hair out of my face, curiosity temporarily overriding my nerves. "Hello?"

Footsteps approach from downstairs and Jax tenses as an older woman passes quickly, head bent. He doesn't relax until she's long gone.

I'm on the verge of repeating my question, irritation gnawing at my skin, but Jax trips into me and we crash to the landing floor. I keep the flower extended away from my body to avoid it being crushed. A few petals fall to the floor.

"Take this, keep it out of sight at all costs," he breathes into my ear. A slight bit of pressure from him against the palm of my hand and I can feel the shape of a cool vile. Then his weight disappears and he's hauling me to my feet. I keep the vile pressed against my chest.

"What the hell was that?" I hiss, still jittery.

He hardly glances in my direction. "Hmm? Oh yes, sorry about that, I must have tripped over my own two feet." His strides become quicker and any follow-up questions are lost.

Neither of us speak until Jax stops in front of a door on one of the lower levels of the building labeled eight-seven-eight. The hallway is plain and too bright, the fluorescent lights buzzing over our heads. He pulls a small plastic card from his pocket and inserts it into a device on the door handle. A green light blinks to life with a click.

"After you," he says, pulling open the door.

I peek into the room, and there she is.

"Selena!" I shriek, tackling her off the side of her bed. She hugs me tight, laughing and crying and everything in between.

"What are you doing here?" she asks in disbelief. *"How did you get here?"*

"They're keeping me upstairs. I have a lot to tell you, but, here." I offer her the tired sunflower, a little wilted now. She takes it incredibly carefully, a spark of joy coming to life in her eyes.

When we were apart as kids, Selena was placed in the care of a couple whose previous child had passed extremely young. They resented her, but they never hurt her. She became very isolated. But she found solace among their gardens, hidden by the shade of the trees and the songs of the birds.

Her room is completely white, lacking any color or personality, and maybe she'll feel a little better with something she knows.

"It's lovely, thank you Corinne." A few more tears leak from her eyes and she wraps me in another tight hug.

"Corinne," calls Jax, clearing his throat. "Sorry, but we should get going."

Selena eyes him suspiciously, but turns back to me with a watery smile. I embrace her again, and tuck a strand of hair behind her ear, promising to try and come back soon.

Outside in the hallway, I try to hide my tears from Jax. He has enough grace to pretend not to notice, at least.

"Wait, Jax." I chew on the inside of my cheek, unsure whether to ask or not. He meets my gaze steadily, waiting patiently. "I heard that Rowan and River are here, too. Could I just see them to make sure they're okay?"

Jax sighs, checking his watch. Something softens in his eyes, and he nods, glancing down the hall.

"Just for a minute, though."

"Thank you."

Room eight-seven-nine is Rowan's. When I step in, he's sitting against the wall, eyes shut. He cracks one open in irritation when the door closes behind me, but it dissolves when he processes who it is.

"Corinne?" he exclaims. I give him a small smile as he gets to his feet and walks over. I don't know whether to give him a hug or something else. A handshake is too formal. We end up just facing each other without saying anything.

I cough. "I just wanted to make sure you all were okay."

"River and Selena are here, too?" he inquires.

I nod, saying, "They're in the rooms on either side of this one. I'm going over to River's next."

"They let you out to talk to us?" There's a tone of suspicion in his voice, and I don't like where it's going.

"No, well, kind of." I look away from his pale green eyes and then back with lots of effort. "I'm not being kept down here. The person in charge of this place needs my help with something, so I have a room upstairs."

"You're going to do it? Corinne, these people kidnapped us, I hope you remember."

"I know, but I don't know what other choice I have."

A tense silence falls, and Jax pulls the door open again, holding it with his foot.

"Time's up," he says.

"Who's that?" Rowan's eyes narrow at Jax. The latter smiles tightly at him and takes my hand, guiding me to the door.

"I have to go Rowan, I'll try to come back at some point," I sigh. I really do not have the energy for his attitude right now. Rowan turns away without a goodbye and I can't help leaving without feeling like I said something wrong.

Opening River's door reveals the sound of the shower running from the attached bathroom, so Jax just takes me back upstairs.

"I'll let Mr. Dolion know that you're ready to talk to him now," says Jax. I nod, exhaustion weighing my eyelids. He gives my hand a quick squeeze before closing my door.

## Chapter 8

# Corinne

We're back in the same office as before, with the too-soft chairs and the hallway leading to the small medical room where I woke up. Pierre has another cup of tea in his hands.

"How are you feeling?" he asks kindly.

"Better, I suppose."

"That's wonderful news. Have you any questions about my offer?" I consider for a moment, watching his slow, precise movements.

"Yes, actually." Pierre leans forward ever so slightly. "If Mutes—if the Changed are so terrible and manipulative, how come you want to help them—help me so badly?"

The only reaction from him is a small twitch at the corner of his lips as he responds, "I want what's best for the Changed, for them to safely receive treatment and be integrated back into society. It's what this organization is all about. You've seen the way people treat them, haven't you? If they were to be permanently and effectively cured, well—"

My heart sinks to my toes. He has a point.

How would Ella react if she knew Selena and I were Mutes? I can see her face, the one that kissed away our tears when we had nightmares as younger kids. Or laughed the hardest at her own jokes. The living embodiment of optimism and kindness, that face twisted with disgust and horror at the truth of us.

"You see, don't you. What I'm trying to do here is something that our government sees as a waste of money and resources. They've found a scapegoat to focus they're frustration on while simultaneously making the public believe they have their best interests at heart. But it's all a lie, and I believe you've known this for some time now."

The cameras on every street. The constant "vitamins." The posters and notices advertising huge sums of cash for undocumented Mutes. So many ideas and memories collide in my head, all trying to be heard at once until I silence them with my voice.

"Okay."

"Okay—as in you are willing to stand beside me?"

"Yes." I force the word out before I change my mind. Something is still missing from his story, but I can't find it. It all fits.

"That's wonderful," Pierre sighs, his face splitting into a grin. He has too many teeth. "Why, I can't even begin to express my gratitude. I'll have Jax bring you back to your room and we'll celebrate tonight. What might I do to honor your willingness?"

Excitement bubbles in my chest but I force myself to keep a straight face. I say, "I want Selena to move up with me. The boys, too."

"Yes, that's fine," he says, waving his hand. He's distracted, setting down his cup and rising to his feet. "I'll make it happen. You made the right choice, Corinne."

Jax steps into the room just as Pierre leaves. They exchange a quick glance.

"So you agreed." It's less of a question and more of a statement. A tinge of disappointment laces his words, but his face is unreadable.

"I did."

"I assume you know your way back to your room? I'll retrieve your sister."

***

Selena and I sit on my bed while she Dutch braids my hair, just like we used to do when we were younger. The feel of her quick fingers in my hair is comforting, familiar.

"Tell me again what happened?" she asks.

I sigh, but smile, recounting what I've learned so far. She listens quietly, absorbing the news that Pierre believes us to be Mutations. She took it pretty well the first time around, but she's been a little more withdrawn since.

They'd removed the double bed from my room by the time I returned after talking with Pierre. Two twin beds now sit next to each other, and I put both vases of flowers on Selena's nightstand. She'd spent the first five minutes with me rearranging them in their water and fussing over how they weren't cut correctly, and eventually moving them next to the window.

A tentative knock comes from the door. Selena pauses her work as Rowan and River step into our room. Rowan's eyes go straight to mine, and I can feel the disappointment radiating from him.

"Explanations now, please," requests River, sitting on the edge of Selena's bed. Rowan remains standing, arms folded and leaning nonchalantly against the wall.

"Perfect timing." Selena smiles. "Corinne was just telling me again. Start from the top, chosen one."

I roll my eyes but start again from when I woke up. I leave out the part about the vile from Jax, its weight still heavy in my pocket from the secret meaning behind it. I hate lying to my sister, but I can't sort out Jax's intentions, and until then, the vile and its mystery contents will stay out of sight.

Once I fall silent, Rowan blows a breath out through his mouth, shaking his head. River gives him a stern glance and turns to me.

"That is one hell of a story. I see why you agreed. But Rowan has a point with his hesitancy to trust that man."

"I know, but I didn't really have any other choice. I mean, there was a room just down the hall the entire time where he could have just strapped me in and taken what he needed."

"Entirely fair," he responds. "Although I have to wonder what he meant by celebration."

River hardly finishes his sentence before another knock sounds from the door and Jax pokes his head in. Rowan avoids his gaze and examines the ceiling.

"I've got some papers for you, Corinne," he says, trotting over. He hands me a cream-colored folder and nods at it. "Just some contracts to sign and some more information about tonight. Mr. Dolion is allowing you to bring one of your friends here with you."

"I'll go." Rowan pushes himself off the wall and subtly places himself between me and Jax. I stand up as well, moving in front of *him* and crossing my arms.

"He said *I* get to invite someone," I remind him. His attitude is *really* starting to get on my nerves. "You're acting like a kid, Rowan. What is your deal?"

"What's my deal? This entire goddamn situation! We get snatched and brought to this place in the dead of night. They ransacked our homes, and you just want to waltz into their arms?" He grabs my shoulder to try and move me away from Jax.

"Don't you fucking touch me!" I seethe, throwing his hand off me. His eyes go wide. I grab his collar and pull him down so we're eye to eye, noses inches apart. "Need

I remind you that you're the one who followed me into the woods? *You* hopped the fence and *you* abandoned your lovely little home in that city. I owe that place nothing."

He stumbles back when I let go, face blank.

"Fine then. Remind me next time we get kidnapped to play damsel in distress with the captors' workers and maybe things will work out just fine," He spits. I glare at him as he strides out of the room and into his and River's.

Selena sits quietly behind me and River sighs deeply. Jax's lips are pressed into a thin line.

"I can go," offers River. "Unless you'd rather bring Selena."

"I'm good. I think I'd rather sleep." My sister laughs lightly, trying to lighten the mood.

"Alright then, I'll let Mr. Dolion know your decision. First you need to sign some papers, though." Jax nods at the folder in my hands. I flip it open and pull out a stack of crisp pages, filled to the margins with words.

"Jesus," I mutter, scanning the information.

"It's a lot of standard stuff. Just consent to have your medical records looked through, etcetera."

I try to read through it all anyway, even the fine print. Other than some strangely worded agreements or the occasional addition of an improbable scenario, it seems legit. While I go through signing with a little ballpoint pen give to me by Jax, he and River discuss protocols for the celebration that evening.

I've just signed the last page and slipped the papers back into the folder when another sheet falls out. I pick it up, glancing at the two still deep in conversation. Selena peers over my shoulder. This paper is folded in several places and handwritten, messy, like someone had to get their thoughts down quickly. Scanning the words sends my stomach twisting into a cold knot.

*-They had children. ~~3 girls?~~ 2 kids total (genders*
*unknown) Might be a lead→look into it*
*-Removal would cause death of the brain.*
*-Why are some so much stronger? →outliers, freak*
*accidents*
*-Have to collect as much variety as possible. Can*
*one body hold all?*
**Call Candol @ 9** *no new leads*

There's much more, both sides entirely covered in scribbles, but Jax has noticed the paper and snatches it from my hands.

"Whoa, must have got added by accident. These are just some of Mr. Dolion's notes. He's pretty forgetful sometimes." He smiles at me, but it's forced.

"Jax, what did that say about brain death? Pierre said it would be fine," I say slowly, getting back to my feet. Jax shakes his head, looking a little green.

"Don't worry Corinne, these are outdated. You should start getting ready for the celebration. Have you finished signing?" I stare at him, extending the folder. His dichromatic eyes dance around the room, but his smile remains intact.

"Alright Jax," I murmur. I watch him fumble his way to the door and out of sight.

*Chapter 9*

# **Corinne**

I stare with pursed lips at the invite Jax had given to River for the celebration tonight. It's a formal event, the theme: Masquerade.

"Where am I even supposed to get a dress?" I mutter to myself. Unsure what to do, I glance at the clock. It reads 4:36; the party starts at six. An hour and a half. I smile softly, thinking of Ella. She would have the time of her life dressing me up for an event like this.

I shower quickly and cross my fingers that my hair will dry in time. When I come out of the bathroom, Selena is standing next to a clothing rack on wheels in the middle of the room.

"Someone dropped this off while you were in there," she says, eyes glued to the rack's contents. Several dresses hang from the rod, all stunning in their own way. I join my sister with examining them all, eliminating all the pieces with open backs or no shoulder coverage.

"I don't think anyone will really mind," Selena murmurs, referencing the birthmark.

"I know, but it makes me feel better." I smile, already tired thinking of the evening ahead. She squeezes my shoulder and we keep sorting through the remaining dresses.

We finally settle on one that would have sent Ella

absolutely feral. A rich, midnight blue, all silver trim. It's soft and silky, sporting a Queen Anne's neckline and a skirt that tightens around the knees before flaring dramatically. It's a little form-fitting, but it's about my size and it'll do fine. Selena re-braids my hair just before six and hastily curls it around my head in a crown to finish it off.

"Thanks, Leenie," I say, giving her a quick hug before heading to the door.

River is already in the hallway, Jax next to him. He's talking to Rowan, who's inside their room. The latter catches sight of me and jogs outside with us.

"Corinne, can I talk to you for a sec?" he asks, sighing. Jax checks his watch and gives me a nod and I follow Rowan into their room. River shuts the door after us.

"You look nice," he states, fidgeting.

"What's wrong?" I ask, bracing myself for another outburst.

"Look, I just wanted to apologize for earlier. What I said was brash and insensitive, and I know you're just doing what you need to."

I raise an eyebrow at him, scowling. "Did River make you apologize?"

"No—well, yes, but I mean it, seriously."

"Rowan, can we talk about this later?" I shiver, and my mind is drifting.

Rowan visibly deflates, looking distressed. He clasps his hands in front of him, saying, "Fine. Just—be careful tonight, please."

I nod, touching his arm briefly before stepping back into the hallway.

"Let's go."

## Chapter 10

# Corinne

Jax stops in front of a large set of double doors, the sounds of conversations and muffled laughter filtering into the corridor.

"Don't forget these," Jax reminds us. He hands us each an elaborate mask, silver in color to match our outfits. "And remember, just make small talk, humor people, you know. Mr. Dolion likes to show off his accomplishments, so just stay near him, dance a little, and then you can leave. I'll be around the party, too, so find me when you're done."

The doors are opened by two people in white clothes, workers here, Jax tells us. They're everywhere, holding doors, taking coats, serving drinks and snacks. He says they're paid extremely well, and given food and board both inside and outside of the facility.

The room on the other side is massive, elaborate columns surrounding the inside walls. The ceiling arches high overhead, dotted with several extravagant chandeliers. All around us, people flow too and fro, talking to each other, sipping from crystal glasses. And the masks. Masks of all sizes, shapes, and colors. Masks that match the outfits of the wearers and masks that greatly contrast them.

Pierre is easily spotted, wearing a scarlet eye mask. Several black feathers extend from the top and curl around his slick hair.

River offers me his arm and I link mine through his. We make our way slowly towards Pierre, who is surrounded by several other costumed partygoers. He notices us right away.

"Why it's the star of the show herself!" he gloats, pulling me towards him. I lose my hold on River. "I see you found a suitable dress from the selection?"

"Yes, it's lovely," I murmur, scanning the crowd. Pierre seems to have a fondness of all things extravagant, most of them wearing eye masks like mine and Pierre's, but some that cover their entire faces, making any distinguishing features invisible. Pierre's grip on my arm is tight, but his smile is joyful and at ease. River and Jax have disappeared, lost in the throng of people.

"Corinne, darling, meet my sister, Arcane. She runs the sister facility to this space over in Linaria."

A slender woman with olive skin approaches. She's wearing a pure white gown, layer upon layer of gossamer fabric making the skirt billow out in a graceful waterfall. With the plunging neckline and no straps, it's a wonder that it stays where it is. Her mask is a mirror of her brother's, only in white and silver. She and Pierre look incredibly different at first glance, but they have the same air of power and steadiness.

"It's wonderful to finally meet you, Corinne," titters Arcane. Her voice is breathy and strangely compelling. I notice a nearly empty glass of champagne in her hand. "I've heard quite a bit about you, and I must say you look just *darling* this evening!"

"Thank you, ma'am. You look lovely yourself."

"Oh, why, you're too kind. How old are you dear?"

"I'm eighteen."

"Ah! The same age as my daughter, you must meet her,

she's around somewhere. Why, right there. Breanna! Breanna over here!"

Breanna is slightly shorter than me, wearing a rosy pink dress with an empire waist. She has the same tanned olive skin as her mother, and her earth-colored hair is twisted up in an intricate bun. She looks at me with a mixture of fear and envy, the gold pearls studding her mask glittering in the dim lighting.

"I must speak with a few other guests, but I'm sure we'll be seeing plenty of each other in the future. Ta-ta!" sings Arcane. She gives us a fluttering wave and disappears. While Pierre is serene and unassuming, Arcane is a whirlwind of a person, flitting between people with ease and impact.

"Why don't you go off and dance," suggests Pierre softly. "Relax a bit. I'm sure you'll feel better once you mingle with a few more people. Breanna, will you take her?"

He hands me a glass filled with champagne as I slip into the crowd with his niece.

"Don't get too comfortable," Breanna hisses in my ear. And then she's gone. Fine.

Unsure of my destination, I sip the dry, bitter drink delicately, trying to look occupied. An arm loops lightly around my waist, and River is there, guiding me along.

"How'd your little chat go?" he murmurs, calculating eyes lost behind his mask.

"Fine, but strange." I find some comfort in River's presence, knowing I'm not entirely alone in this ordeal. "What do we do now?"

"We dance." He smiles slightly at the dance floor and we blend seamlessly with the revolving cycle of people.

The music is a steady thrumming that I can feel through the floor as I swallow another dreg from my glass. It's a grounding noise among all the floating voices. Neither of us know the specific dance to match the song, but no one seems to notice as long as we keep moving. Eventually everyone switches partners and I get pulled away, finding myself face to face with Jax.

"Having fun?" He smirks.

"Oh, yes, lots," I mutter, glancing over my shoulder. Pierre is where I left him, chatting with guests and occasionally gesturing in my direction.

"Corinne, is that vial still on you?" Jax asks. His tone is different, urgent, tense.

"Uh, no. I left it upstairs. Why?"

He purses his lips. "Nothing, never mind, you'll be fine."

Before I can push for answers, we switch partners again, and I find River.

"How much longer do we have to be here?" he asks under his breath. I don't answer, head spinning. I lift my glass to my lips, fingers trembling. I grimace as the last of it goes down, tickling my throat. A server passes with a tray and I exchange my empty cup for a full one. The words from the notes fill my head, words blending together on the memory. What did it mean? Who was Candol? Who were the two girls he mentioned?

I chug my glass, grabbing another from the next server to pass. We switch.

"Enjoying the party, darling?" Pierre's blood-colored mask swims in my vision, his too-large grin seeming unnaturally bright in my muddled sight.

"Great..." I mumble, finishing off my glass.

"Go easy on the drinks, darling."

"Sure."

Back to River.

"Jesus Corinne. We should get you back," he says, grimacing. I take another sip from my glass, and he takes it from my hand. "Alright enough of that. How many did you have?"

I shrug, leaning heavily on him. He grunts with the effort

of keeping me upright and calls Jax over. They exchange a few words that I can't make out. Jax leaves. The music fills my head. People and colors blend in my vision.

We're in the hallway now, me, River, and Jax. They each duck under one of my arms, River slinging the strap of my mask over his head so it hangs around his neck. Jax checks my forehead as we head upstairs.

I can hear them whispering, and my name comes up several times. Moments later, Selena's face appears, looking blurry. We're in my room. Rowan's there, too. He and River start arguing while Selena brings me to the bathroom and gets me out of my dress. Soft clothes. Jax is back now, holding the vile. How did he know where it was? He makes me drink it and it takes all my strength not to spit it out.

"What is that?" I complain, wiping my mouth.

"One of your glasses was spiked."

"With what?"

"Something that works quick, probably ketamine or something else of that sort. A couple glasses of champagne won't do that on their own."

"Who?"

"Who did it? No idea. It could have been anyone."

My head is already clearing up, words making more sense now. At the very least, the world has stopped spinning.

I process Selena's presence next to me, concern radiating from her. Rowan and River are still arguing.

"I'm fine now. I'll be fine," I say, pushing myself unsteadily to my feet. The boys' voices are making my head pound.

When Rowan sees me, he stops talking. River looks exhausted.

"My god, Corinne, are you okay?" he presses, walking over.

"Fine, fine. What's all the noise?"

"Nothing, don't worry." He gently tilts my head up, looking into my eyes. "How many did you have?"

"A couple."

River approaches, saying, "It was my fault, so I'll sleep on the floor in here in case you get sick. Selena shouldn't have to clean anything up if worse comes to worse."

"Don't be ridiculous," I slur, swaying. "It was nobody's fault but mine. I shouldn't even have had any in the first place, I just got carried away."

"He's right though, but not for that reason," adds Jax. "Honestly I think you should all sleep in here just to be safe. Someone spiked Corinne's drink for a reason."

"Selena, it's your call," I say, squeezing her hand.

"Go grab some blankets." She gives me a knowing smile. "The more, the merrier."

## Chapter 11

# Corinne

I roll over and glance at the clock on the nightstand. 2:46 a.m.

I listen to the noises in the room. Selena's light snoring from the bed next to mine. The occasional rustle of blankets as one of the boys turns over on the floor. As my eyes adjust to the dark, I notice Rowan's blankets are empty. Panic rises for a moment, and I sit up straight, scanning the space.

Light spills under the bathroom door and I hear the sink running for a moment. The door opens and Rowan's silhouette appears in the doorframe. He pauses, clicks off the light, and pads over.

"Can't sleep?" he whispers. I shake my head, scooting over and patting the mattress next to me. He sits down, one leg hanging over the edge.

"I have a little bit of a headache," I admit. In reality, it's a full-on migraine that feels as though it's knotting my nerves into little yarn balls. His eyes shimmer with amusement and something else; concern maybe. I pause, unsure what to do with his gaze.

"I wonder what from."

"Funny. That all you needed?"

"No, just trying to lighten the mood." He's quiet, thinking. A light burning is all that foreshadows the unprompted tears, and I wipe them away viciously. He notices and moves closer.

"Did I say something?"

I snort, laughing quietly, but through the tears it sounds flat. "No. Just—everything."

I feel him adjust so he's sitting next to me instead of facing me. Tentatively, he takes my hand and winds his fingers between mine, holding on like a lifeline. Or maybe that's me who's holding on so tightly.

My chest tightens as my mind descends towards chaos, torn between wanting the comfort and the fear of getting too close.

"Do you want to talk about it, or be distracted from it?" he intones.

"Distracted," I whisper. Rowan carefully untangles his hand from mine and wraps his arms around my shoulders, pulling me close. I inhale sharply. This isn't what I expected.

"My mom used to ask me that question when I was upset," he murmurs. "If I wanted to talk about it, we'd talk. If I didn't, she'd wrap me in a blanket and we'd sit just like this. Either I ended up talking about whatever was bothering me, or I'd fall asleep." He laughs quietly, and the noise fills my head. The steady rhythm of his heartbeat and the rise and fall on his chest lulls me into a space somewhere between sleep and consciousness.

He doesn't say anything else, only traces his fingers over my shoulder until I fall back asleep, dreams plagued by sheets of notes.

*Chapter 12*

# Selena

Weak sunlight pours through the window, illuminating the dust floating in the air. It takes me more than a minute to remember everything, and I swallow the tears rising to the surface as it all comes back.

Glancing over at Corinne, she seems to be reaching for someone in her sleep. Rowan's blankets are neatly folded and stacked, and he's asleep in one of the chairs near the bathroom, next to a small wooden coffee table.

I slide out of bed, remaking it to the best of my ability and tiptoeing over to the bathroom. I find a toothbrush and a bottle of toothpaste under the sink, as well as a pile of washcloths.

After cleaning myself up, I walk back outside and over to the window where I put the flowers. I arrange and rearrange them, trying to distract myself until the others wake up. It doesn't take long. Rowan wakes from my fidgeting and River is up next. Corinne rises last, grimacing at the bright sunlight.

"What's on today's agenda?" she asks, stretching. Her eyes go to Rowan, whose gaze is already on her.

"Hopefully," says River, "no more parties."

A knock comes from the door. "Jax?" Corinne wonders

aloud. River moves to open it, revealing a girl perhaps a year or two older than us. She blinks, and smiles sweetly.

"I'm here for cleaning," she informs us, stepping in. When she notices the blankets on the floor, she frowns. "Were your beds unsatisfactory?"

"Oh, not at all," hurries Corinne. "Our friends slept in our room last night."

"Was something the matter with their room?"

"Not that either. We just—we had a bit of a scare last night."

I take in her presence, her flawless dusky skin and pale gray eyes, so shiny they look silver. She's pretty short, too, shorter than Corinne, with delicate features. But there's an air about her that suggests she's seen more than most.

"Oh. Alright then. You're Corinne, yes?" she inquires.

Corinne masks her surprise well, responding with, "Yes, and you?"

"My name is Lilac. I saw you last night at the party. Quite the favorite with Mr. Dolion."

"Ah, the party," Corinne echoes, blushing. "Not my best moment."

"But certainly one of your last."

The air in the room goes still, fear's icy fingers touching every one of us.

"What did you say?" I whisper. My sister is frozen, staring at Lilac with wide eyes.

"I said 'but certainly one of her last,'" she repeats. Her smile disappearing as she addresses me. "It is very unlikely that she will survive the procedure."

"Whoa, we were told she was being cured," interjects Rowan. River's gaze skitters back and forth between us all as the scene unfolds. Lilac clears her throat.

"Not quite. To remove the mutation means to remove pieces of the brain stem. It will result in brain death. He will try to isolate the corrupted genes and amplify them within your DNA before extraction. If he plans on using it, it must be potent. Often too potent for the original host to handle."

Corinne collapses onto the mattress, head in her hands, unblinking.

"What have I done," she whispers. "Jax told me the notes were outdated. They didn't matter. Why would he lie? The vile, why would he give me the vile?"

I move to her side, holding her head against my chest and trying to calm her down. It's mostly pointless; I can see the hysteria in her eyes.

"How do you know this? Why are you telling us?" I ask, my voice quivering.

"I was there when he figured it out. As for why I am divulging this is for personal reasons that do not concern you."

"It does if it's her life on the line!"

"We have to get out," declares Rowan, already on his feet, scanning the room. "I didn't like this place for a reason. It was too perfect."

"Hold on," I say, stroking Corinne's hair. "Just hold on. You're getting yourself worked up. We don't know the layout of this place or where we are once we get out. We have no supplies and no destination. Kleka could be wiped off the maps for all we know."

Rowan groans in frustration, running his hands through his hair as he thinks. River still only watches, holding his tongue. Corinne sits up slowly, looking again at Lilac who still stands next to the open door, hands folded in front of her.

"You know how to get out, don't you?" she asks, something in her voice changing.

Lilac nods.

"How?"

"First," Lilac exclaims, her high voice startling us all, "I'm coming with you. And so is a friend." All of us nod. I suppose it's more than fair, but that's a lot of people. "Second, I have information you need, so I'll have to find time to tell you. And third, it *will* take time. From what I heard Mr. Dolion speak of last evening, your abilities have not yet developed, Corinne. That's good. It *buys* time. I have been waiting for someone like you for six years, so we will have to trust each other. Is it a deal?"

*Chapter 13*

# Corinne

Day four of practice.

Pierre has been calling me down for five hours daily to start developing my abilities. The first two days, nothing happened. On day three, I felt like my vision was a little sharper, my hearing a little clearer. He thinks I might have enhanced senses. When he said it, he was hesitant, almost disappointed. I guess he thought our first discovery would be bigger.

"Focus, darling, look for the warmth," he murmurs, clasping my hands between his. This is how it goes, every day. Focus, breathe, listen. Breathe, focus, feel. Over and over again.

I keep my eyes shut tight, thinking of the sun, and campfires, and hot sand until I feel a glow inside my chest. I visualize myself dipping my hand into the light, feeling the warm air soaking into my skin.

A switch flips.

Pain, nothing but pain. I can hear the individual strands of hair on my head shifting against one another. The beating of my and Pierre's hearts sounds like cymbals in my head. The weight of my eyelashes and the feel of each fiber in my clothing feels like thousands of ants wielding pins. I can see the different shades of black in Pierre's eyes as they shift from iris to pupil. Even the air has texture. It's too much, everything all at once.

Pierre's fingers brush my shoulder and live flames move underneath my skin. I scream I think. Everything is drowned out. I just hear white noise.

Then the taste of lemon juice mixed with salt like hellfire pours down my throat.

I black out only for a moment before coming back to my senses—my *normal* senses. Mostly normal anyway. The light is still too bright and I'm still too aware of my clothing chafing against my skin.

"Are you back, darling?"

I push myself up; I must have fallen. Pierre is watching me with curious eyes, as if I'm his little lab rat who has just done a strange new trick.

"Fine," I mumble, rubbing my eyes.

"I'm terribly sorry, I had no idea that your first full contact would have you act up so strongly. Rest the remainder of the day and we'll resume tomorrow."

"What happened?"

"Our suspicions were correct. You possess the ability to enhance your senses. Unfortunately, they all went full power at exactly the same time, and you were probably slightly overstimulated. I had you swallow one of the vitamins you used to take in Kleka to shut them down before you passed out entirely."

My head is still spinning as I stumble back to my room, feeling my way along the wall. The coarseness of the paint under my fingertips is sharp and clear.

Selena is lying on her bed with a book in her hands. It's clear she isn't really reading, just skimming. When she notices my presence, the book is placed face-down on the bed.

"I'll grab the boys."

***

"Tell me again?" requests Rowan.

"Just, an overload. I'm not sure how else to say it," I admit. I'm not too inclined to relive those few seconds, either.

River and Selena sit back and look off into the distance, eyes unfocused.

A slip of paper slides across the floor from under the door. All four heads turn. I move to grab it but River beats me to it; he has incredibly quick reflexes.

"It's from Lilac. She's going to stop over later to let us in on some details regarding how she thinks we can get out. How much longer do you think we have, Corinne?"

"Until—?"

"Until Pierre decides the time has come to start planning for extraction." The words echo in the following silence. None of us want to consider it, least of all me.

"I'm not sure," I murmur.

"It'll work out," Selena assures me, squeezing my hand.

The four of us wait around the room for a few hours until Lilac knocks on the door and lets herself in. She's no longer wearing her work clothes, but true to her name, a delicate purple shirt and a white tea-length skirt that flows around her knees.

"Sit," she requests, perching on the edge of one of the beds. Her hands are folded neatly on her lap. Her thin fingers are knotted loosely together.

We pull over the four chairs that are scattered about the room and place them in a clumsy semi-circle in front of her.

"Before anything else, I want to say sorry, Corinne. I must have given you a scare last time we spoke. You don't have to leave if you'd prefer to stay. I was pushy. It's up to you and your friends," she says.

"It's tricky," I admit. "Believe me, I don't exactly want

to be here. But—where would we go? I mean, we know nothing about what's happening in Kleka. We don't even know where this facility is located. And—honestly—he has a sound goal. If he could create a cure for all of the Changed with one mutation, I'm sure I could convince him to keep looking for another, someone willing to die for the cause."

"No way," argues Rowan. "We're not staying here. You're not staying here. You could *die,* Corinne."

Lilac lays a hand on his arm, saying, "Let me handle this." She turns to me, silver eyes exploring my face. "Let me tell you about this place. I was brought here eight years ago by a team of hired bounty hunters. Not hired by the government, but by Mr. Dolion. I was eleven.

"He rounded up hundreds just like me of all ages. I saw a girl who was only six, her abilities just starting to show themselves. She made the most dreary things into the most beautiful, colorful objects with a tap of her finger. But now she's dead, her colors stolen, stripped from her very skin.

"Mr. Dolion's pristine facility wasn't always so nice. We were the first test subjects, his lab rats. He performed experiments on every one of us, relentlessly looking for a treatment. I remember the first person to respond positively to the tests. He was glorified, moved into the closer circles of Mr. Dolion's favorites. He was finally making progress. Until that successful patient's abilities returned so potent that he destroyed himself. He cooked from the inside out, and also burned down a good chunk of the building.

"Mr. Dolion's labs may seem clean and tidy, but they're anything but. Changed like you and me are rounded up and brought here, given treatment and used as guinea pigs for his newest ideas. Once 'cured', they're given a place to stay. And most do stay. Most want the security that 'normalcy' so falsely offers. People are free to leave, of course, that's what he says. I made a friend about halfway through my stay here who once cured, asked to leave. I never saw nor heard from her again. Since her disappearance, I've been waiting for someone like you. Mr. Dolion has, too. He needed someone with such a strange and powerful mutation to create a permanent cure. And you stumbled right into his grasp.

"But the thing is, Mr. Dolion doesn't only want to create a cure. It's on his agenda, but not his priority. Ever since he began his work, he has started collecting as many powerful mutations as possible. He calls them Forces because they're entirely random and so dangerously potent. And you were a lead, a chance, an accidental discovery. He brought you in, ran the standard tests, and would have sent you down to the labs had he not discovered the discrepancies in your DNA."

Lilac's voice fades away. She has told her part, and waits for our reactions. Selena is the first to react.

"Why the collection? Why keep all the Forces after curing them?" she asks, her gaze distant.

"Just another of the many missing puzzle pieces," she sighs. "But they're—different. Cured and yet quiet, subdued somehow. The mutations are only switched off, not removed in these 'cures'. It would take another, more difficult, reversal surgery to reactivate them."

"What about your ability?" inquires River.

"I used to be able to hear the trees speaking to one another, to me. I used to be able to hear the songs the wind would weave, but I can't anymore. It was taken from me."

My own body feels heavy, loaded with lead. Lilac is right about the normalcy. It smothers you, convinces you to stay. The feeling of security, a safety net, it's all spider webs and smoke.

"So where is this place? And how has no one noticed the disappearances outside?" I voice my questions to Lilac, feeling sick to my stomach.

"The facility is located at the bottom of what used to

be called Lake Superior. It's just another nameless body of water now," she informs me.

"How? The windows—"

"Artificial lights and holograms. Confuses the mind. As for the disappearances, they were all Mutations. People notice, but no one cares. Less trouble for the Unchanged."

"So we get out, expose this place, and shut it down," presses Rowan. "*Someone* has to care."

Lilac frowns slightly. "Mr. Dolion is employed by the government. His work is funded, supported. But he despises the system, always has, and that is the part that confuses me most."

## Chapter 14

# Corinne

Lilac gave us a map of our floor of the building before she left. "I have to report back to work," she said. Her absence would be noticed and reported.

I scan the paper again. There is a blue X marking our rooms, a red one blotting out Pierre's private office, and a half dozen green circles around each service elevator. Since the facility is at the bottom of a lake, the only way in and out is through six massive elevators. They're used to get people, food, medical supplies, the works in and out. The seventh elevator is in Pierre's office. It is probably only big enough for him and some security in the case of an emergency.

Lilac also told us that we wouldn't be able to meet the other escapee until we're actually in the process of getting out. It's too risky otherwise.

As for the getting out itself, getting to the elevators is step one. Traveling in a group of four is too obvious, so we'll have to stagger our timing and be familiar with the route. Step two is getting on the elevator and staying out of sight. There are the security guards, too, of course. Everyone who comes in and out is recorded and checked for ID. We'll have to hide in cargo boxes or something before they're even loaded. It's perfect, actually, because once supplies are shipped down, the crates are emptied, sorted, and then sent back up to be reused.

Then there's where we go after we're out. Lilac claims she knows a place where we can hide, bide our time. It's not a promise, and it's not pretty, but it's all we have right now.

Selena pulls me from my train of thought with a tap on the shoulder. "How are you holding up? Do you want something to eat?"

"I'm fine, just exhausted. The lights are still a little bright. And I'm anxious. Okay, maybe I'm not so fine," I laugh, a quick, short release of sound. Selena smiles and tugs on my braid, saying she'll go find something to eat.

River has been rather withdrawn as usual, lost in thought. He does that a lot. But Rowan is like an apprehensive cat, pacing, looking out the window, sitting down for a minute then standing back up to check the time. He must feel lost. He has nothing to do, and it makes him antsy.

"Rowan, could I get your help for a minute?" I ask. Maybe he just needs a distraction, something to focus his mind. He moves quickly to my side, bouncing on the balls of his feet.

"How goes the plan, chosen one?" he asks, a smile flickering over his lips.

I sigh. "Not great. I still don't like the fact that we have nowhere to go."

"Once we get out, we can go back to Kleka, scope it out. I think though that we have to have faith in Lilac. She's been here way longer than we have, and if what she said earlier is true, she probably hears a lot about the goings-on outside from new Mutes."

"I suppose."

"Hey," Rowan glances at the maps again, "do you want to take a walk and scope out the place in person? It might do us some good to get familiar with the route."

I nod, pushing my chair back and stretching. My neck

feels stiff from leaning over the table for an hour. It's a good idea to look around, and no one should think anything of it. Pierre gave me the rest of the day off so I don't have anything planned until tomorrow's practice. I glance once more at the map, committing the turns to memory before we head out the door.

River doesn't even glance up at us as we pass.

Rowan and I make small talk as we walk. Several workers pass, throwing us curious glances, but no one stops us. There is no sign of Lilac or Pierre.

The loading dock area is enormous, at the very least the size of a football field. I've never actually seen one in person since it's a dead sport, but I know they're supposed to be huge. Rowan and I stand in a hallway outside, peeking around the corner. Giant crates and cargo boxes litter the space in a seemingly organized chaos. People hurry in between, barking orders and moving supplies. On the walls on either side of the room, six massive lifts open and close as materials are moved up and down through the water.

"Look at the guards," whispers Rowan. I jump; I thought he was farther behind me. I turn my attention to the people in all white standing at lift entrances, calmly strolling the space and occasionally speaking to a worker.

"Weren't the people we saw in Kleka wearing black?" I ask.

"My thoughts exactly. I'm thinking there are different groups with different jobs. The ones in white stay in the facility, and the ones in black are the people who go out to round up Mutes and ransack towns."

It shouldn't be funny, but the whole situation is so ridiculous that I can't help but snicker. Seriously, a mad scientist performing lethal experiments at the bottom of a lake. It's crazy. And it finally hits me how real this whole thing is, that if we don't get out, we could all lose our lives. If I had remained ignorant of the outcomes and died during extraction, would the others be sent down to the labs? Picked apart like pomegranates?

"What?" Rowan grins, elbowing me.

"Just—look at all this. Only what? A week or so ago? You were about to interrogate us for wanting to leave the city."

He smiles again, then casts one more look into the loading dock before we start heading back.

River is gone by the time we return to my room, and Selena is nowhere to be found.

"So, how do you propose we get out?" I ask once we're both seated. Both our legs bounce up and down in a frantic rhythm.

"I suppose our only realistic option is to get in one of the crates. Now that I think about it, it's perfect actually. Because they send empty crates back up, we just have to make sure that we're not all in one crate so it isn't strangely heavy." Rowan stares intently at me, waiting for a response. The cornhusk green of his eyes is bewitching, shifting in the afternoon light.

"Your eyes are really pretty," I blurt out.

Rowan draws back, surprised, then laughs. Embarrassment surges underneath my skin as my brain catches up to my mouth, but his smile distracts me. One side curves up and the other down, making him look like he has a secret.

"What I meant—I mean—I've never seen the color before," I stammer.

"I guess it's not a very common shade," he muses, leaning back in his seat.

Selena saves me by tripping into the room, barely keeping a tray level in her hands. I spring to my feet and steady her.

"Sorry, it took a while to find someone." She sets down the tray on a side table and sits on the edge of the bed. "Did you two scope out anything?"

"Yeah," says Rowan, yawning. "We checked out the loading dock. Figure we'll have to split up into twos or something and hide in the empty crates that get shipped back up to the surface."

Selena nods, and then wanders over to her flowers by the window. Silence falls.

***

Three days later, another slip of paper slides under my door. Rowan and River are in their room, and Selena is in the shower. It has only two words written on it:

*Tonight. Midnight.*

I suck in a breath and tear the note into pieces.

Trainings with Pierre have only gotten more intense, and I hardly have control over my enhanced senses. We've been trying to isolate the senses, to amplify only one at a time, but it hurts. He's frustrated, too, although he hides it well. Panic grips my stomach. Will I ever get the hang of my abilities without his help?

*Stop. Don't let his honeyed words get inside your head.*

I walk to the window and shut my eyes, holding my breath as long as possible. When I let it go, I try to let the silence become tangible, let the quiet slide between my fingers. It's one of the methods Pierre's been having me try to find sounds that normally aren't audible to the average human's ear. But that's all I hear. The quiet.

There's a pressure on my waist, a warm hand with steady fingers.

Fear seizes my heart, and launches it into my throat. Instincts take over as I whirl around, swinging a fist at the person behind me.

Rowan dodges and misses the brunt of the punch, but I still barely catch his jaw.

"Damn, you're quick. I didn't mean to scare you, sorry." He winces as he flexes his jaw, the skin already beginning to redden.

"Oh my God, I'm so sorry," I gasp, cringing. "It's a reflex." I kneel down and tilt his chin up to get a closer look. "It'll probably bruise."

"Don't worry about it."

My hand lingers on his jaw for a moment before I let it drop.

"What are you doing in here, anyway?" I ask.

"I knocked, but no one answered. River's walking around, and I didn't really want to hang out by myself." He smiles.

"Well, get ready, because we're getting out tonight."

## Chapter 15

# Corinne

At night, the stark, fluorescent lights of the hallways are dimmer. Footsteps are few and far between, replaced by a steady humming of pipes and the building settling. Selena and I walk briskly, sticking to the shadows just in case.

Rowan and River left a half hour earlier, and Lilac and her friend will be at the dock in twenty minutes.

The massive room and its enormous crates is still busy, but much quieter than during the day. Selena and I walk with purpose down the aisles. There's no way to sneak around, so the hope is that if we look like we're supposed to be there, then no one will bother us.

"You two, these crates are due for departure in thirty minutes, what are you doing in here?" The man who spoke the words walks towards us briskly, head high. He's wearing a white uniform; security.

"Just learning the layout," I say.

"This area is off limits for non-essential workers."

"I'm not a worker, sir. My name is Corinne." Recognition flashes in his eyes and he nods, business-like.

"My apologies. Feel free to look around. Just make sure you're gone before *they* start moving the crates." He smiles slyly before continuing on his way.

Once he's out of sight, I lean over to Selena, whispering, "Who's they?" She shrugs, lips pursed.

We wander the area, weaving between crates as we look for a quiet place with no one around. Finally, it happens. We're shielded from the cameras and two workers are unloading one of the last crates. When their backs are turned, Selena and I slip into the space, ducking behind some empty cardboard boxes just as a horn blows.

"That's our cue," one of the workers sighs.

"Wait, give it a moment. Dolion is on his way."

"At this hour? The Souls are about to be let out."

"Must be important then."

A pause, then footsteps. Pierre's voice joins the two outside, and I freeze. I can feel my heartbeat in my ears. My breathing is shallow.

"This is the last one, correct?" he asks. There's a note of urgency behind his honey words.

"Yes, sir. Just finished unloading."

"Perfect. This will be the last outgoing shipment for a little while. The facility will be in temporary lockdown as we approach the operation. No one comes in or out after this shipment."

"Fine. We'll see to it."

Footsteps recede, and I let go of a breath I didn't even know I was holding.

"I'll do one last scan of the crate, make sure we didn't miss anything in here."

And just like that, the dissipating fear returns full blast. The worker steps into the crate and starts shuffling the boxes around.

"We got everything, relax."

"Just making sure." The box above my head moves and I see the man's hand. I shrink back against the wall and floor, making myself as small as possible. Selena is across from me, eyes wide and frozen. I press my hand hard against my mouth to stifle the sound of my breathing.

"Seriously, Joe, come on. I don't want to be in here when they let the Souls out."

Joe pauses, then sighs. "Fine, but if the count is off, don't blame me." His hand disappears and when the crate is closed, the sound of their voices can no longer be heard. I release my shaking breath, collapsing in relief.

"You think Lilac and her friend got here on time?" Selena whispers, scooting over to my side. I wrap my arm around her shoulders and hug her tight.

"I hope so. We don't have anywhere to go if they don't make it."

She squeezes my hand and pulls back.

Jax crosses my mind just then, and I'm not sure why. A pang of guilt makes me cringe. We never told him we were leaving. Sure, he works for Pierre, seems pretty close to him in fact, but he seemed like he trusted us. I wish we could have brought him in on this.

All of a sudden, an ear-splitting shriek echoes through the loading dock, but it is muffled and distorted through our metal confinement. I push myself up to my knees, peering through a rusted-out hole in the side of the crate. Tall, skinny creatures pour into the room, lunging at each other and lifting the empty crates like they weigh nothing. I recognize them as the same nightmarish monsters that we saw in the forest outside of Kleka. One of them reaches for our crate, sending Selena and I tumbling when we're lifted off the ground.

The crate is stacked among others, presumably in one of the gargantuan lifts. I slam into the floor as we're set down, seeing stars in my vision. The sounds of metal sliding on metal echo all around us as more crates are stacked on top of each other.

Once the clanging stops, we start moving up, the lift whirring and straining. It's dark inside the crate, and neither of us move. Only a couple minutes pass before we jerk to a stop. I struggle to the peephole in the wall, my head still throbbing.

The lift doors are open, and more Souls are pacing anxiously outside. Moonlight—real moonlight—streams in, illuminating their features.

Their eyes are like curdled milk and stare blankly ahead, two slits roughly in the center of their faces serve as a nose. Each bone is a prominent crease or lump in their distorted, stretched out bodies, and when they open their lipless mouths, I'm greeted with rows upon rows of sharp, needle-like teeth. They protrude from the Souls' smooth, round heads. Icy fear trickles down my spine.

"How do we get out?" whispers Selena. It's a solid question, one we didn't consider. The latches are on the outside, and who knows when they'll open the crates again. They might leave them in here until they're needed again. Pierre did say they'd be pausing all shipments.

But it turns out we don't need to worry because through the hole, I see one of the Souls rush another, screeching. The two start fighting, swinging their long arms at each other's heads. More of the monsters join, apparently taking sides until nearly all of the ones I can see are shoving each other around.

The first two stumble towards the piles of crates. One of them grabs the second by the shoulders and hurls it into our pile. I'm thrown from my lookout point as our crate slides off its perch with a metallic shriek and tumbles to the floor of the lift. The door buckles and pops open when we land. More crates are knocked over as the fight escalates, and somehow we manage not to get crushed.

Selena drags me to my feet, shouting something I can't

hear. We make a move towards our now open door, but a Soul's face blocks it. It stares at us, grinning, and begins to reach into the crate with an outstretched claw. We scream, stumbling backwards to avoid its talons.

There's a blur of movement. A second Soul barrels into the first one from the side, sending them both into yet another stack of crates.

There's a ripping sound before the two disappear from sight, a crack and something splatters against my face. I flinch and look down. Black blood stains my clothes and skin. One long, snake-like arm wraps around the edge of the crate. It is bent and disfigured. I drop to my knees and clamp my mouth shut to stop the bile. Bone protrudes from the shoulder area, sinewy muscle dangling in tattered strips from the torn flesh.

"Corinne, we have to go!" Selena screams. She tugs me to my feet again and we sprint for the opening of the lift. I set my sights on the tree line, just a hundred feet from the door.

A piercing alarm goes off and I flinch, nearly falling over. Dozens of people in white stream in from side doors, yelling orders and dodging rogue Souls. I do my best to ignore them and focus on my destination.

We reach the trees, panting and shaking and covered in sticky black blood. Selena collapses against a tree. I can barely stay upright. Branches snap and the boys appear. I grab Rowan's shirt as he flies by, halting him. River notices and spins around, dropping low to stay out of sight.

I can distantly hear the breaking of waves, and barely make out a strip of water, black in the night. The moon glistens and scatters over the unruly surface.

"Thank God you made it," I exhale. "How'd you get out of the crate?"

"Don't really remember. It was mostly a blur," Rowan

says. River casts a look his way, and I note the faint smell of burnt—*something*. "You?"

"Our crate got knocked off and the door flew off," says Selena, leaning her head back. "Did you see Lilac at all?"

Just as Rowan shakes his head, Lilac stumbles into sight, gasping for air. Another girl follows close behind, and my blood runs cold.

"Breanna?"

## Chapter 16

# Corinne

Arcane's daughter. Pierre's *niece.*

"What the hell is she doing here?" I ask, shooting to my feet.

"Relax," says Lilac, stepping between us. "She's on our side."

Breanna glares at me, arms crossed defensively. The intricate hairstyle is gone, her short, brown hair brushing just past her shoulders.

"Who is she?" asks Selena, standing next to me.

"Pierre's niece. Her mom runs another lab in Linaria. I had the pleasure of meeting her at the masquerade event. Was it you who spiked my drink?"

"So what if it was? The party was boring. Everyone would have come to your aid anyway," she scoffs. "Pierre's little chosen one."

"It's not like I wanted to be kidnapped."

"Maybe not, but you sure took advantage of your status." Lilac grabs both of our wrists, yanking us to her.

"If you're done bickering, let's go. The longer we stand here, the more likely it is that they'll find us. If Mr. Dolion hasn't discovered your absence already, he will very shortly," she hisses. Breanna twists free of Lilac's grip and shoots me another death glare.

The shriek of a Soul reaches us, getting louder by the second.

"Scatter!" shouts River. We all book it into the trees just as a Soul bursts into the space, milky eyes blazing. Its arms swing wildly as it searches for anything to grab.

Selena screams as it catches her by the leg and drags her backwards. She tries to twist her body out of its grip, but the monster is too fast. It holds her by one leg upside down in the air as she struggles like a caged animal. But it's no use. The Soul backhands her with its ginormous clawed hands and her eyes roll back in her head. Her body is now as limp as a rag doll. The sharp, black claws leave three long gashes across her face. Her scarlet blood stains its hand as it drips onto the dirt below.

I scream, doing a full one-eighty and running back to my sister. But River is already there. Somehow, he has scaled one of the trees and now lunges for the Soul's head. I notice the sharp rock in his hand just as he drags in across the neck of the creature.

Selena drops like a stone, and I reach her just before she hits the ground. My breath is knocked out of my body, but Selena is safe. I try to wake her, but she's out cold.

I haul her over my shoulder fireman-style and move away from the Souls as quickly as possible. River drops from its back and follows closely. The Soul retreats into the open area in front of the lift, its screams quieting with the distance.

We regroup several yards later and silently continue deeper into the trees until Lilac changes directions, going left. More walking.

Day begins to break. Hesitant ribbons of sunlight break through the treetops and scatter fragments of gold light on the forest floor. We stop for a moment, and I set Selena down. She groans, slowly coming back around.

Her face is swollen where the Soul broke skin. Blood has dried around the cuts.

"The trees are moving," murmurs River. Everyone stills,

listening. We hear the creaking of wood and groaning of the dirt as it releases the roots of the trees. A quiet wind pushes the leaves around and cools my skin. The silence feels stifling after the raucous.

"There's a little town on the shoreline a little further South," says Lilac, kneeling next to Selena. "We'll want to get her some medical attention to avoid infection."

The streets are still vacant when we reach the town. An early morning mist has settled over the place. Sealing it off from the rest of the world, and yet so close to Pierre's labs.

We wait on one of the floating docks while Lilac stops in at the pharmacy. When I ask her how she'll pay for things, she reminds me that the workers in Pierre's camp are paid for their service even though most don't ever have reason to use the money. I sit with her when she returns, cleaning around Selena's wounds with hydrogen peroxide and covering them with a bandage.

"I also picked up some painkillers if it bothers her too much." Lilac hands me a little pill bottle and I tuck it in my pocket.

Selena stirs again, eyes fluttering open. We smile at each other and I kiss her cheek before going down to the water. I wash my face and arms, trying to clean the black blood from my skin. Even when it's gone, my skin burns.

Rowan calls me back up a moment later.

"People will be getting up soon, and Lilac's getting anxious," he informs me. Once she's assured Selena is feeling more stable, she herds us towards the street again, then into a tiny alley between two brick buildings. A slight depression in the asphalt holds a storm drain, which Lilac removes.

"Please, please, please," she mutters, peering into the darkness. "Looks like the rumors were true. There's a ladder on the side, so take turns going down and hold on tight. It's probably slippery."

Selena is the first one down with River supporting her until she grabs the ladder. He follows closely. Rowan, Breanna, then Lilac. I'm the last one, pulling the grate back over the opening before descending.

The ladder isn't too long, but my foot slips on one of the last few rungs and I drop to the ground off-balance. Rowan's arm steadies me. I can barely make out his face in the fractured light from above, and the rest of the space is lost in darkness. The echo of Lilac's voice gives me a clue that we're in a tunnel system of sorts.

I find my sister. "You okay?" I ask.

"It stings a little, but not too bad," she croaks, smiling weakly. I squeeze her hand in relief.

"There should be another passageway in here. Look for any side doors or trapdoors. I'm not really sure," she says.

"What about a boarded-up hole in the wall?" inquires River. He is in fact examining a hole in the wall, about three feet up from the ground and blocked off by a sheet of damp, rotting plywood. He rams his shoulder into the center, breaking it on the first try and prying off the edges.

Lilac leads this time, hoisting herself up into the tiny tunnel. Rowan shrugs and hops in next. I follow, inhaling a lungful of stale dust. The space is cramped and I feel suffocated on all sides. Little rocks and broken glass prick my forearms as I shuffle along.

A deep rumble grows, getting louder. I can feel the reverberations in the ground all around me, and my heartbeat picks up speed. My body freezes, limbs locked. Cracks spider-web across the ceiling, dropping dust and pebbles.

"Turn back!" yells River, cursing. I twist my body in the direction we came from, but my body isn't responding to my thoughts.

"Keep going, Corinne!" coughs Rowan, now behind me. "The tunnel's collapsing!" I jerk forward, shaken from my trance. The sound of crumbling dirt and rock shakes the passage, and I whirl around for the second time. I can see the rock falling behind us, closing in and thickening the air with dust. I grab Rowan's hands and haul him forward, the rubble just barely missing his legs and skidding to a stop inches from us.

My arms are locked around his waist, both of us breathing heavily. My heart is racing at an inhuman speed, the brush with death sharpening my senses and making me jittery.

"Thanks," he whispers hoarsely, climbing off and helping me sit up.

"Anytime," I assure, taking in a gulp of air. Bad idea. Dust and particles of rock make their way into my lungs and I cough.

"Where's Lilac?" asks Breanna, voice panicked. I peer behind Rowan, but there's nothing but the new wall of the rock. My heart sinks.

"She was ahead of me," Rowan exhales, dragging a hand over his face. "Goddammit."

Breanna squeezes her eyes shut and chokes on her tears. My eyes prick and I swipe at my face viciously.

"What do we do?" Selena asks, expression distant. Looking around I notice that the dirt has shifted to reveal an opening in the side of the tunnel. I can see a wall maybe four feet in front of it, but only darkness below. Selena is sitting right in front of it.

I call out to warn her, but it's too late. She leans back and disappears, her screams echoing as she plummets down the gap.

"Selena!" I yell again. I edge towards the opening, peering into the darkness. I blink, and then something clicks. Vertigo poisons my mind, barely able to keep my balance as my vision lengthens and sharpens.

I can see all the way down, even though it should be pitch

black. I gasp as I struggle and fail to regain control of my senses. It's water, and I whimper in a mixture of relief and concern when I see my sister swimming towards a not-so-distant shore. I'm not a very strong swimmer. "Rowan, can you see what's down there?" I ask. He moves to my side and looks down, squinting.

"No, why? Can you?" I nod, chewing my lip nervously.

"It's a thirty-to-forty-foot drop, but we'll land in water. There's a shore maybe ten yards to the left. Selena's there." River looks at me like I've grown a second head, and I take a deep breath. "Fine. I'm going. Come or don't, it's your choice. But Lilac got us this far, and I'm not letting it go to waste." And before I can change my mind, I swing my legs over the edge and push myself over.

## Chapter 17

# Corinne

It feels like I fall for hours, but only seconds at the same time. I slam into the water feet first, which feels like hitting a brick wrapped in sandpaper. My legs collapse beneath me, and I sink into the water, kicking hard before bursting through the surface, gasping and coughing up the briny liquid. Treading water, I scan the space with my unnerving sight until I locate my sister.

I paddle/flail towards her, and haul myself onto the shore. Shivering and still fighting for air, I yell, "It's safe, c'mon!" I hope they can hear me, wherever the hole is. A few seconds tick by and I begin to worry that they've left us. That is until I see Rowan fall steadily towards the water, which splashes at contact. He pops back up in a few seconds, and swims over to us. Selena and I help him onto the shore and he lies there for a minute, regaining his breath.

I see River come down next, a silent dart plunging below the surface. Breanna follows soon after, sliding cleanly into the dark liquid. We're in a cave, which I notice because of the absence of light, and the stone walls are slick under my fingers and made of gypsum, giving the dark space an eerie glowing quality.

Once everyone has reached the shore, Selena asks, "So what now?"

We're clearly in an underground lake, with separate tunnels branching out in all directions. My eyesight is unnaturally good for the obvious darkness down here, everything cast in an eerie green glow. "Selena, how many fingers am I holding up?" I quaver. I hold up three fingers a few inches from her face and she reaches blindly for my hand.

"It's too dark to see anything, Corinne," she murmurs. It's silent for a count of three before she continues nervously. "How many fingers am *I* holding up?" I immediately see her hold up two fingers.

"Two," I say. She holds up four fingers now. "Five. Three. Two. Four. Five. One."

Her mouth opens wider after every correct answer, and the others look a little nervous. "You got all of them right," she breathes. I shift my weight, uncomfortable with all the attention. "How?"

I shake my head, still trying to figure that out myself. "I guess Pierre's training is working at least a little bit."

We move down the tunnel closest to us. Since I'm the only one who can see, I lead the way. Glancing around, I take in all the water dripping from cracks in the ceiling, and the little puddles and streams they form on the stone floor. I shouldn't be able to see all of it, but here I am in that very situation. Rowan quickens his pace to walk alongside me.

Breanna sniffles loudly from the back of the group, and I have everyone pause for a moment to catch their breath. Lilac's death still hasn't processed, but I can feel the grief settling in. As much as I dislike Breanna, I feel bad for her. Lilac was probably her closest friend.

While everyone rests, I walk a ways down the tunnel alone to scope it out. Maybe there's another side tunnel or some sign of life.

I swipe at the tears on my face again and almost trip over

a rotund object on the ground. It clatters against a wall and I glare at it before I can process what it actually is.

Screaming, I stumble backwards and away from the skull, its black empty sockets staring lifelessly back at me. I press a hand to my mouth and squeeze my eyes shut, but the image of the bald, white head is ironed onto the back of my eyelids.

I fall when I step on another one. When I open my eyes, I find myself in a side room, dozens of skulls surrounding me. They are cracked and yellowed. I scream again, backing myself into a corner as far away from them as I can get. The hollow voids in their faces follow me, eyes closed or open. My resolve cracks and I sob, curling into the fetal position and rocking back and forth like Tarissa did in the police station.

Warm hands pull me up, and I thrash around, trying to escape. "No! No, lemme go!" I scream, kicking my feet out and scattering the heads which clatter against the walls and each other. "Let go of me!"

"Corinne, stop!" yells Rowan—I recognize his voice now. "Hey, come on, pull it together!" His voice is softer now, but not any less stern.

I stop, and lean heavily on Rowan, still crying my eyes out. I don't want to break down in front of him, or any of them for that matter. "Why?" I sob, clinging to his shirt. He folds me into his arms and pulls me close, and I resume trying to free myself, but now for entirely different reasons.

He rubs my back until the tears relent before speaking again despite my protests.

"I don't know. But we have to keep going. We have to get out so that we can expose Pierre's work and get his work shut down. Otherwise, more people will end up trapped in contracts like yours or have their lives taken trying to get out," he murmurs, his chin resting on the top of my head.

I take a shuddering breath, closing my eyes and focusing on his words.

We stand there for another few seconds before I move again, drawing back. I'm glad he can't see the state of me, crying and unstable mentally and physically.

"C'mon, the rest of the group's waiting for us."

The skulls still stare at me, jeering, but I know we have to keep moving forward. So, I take a deep breath, wipe my eyes, and paste a smile on my face. Who knows what kinds of monsters created that room of human remains. I swallow and let Rowan lead me by the hand, more for him since he can't see anything, but it still comforts me.

We merge with the group, saying nothing. *Keep moving. We're almost there.* Almost where? We have no home—the state of Kleka's infrastructure is unknown to us—no destination and no purpose.

I get my answer when the tunnel opens up into a huge cavern. The walls are slick with sludge and the smell of rotting corpses rams into me with the force of a charging elephant. Breanna throws up behind me, the stench of vomit mingling with the scent of death.

The floor is littered with human bones and skulls, and even some skeletons still clothed in flesh, their decaying bodies twisted and bent, a jumble of decomposing limbs. I feel as if I'm going to be sick as well when my sharpened eyes zero in on the rich, brown skin of a girl with silver eyes sprawled but a few yards in front of me.

Lilac.

*Chapter 18*

# Selena

I pick up on the smell of rotting bodies immediately, but my vision annoyingly still hasn't adjusted to the darkness. I know Corinne can hear and see perfectly, which frankly, worries me. I don't want her to feel alone in her trials.

Corinne gasps, and I know something must be wrong. All I can see are faint silhouettes and a large mound ahead of us. A figure lays inert on the floor in front of Corinne, and I squint my eyes to try to make out any distinguishing features.

"It's Lilac," Corinne croaks. "She—she's here."

My head spins and I shake my head. An image of what she must look like pops up in my mind—limbs bent and blood dripping from her lips; eyes wide and glassy with her hair splayed out all around her. I cover my face with my hands, trying to block out the mental picture.

"Is she alive?" Breanna whispers.

"I can't tell. It looks like she's breathing but—" A pause. "She has no pulse." A ghostly moan echoes down the passage behind us.

"Souls," says Breanna immediately, Corinne getting to her feet where she had been kneeling to try and get a better look at Lilac. "We need to get out of here. We'll have to come back for her." No one protests despite the despair in Breanna's voice.

"There!" whisper-yells Corinne. "There is a passage on the other end of this cavern. But—we need to climb over the pile of—of bodies." I go as still as stone. Pile of bodies? I look up and squint my eyes again, taking note of the mass of black in front of us which the smell seems to be originating from. So I steel my nerves, and begin to climb.

The others follow reluctantly, the howls behind us growing louder by the second. Bones shift loose as I go higher, and I slip multiple times. River is right behind me, and he steadies me by resting a light hand on my hip.

We reach the other side of the pile which, thankfully, isn't as large as I had anticipated.

I follow the sound of Corinne's footsteps as she moves around, and then a tiny flame appears, illuminating her face.

"There was a lighter on the floor," she murmurs. Rowan goes to her side, and I allow a small smile at the sight of them standing next to each other, even if Corinne is almost imperceptibly inching away.

"Where to now?" he asks Corinne, who's still clearly rattled.

"Um—here. Over here," she says, moving towards my right. I stay near her, the thick darkness seeming to reach for me. I hate the dark.

The lighter casts shadows on the wall. They appear to be dancing like drunken devils. I can now make out an opening roughly thirty yards away.

The Souls call out again, their ghastly chorus chilling me to my bones and shaking the stone walls around us. I had almost forgotten about them.

"We need to get into the tunnel!" exclaims Rowan. No sooner does he say that than I happen to glance back to the mound just in time to see four, five, no six, slim creatures reach the top. They are so white they look like they're glowing against the darkness. I can't tell if they have any weapons in their hands, but I think it's safe to assume they don't need them.

"You guys, I found something!" Breanna shouts, barely audible. She's already in the tunnel. "It's some kind of lever!"

"Then pull it! Maybe it'll help us somehow!" hollers Rowan.

"No! We don't know what it does, don't touch it!" Corinne screams. But Breanna must have already pulled it because the rumbling grows louder and I vaguely see some sort of barrier slowly lowering from the ceiling. "Okay, never mind, just run now!" She doesn't need to tell me twice.

The door closes faster, only ten yards left. I'm falling behind, and I push myself to go faster. Six yards left. River and Rowan make it in. Three yards. The door is three feet from closing and Corinne dives under. Four feet away I drop and slide, just barely clearing the slab of stone. It slams shut behind me, pulling out a few of my hairs. We all pant in the darkness, nobody saying a word as we try to catch our breath.

"That—was—way too close," Rowan gasps.

I think the others nod, but it's hard to tell so I get slowly to my feet and move to Corinne's side to take her hand.

"Well hello," says River. I freeze. Not Corinne.

"Wrong person," I mutter, releasing his hand and going to the real Corinne. I brush her arm and she intertwines her fingers with mine.

"What's our next move?" asks Rowan. "We need to get out of here."

"No shit, Sherlock," grumbles Breanna. "And how do you propose we do that?"

Rowan shifts his weight and says, "Corinne can see perfectly down here. Anything stand out to you?" he asks my sister. I can sense the tension between them.

"Yeah—" she starts hesitantly. "There's a fork in the tunnel just ahead of us. The left passage looks fine, but the right looks different, like—" Her words trail to a stop.

I go to stand at the fork, and peer into the darkness.

"Where's your lighter, Corinne?" I ask.

"I dropped it when we ran, I think." Breanna sighs in frustration.

"I say we listen to Corinne," comments Rowan. "It's honestly our best bet with her enhanced senses."

But River doesn't so readily agree. "I think we should go right. If it gives off a bad aura it's most likely where we need to go." He's sort of got a point.

"Can we just decide something already? We need to get help for Lilac!" strains Breanna, "I'm going with River. Corinne having fucked up night vision doesn't mean she's qualified to get us all killed. It's not even fully developed. No offense, of course." She uses the 'no offense' as if it makes everything better. I cringe at the harshness of it.

"Yeah, no offense taken," snaps Corinne. I can hear in her voice that she's gone. "I'm just *praying* for your validation. I want to get out of here as much as you do so don't start pointing fingers." A slight tremor goes through the cavern, but Corinne and Breanna don't seem to notice.

"Sorry, let me make things clear for you. You should've been the one crushed in the cave-in instead of Lilac and maybe then we wouldn't be in this situation!" screams Breanna. The tremor turns into a violent shudder.

"Guys," I whisper. "You have to be quiet. This place isn't stable." They ignore me, raging over one another and trading insults. "Shut up!" I snap. They stop, staring at me. "Can't you see it's dangerous here? Look!" I point up to the cracks that I can hear spider webbing across the ceiling as dust coats my shoulders. The intersection shudders again.

"Sorry," Corinne whispers timidly, eyes glued to the

ceiling. She probably can actually see them. Breanna just folds her arms and turns away, huffing.

"Okay. Which way are we—" I'm cut off by a series of loud bangs on the stone panel behind us. The Souls have caught up to us.

"Shit—they're going to collapse us in. We need to go *now*," says River, moving to my side and pulling me towards the right path.

"No, come to the left!" whisper-yells Corinne. "That way doesn't feel right!"

"We'll be fine, as long as we're together," replies Rowan in a soft voice. "There is always power in numbers." Another dozen or so thumps shake the tunnel violently, and we all fall to the floor gasping. I hear the door behind me begin to split while dust rains down on us like Mardi Gras confetti.

"Fine go right—" Corinne hesitates. "But I'm going left."

"What, no!" bursts out Rowan. "We are absolutely not splitting up!"

Corinne backs away, glaring at Breanna. "Well, I'm not going right; especially not with that bitch."

"Why you little—" growls Breanna, lunging at my sister. I step out of River's grasp and between the two of them before a brawl can start.

"Hey, both of you cut it out. Let's just go left okay?" I say, attempting to calm them down.

"No way!" snaps Breanna, turning around and stomping back to River's side.

"Well, we have to go!" yells Corinne. "This place is caving in as we speak!" As if on cue, chunks of rock fall from the ceiling, and she jumps backwards just as a piece the size of her head smashes into the spot where she had just been standing.

A scream escapes me as a section of the door is punched through, then a clawed hand starts flailing around in the dark. The Soul who broke through shrieks bloody murder, turning my blood to ice water in my veins. I'm about to physically drag Breanna and River to the left just to pacify my sister when it happens.

The stone above our heads collapses, sending rubble, dust and dirt crashing down on us. Rowan and Corinne dive to the left, jagged boulders missing them by mere inches as they're pelted by smaller bits of rock. River and Breanna sprint to the right before getting flattened, and I have to make a decision *now*. Time slows and stretches as my eyes dart between my sister and River, both screaming at me to run through the blood pounding in my ears. I turn to see Corinne with tears running in rivulets down her cheeks, and in that moment I make the worst decision ever. I run to River.

# Chapter 19

# Corinne

"She chose him over me," I whisper, my voice nothing but a ragged version of itself. "I, I—" I sit down carefully, the dust settling in our now sectioned off corridor. Rowan sits next to me, and I wrap my arms around my knees, staring unresponsively at the floor and muttering words I can't even make out.

I come to a standstill when Rowan presses a hand to my back, and starts rubbing it in circles. I close my eyes as pictures wash through my mind. Pictures of things I don't remember experiencing. A wordless, soundless anger envelops my thoughts. How could my own sister abandon me like that?

I get up to pace back and forth, unable to voice my feelings. The outrage towards Selena just grows and grows until Rowan gives me an outlet.

"Hey, it's going to be okay. We'll find them again," he whispers. I stare at him.

"How can you say that?" I explode, furious. He looks confused and shocked.

"Say what?"

"That it's going to be okay! It might get better for you, but the abilities that are supposed to be my greatest asset are all screwed up for all I know! You saw the doubt in their faces when I could see things I couldn't before! And I've just left the only place that could get them straightened out." My voice rattles around the empty space.

"Actually, I couldn't see their faces, it was too dark for me." I bury my face in my hands. "But—but hey, that's not the point. Your abilities have been insanely useful so far," he says, trying to backtrack.

"Great, I'm a tool," I say bitterly.

"No, that's not what I meant and you know that." He takes a deep breath. "I understand how you feel, so sit down and let's work this out."

"No," I whimper, my anger burning up. "I don't want to talk about anything, I just want my sister back." I'm shaking—but at least it's not because of tears. I cover my face and try to slow my breathing.

"We can't do that until you sit down," he says, his voice strained. "You're being stubborn and irrational, and it's not going to get you anywhere."

"I really don't give a shit. I can't get a hold on this ability and all I wanted was to get out of that suffocating city. You don't have to put up with the frustration of being unable to control your own fucking body!"

Rowan looks away and closes his eyes tight, raises his hand, then snaps his fingers. I cover my mouth when a flame the size of my pinkie finger flares up in his open palm, feeling unable to tear my eyes away from the flickering column of heat before he closes his fist and the light goes out, leaving us in complete darkness again. Well, not for me.

"Rowan," I whisper. There's nothing else to say. He meets my eyes again, tears now running freely down his cheeks and leaving lines through all the dirt on his face. Puzzle pieces click in my head. The way his skin is always a little too warm, the smell of melted metal outside of the lift.

"It's okay," he mumbles, scrubbing at his face.

"How—" I start, struggling to find the right words. "How long have you known?"

"Since I was six." He stares at the ground now, arms limp by his sides. I slide to the ground next to him, taking his hand and holding on tight.

His eyes widen slightly at the touch, and I tentatively start moving my thumb in small circular motions on the back of his hand. His eyes close and he leans his head on my shoulder.

"I'm sorry," I murmur, hating myself, and my words, and my unchecked anger.

"It's okay. It happens. We move on."

"But—"

He lifts his head and tilts my chin so I'm looking at him. He searches my eyes, thumb brushing away the burning tears there. I close my eyes and rest my forehead against his.

"It's *okay*. Besides, better you let it out than hide it." The feel of his hand cupping my face is grounding, a tether, and I lean into it.

"We should get some rest," he says quietly. I nod, and before long hear Rowan's soft snores. I allow myself the smallest of smiles, however sad, and lean my head back against the wall, still rubbing my thumb along his hand, which is gripping mine like a lifeline. My eyes close slowly, drowsily, but it still takes many long minutes for sleep to find me. When it does, it's light and paranoid.

✶✶✶

I'm awoken by my stomach growling, and I feel Rowan stir in his sleep. My shoulder throbs from him leaning against it all night—or day; it's impossible to tell down here—but I don't mind. He needs the rest as much as I do.

We wander the tunnels for what feels like days, hungry

and thirsty, completely lost, searching for the others, and waiting for one of the tall, slender monsters to round a corner and snatch us up. The tunnels have to intersect in more than that single spot, so we hold out hope. Every time we round another corner in the maze-like tunnels, my spirits sink lower with the empty corridor ahead. Eventually we think to use the follow-the-right-wall trick to hopefully run into something useful. Such as an exit. It's not until hours after starting our new tactic that we take another break from walking.

My words die in my throat and I squint. Something's off. Then I realize what it is. I'm squinting because something's brighter than before. I shake Rowan awake—he had fallen asleep while we rested—and he snaps to attention, looking around.

"What is it?" he asks carefully. I point giddily to the end of the insanely long corridor we're in, to the tiniest pinprick of light at the end. A way out. Before I can say anything, I feel like I'm hurtling towards the light until I realize that I'm not moving. My vision is. I zoom in impossibly far until my eyes focus on the source of the dim light. A staircase winds around a stone column, and a thin, hazy light shines from above.

I shake my head, and zip back into perspective. I realize Rowan has been talking to me.

"What's up?" he asks worriedly.

"It's a staircase at the end over there. The light's coming from up above."

It's quiet for exactly six seconds until Rowan stands up and brushes his pants off.

"Well then, we better get moving."

I stare at his hand, which he's holding out for me to take. Finally, I do, and he pulls me up as we start walking in an only slightly awkward silence. I count each minute as it passes, but the stairs only seem to get further and further away.

We reach the end of the hallway after a solid fifteen minutes of walking, but as soon as I put my foot on the staircase, the step sinks into the ground and a stone door drops behind us with a resounding boom.

"That can't be good," Rowan mutters. I can see the uneasiness in his features. It's justified when dozens of slots open up in the walls and water begins to cascade out, sloshing around our feet.

"Go, go, go!" I shout with increasing panic. We sprint up the stairs, every step that we touch rising up behind us, blocking us from any possible way of backtrack. Rowan grabs my hand again and pulls me along, trying to keep us on the same step. With the water streaming down the stairs and the rising steps holding in any water that does reach us, we just barely stay ahead.

And the water's gaining.

We run up the spiral so fast that I begin to get dizzy, and my legs burn like hell, but there's no way we can stop. So I run faster, heart pounding and chest constricting. Rowan doesn't let go of my hand. My breathing is labored, the water up to our knees despite our constant movement.

Finally, a warped, wooden door appears above us. Rowan tries to twist the knob but it's locked. He curses colorfully and rams into it with his full weight behind one shoulder. The freezing liquid is now up to our waists. He yanks me inside and tries to close the door behind us, but the influx of water is too great and we're pushed back, chest deep now. A ladder stretches up and up behind us, and I wordlessly pull him to it.

He pushes me up first, so that the water now rests at my waist again and his chin. The slick metal rungs are slippery and I almost fall several times, but he and

I climb above the water and slowly leave it behind. Not completely though.

Several minutes pass, my arms and legs shaking from the strain, until we reach a cold metal platform, with another shabby looking door at the far end. I push it open, feeling depleted, expecting another ladder or staircase and my only thought being the need to get away from the water, away from the stairs.

It's a shed.

I stare in confusion for a moment at the rakes and shovels and the wheelbarrow next to us. Overwhelmed and freezing, deprived of food and water, I collapse into a freezing, trembling heap on the floor and watch the world fade away.

***

I wake up under a heavy blanket, my head settled in Rowan's lap and his hand in my hair. I sit bolt upright and stare at him.

"It's okay, you curled up like that and I didn't have the heart to move you," he says, smiling sheepishly. Heart still pumping adrenaline, I rub my eyes and peek around. We're in a sprawling living room, with pale gray couches and a cream-colored rug. Serene paintings hang on the walls, and an intricate crystal chandelier dominates the center of the ceiling. I'm covered with a white, wool blanket. I cringe at the dirt on my clothes, now rubbing onto the fabric.

I startle when a man and a woman walk in, both of them wearing simple gray clothes.

"Where is the rest of your group?" asks the man when he and the woman reach us.

I'm still in a sort of shock, and all I can get out is, "The rest of the group?"

The man bounces on the balls of his feet until the woman

rests a hand on his forearm. "You are Corinne and Rowan, yes?" she asks, her soft voice matching her kind brown eyes. I'm about to ask how they know our names but Rowan steps in.

"Yes, that's us. We were split up from the rest of our group in the catacombs. Can you help us find—" his voice hitches and stops as he stares at something on the woman's shirt. "You—you're part of Lotus Protection?" he stammers. "I didn't think they actually existed—"

I follow his line of sight to the patch on the woman's shirt: a plain gold lotus flower enclosed in a circle. The man has one exactly like it, and I'm reminded of my necklace. I panic for a second. Did it get lost in our frantic race up the stairs? But no, the gold chain is still at my throat, the weight heavy and familiar.

Turning my attention back to the newcomers, I look at their faces for a moment. They seem familiar, but I can't place them. Anyway, a much more important question is circulating in my head right now.

"Um, excuse me, but could someone please tell me what 'Lotus Protection' is?" I ask. They all look at me. The man and woman have a bemused look on their faces, Rowan staring in surprise.

"They're the most undercover Mutation Assistance Association ever," he rushes, incredulous eyes wide. "There are MAA's all over the place, but the Lotus Protection Corporation is the most famous of them all." He turns back to the adults, eyes sparkling with admiration. "I can't believe I actually get to meet you guys. I've always hoped to someday join and help to protect Mutes."

The man and woman smile again, but this time the amusement doesn't reach their eyes. "You will soon get to assist us greatly, but right now we need to get you two cleaned up. It's almost dark and—"

I hold up a hand to interrupt her. "Wait, what about the others?" I ask.

The man speaks first. "A search team is being dispatched as we speak. They will comb the tunnels until your friends are found. They know the catacombs better than anyone." He assures me. Who the hell are these people?

"There's someone else down there who needs help," I rush. "Her name is Lilac, she has silver-colored eyes, you can't miss them. We found her but we weren't sure if she was alive. Please look for her. She was in a big cavern, near a pile of—near a pile of bodies."

She promises to call it in.

"Now, let's get you cleaned up."

I glance at Rowan, but he's too busy staring at the pair to notice me. I shake my head then rub my tired eyes. Worry clenches my gut so tightly I feel sick.

But when I glance up again, Rowan's looking at me, and gives me a small, lopsided smile.

I notice a kitchen to my left for the first time, which opens up into a dining room with crystal cups and plates set up on the table.

"Gigi!" calls the woman, the volume of her voice surprising me. "Come show our guests to their rooms so they can get washed up before dinner."

A girl who looks to be about six or seven with rumpled, black hair bounces over and grins at us, giving us a salute. "Gigi at your service!" she announces. "Come on, I'll show you where you'll be staying for now!" She bounds up a set of stairs in the dining room and my legs turn to jelly, remembering the never-ending staircase we were just forced to climb.

Rowan brushes my hand when he passes me, giving me a reassuring look over his shoulder. I push past the burning in my overused legs and grit my teeth, climbing the thirteen steps to a landing that branches out into three different hallways; left, right, and straight. Gigi is prancing down the one to the left so I follow her. I glance around trying to find Rowan, and he pops out from a closet behind me, tasing me in the sides.

I shriek with surprised laughter, my worry evaporating like water on a dry, summer day. I turn and run away from him laughing. Gigi catches on and joins me in my escape, tugging me into a room on my right, then into the closet of the room. Rowan skids to a stop in front of the door with a huge grin on his face and walks around the room before sarcastically lamenting our absence and leaving again.

Gigi and I laugh until our sides hurt, then lay sprawled on the floor in content silence until the girl tells me dinner will be ready soon.

"We can find your friend and I'll show you guys where you can shower," she giggles, her face still pink from gasping for breath. "After that you can meet my brothers and sister!"

***

The shower is like a slice of heaven, the warm streams of water rolling down my back and clearing out my system. But I still scrub my skin raw before I feel clean enough to step out of the shower and dry off with the fluffy blue towel on the back of the door.

Gigi gave me her bright orange hairbrush before she left, telling me it would make my hair so pretty. I tease it through my damp hair, letting the strands air-dry as I shove on some gray sweats and clip my necklace back on. By studying the design on the pendant, I can confirm that the lotus on my piece of jewelry and the lotus on the shirts of the people downstairs are indeed the very same. That leaves me now to wonder what the relationship is between the two.

I can smell dinner before I even get halfway down the hallway, and the inviting scent drags me downstairs and into one of the wooden chairs. A spread of chicken and vegetables decorates the table. Everyone smiles and chatters away while they devour their food, and Gigi excitedly introduces me to the triplets, Deezy, Duncan, and Dara, who stare at me with wide eyes and open mouths. I learn that the man's name is Ben and the woman's name is Kara. Then she moves on to tell me about how she wants to grow up like me, with pretty hair and a handsome boyfriend. I throw a glance at Rowan, but he just laughs and ruffles Gigi's hair. I stare at my green beans.

"So, any news on our friends?" asks Rowan with a hopeful voice. I can't help but feel a surge of guilt about having forgotten about them. We're being pampered and eating hot food while they're probably dirty and terrified beneath our very feet. The thought turns my meal bitter and I push my plate away.

The smile slides right off Ben's face, and he says, "Not yet. Our team is still looking. But rest assured that you two will be the first to know of any progress." I'm not entirely satisfied with the reassurance, but my restlessness eases a bit. "Well, who wants dessert?"

*Chapter 20*

# Corinne

Dessert is a melt-in-the-mouth chocolate cake topped with fresh raspberries and jam swirled into the frosting. I sigh when I take the first bite. If heaven is real, then this is it. I even ask if I can take a slice back to my room with me as a late-night snack. Ben and Kara happily indulge me and tell us to get some rest. Rowan and I bid goodnight to them, and Rowan gives Gigi a hug. She definitely has a major crush on him. She even gives him a peck on the cheek before sliding off his knee and giggling as she hides behind the couch in the living room.

I can't take my eyes off him with his damp hair, crazy happy grin, and glittering eyes. He looks so happy and carefree that I'm almost envious. He catches me staring and saunters over to where I'm standing near the base of the stairs. I experience a major bout of deja vu back to when he and his brother came up to us at the hospital. It all seems so long ago, though it's only been a few weeks.

"What, you wanna kiss me too?" he teases, poking my arm and bringing me back from my reminiscing. I fan my face and slip into my most exaggerated British accent, pushing aside the risk of delving headfirst into bittersweet memories.

"Oh my, Rowan, how scandalous of you!" I scold, tossing in a smile. He throws his head back and laughs, such a pure unfiltered sound of happiness it confuses me. Eli was always so serious and forced, making this rather new to me.

Two bunk beds sit on either end of the room, with a bathroom on either wall and a large closet next to the door. It's very asymmetrical, and has a much cozier feel than the strict and pristine style of the rooms in Pierre's mansion.

Rowan starts to climb the ladder to the top bunk but I quickly scale the back of the structure and flop onto the mattress.

"No fair!" Rowan complains, his face only a foot away from mine. "How come you get top bunk?"

"Because I was faster," I state matter of factly.

"Pleeeease?" he pouts, giving me puppy eyes. I almost break. Almost.

"Nuh-uh. No way. I'm always scared the top's going to break and I'll be trapped underneath," I say. He snickers, pursing his lips in a poor attempt to conceal it. "It's not funny!" I protest. But he just laughs again and swings back down to the bottom, and I hear the creak of wood and his body settles into the mattress.

Several minutes pass before I muster the courage to say, "Rowan, do you think the others are going to be okay?" At first I think he didn't hear me, but then the mattress shifts again and his voice floats up to me.

"Yeah, I think so. The Lotus Protection is the best of the best, and if anyone can find our friends, it's them."

It's quiet again, and I wait until Rowan's breathing slows and evens out before creeping out of bed. I pause for a second next to his bunk, watching him. He looks so peaceful when he's sleeping, and I envy his ability to sleep so easily.

A slim balcony looks out over the backyard, and I go outside. The warm nocturnal breeze rustles the gauzy curtains behind me. I take a deep breath of the clean air and feel my worries fade away instantly, as if someone clicked the mute button on my mind's remote. I glance up at the cloudless sky, wanting to get higher and see the stars better, so I snag my chocolate cake from inside the room and climb onto the railing. Then I shove the plate onto the roof and do some sort of jump-crawl combo onto the ledge above. Skirting all the windows in case any of them belong to Ben and Kara, it's a careful climb to the place where both the slopes meet in a long, flat strip of roofing tile.

I lay down, taking tiny bites of my cake and gazing at the twinkling stars, then closing my eyes as a flood of images from my past drowns my brain. When I open them again, I search for the familiar constellations, picking out the Ursa Major and Ursa Minor, aka the Big Dipper and the Little Dipper, and Orion's Belt, which I then use to guide my search for the rest of his body. The stars sparkle and dance in the night sky, and I'm just barely dozing off when there's a rustle below me.

I sit up, and my still-activated enhanced vision zeroes in on a figure climbing onto the roof. My heartbeat quickens when I realize it's Rowan, carrying an armful of blankets and some pillows. He crawls up and plops down next to me, catching my eye and smirking in my direction.

"Did you really think you could come up here unnoticed?" he laughs.

I sigh. "And I seriously thought you were asleep." He simply grins again and hands me a pillow and a couple of blankets.

"Here, so you don't freeze to death," he says. I gesture around us to the warm breeze and not a cloud in sight and he rolls his eyes. "Just let me feel useful."

Hesitantly, I tuck the pillow under my head and curl up in the blankets. It's much more comfortable, but I'm not going to tell him that. Instead I turn my face back up to the stars, and get lost in them until Rowan's attention pulls me back. I lay on my side facing him and he does the same. I shiver despite the warmth.

"What?" I ask. But he just studies my face, his corn-husk-colored eyes flitting across it. We hold each other's gaze for another painstakingly long few seconds before Rowan tears his eyes away and sighs.

Just then, loud shouts cut through the night and I spring to my feet. My neat little night vision capability kicks in just in time to see six figures dressed in black racing to the front door of the house. Two of them are limping. One of the sturdier ones is carrying someone, who lies limp as a rag doll. They enter the house and various lights flick on, shortly followed by a shrill scream. Rowan and I look at each other before scrambling back down the roof and onto the balcony. We get inside just as the bedroom door slams open, and Gigi stands there, panting, with a frantic look on her pale little face.

She swallows before speaking. "Your—your friends are here."

We race down the stairs after her, coming to a halt in the kitchen where Ben and Kara are kneeling over whoever was being carried. Rowan chokes as River rushes up to him and wraps him up in a bear hug, a relieved smile plastered on his face. I wait for Selena to come to me, knowing I'll forgive her immediately. But the other conscious member of our group turns her head, and I see that the brown hair belongs to Breanna. Which means the one that's uncon-scious, is my sister.

*Chapter 21*

# Selena

I float around in the swirling blackness, not fighting it as it takes me farther and farther away from the light that is reality. I drift aimlessly, not caring about or remembering anything, not even my name. That freaks me out and prompts me to begin struggling to remember anything from my real life. Then a voice echoes faintly through the never-ending emptiness.

"Selena."

That's my name. I am Selena. And the one calling me is Corinne, my sister. As I remember her, I also remember the guilt at having chosen River and Breanna over her, my own flesh and blood. I don't even know why.

For a moment I wish I could crawl back to my hole and never come out again, but I do, so that I can apologize to my sister.

It feels like there are weights taped to my arms, and my head pounds as I drag myself back to consciousness. Finally, I crack open my eyes and blink rapidly, trying to clear the dancing spots of light out of my sight. Corinne laughs tearfully and wraps me up in a hug, cradling my head.

"I'm sorry," I croak. "I don't know what I was thinking."

"It's okay, it's okay; no harm done," she whispers, smiling. I melt, unbearably relieved that she understands. I take a deep breath and use this chance to look at her face. She seems happier. And clean. I'm suddenly very self-conscious of all the dirt I'm getting on her clothing. But she doesn't seem to care much at all. She also looks—flushed. I immediately look at Rowan, who has a similar tinge of pink on his face, and my eyes widen as I connect the dots.

"Did I interrupt something?" I ask weakly, attempting and failing at a grin. She doesn't seem to understand.

"Not at all," she says quietly, distracted with smoothing my hair away from my face.

"Uh-huh," I say skeptically, lifting an eyebrow. I wince then, hands fluttering to my head where a long gash oozes blood. A worry line appears in my sister's brow. When did that happen?

"Ben? Kara?" she beckons. The two adults talking to Breanna come over and the woman, Kara, examines my wound with a tight frown.

"That wasn't a Soul who gave that to you was it?" she asks. She reaches out to my head but stops just before she touches it. I feel my eyes widen to the size of quarters.

"You know what Souls are?" I ask nervously. She nods, but doesn't give me any further explanation so I push for more information. "How? Who are you?" I grimace as she cleans the cut with hydrogen peroxide and sticks a large patch with some sort of white cream over it.

When Kara doesn't respond immediately, Corinne fills in for me. "They're part of an organization called Lotus Protection. They're one of the most powerful MAA's any-where. MAA stands for Mutation Assistance Association, remember? We learned about them during 'History in the Making' at school," she adds when I stare at her uncom-prehendingly. She looks extremely proud, and Rowan gives her a thumbs up. He and River are deep in a very animated conversation, their hands flying all over the place as they speak. Well, Rowan's hands are flying around, but River is his ever-cool self, getting his emotions back in check quickly.

"Wait," whispers Corinne, glancing around the room again. "Where's Lilac? Did you find her?"

Breanna perks up, expression hopeful.

Kara shakes her head hesitantly, eyes lowered. "The search team told me that they found the cavern you mentioned as well as the mass grave. The place was partially collapsed, and they spent several hours looking, but not a single girl with silver eyes."

Corinne deflates and Breanna swipes at her eyes, the room going silent for a moment.

"We have a lot to talk about, and I want you to tell me everything," says Corinne. "But first can we sleep?" she asks, all excitement gone from her face. I notice the bruises under her eyes for the first time and realize she's probably no better off than we were. I bite my lip, feeling guilty for having kept her from getting some well-deserved rest. Although she didn't look like she had been sleeping prior to our arrival.

She helps me up the stairs, gripping the railing so tight I'm surprised it doesn't splinter.

Our room has matching bunks with gray comforters and white sheets, along with a balcony overlooking the garden out back. The floaty white curtains flutter from the steady breeze coming through the open doors and I breathe in the fresh air deeply, relishing the feel of it compared to the dank, musty air below ground.

"Here, you can have my bunk," offers Corinne, shoving me up the ladder of the bunk on my right. I look around in confusion, noting that there are only four beds.

"Where will you sleep?" I inquire.

"I'll be fine," she promises. "Just get some rest." With that she goes out to the balcony, hauls herself up onto the roof and disappears. I want to talk to her, to join her on the roof, but my body betrays me, melting into the warm clean sheets. Before I know it, my eyelids flutter shut and the dreams take over.

*The cave collapsed, and they were stuck behind a wall of rock, hacking and coughing. Selena pounded on the barrier, screaming that she needed to go back. Too late. They had to move. The shifting earth opened a hole in the wall next to the door they had come through, and the Souls were now able to reach them.*

*They sprinted down hallway after hallway, making more turns than they could count, but they couldn't seem to shake the monsters. Finally, after making a series of five rights then a left, they were able to trick them and take a break from running. Selena doubled over and coughed up bile, the combination of running and feeling as though she had betrayed her sister leaving her with a sick feeling.*

*River silently walked over and let her lean on his shoulder. She put an arm around his neck and he an arm around her waist, hauling her to her feet and giving her his support for a good while as they wandered hopelessly through the labyrinth of stone. They were dirty, tired, and hungry, and they had all begun to wish they had followed Corinne; even Breanna, although she wouldn't admit it.*

*Finally, they saw a light at the end of a tunnel, and renewed by the way out, they ran towards it laughing and smiling. But when they got to the source, they saw it wasn't a way out, but a note laying next to a candle poking out of the eye*

*socket of a cracked, wet-looking skull. Soft tissue
and hair still stuck to it. Breanna screamed, and
Selena had to clap a hand over her mouth to keep
from hurling again. River snatched the note out
of the small niche, and read it aloud.*

Those who seek freedom,
Will never submit.
Those who escaped,
Had to learn when to quit.

*Selena had been about to tear her hair out
with frustration when she was yanked upwards
so violently and so suddenly that she didn't even
have enough concentration to scream. She was
dangling by one foot from a rope anchored to the
ceiling, and she noticed her friends in similar
situations. They were flailing about in her blurry
vision, but the blood was rushing to her head
too quickly and that was the last she saw before
something struck her head and she went out like
a light.*

# Chapter 22

# Corinne

My hands are crossed behind my head and I stare at the stars, looking like diamonds scattered across a blanket of midnight blue. A small noise below catches my attention, and I expect Selena to climb up.

"It's alright, get some sleep," I say, not bothering to turn my head. The intruder clears their throat and I look over.

"It—it's not Selena," says River tiredly, staring at his shoes. He kicks at the roofing tiles before looking up to meet my gaze. That's not a River thing to do. I pick out the details of his face. Dark skin rings his eyes and his lips are chapped and pale.

"Come on over," I say, patting the spot next to me and returning my focus back up to the stars. He comes over and sits, but he still seems tense.

"Corinne, I just want to apologize for—" I hold up a hand, silencing him.

"It's all good. You don't need to say anything. It's fine," I tell him. I don't need anyone feeling guilty on my part, even if his words stung more than a little. He seems to deflate, and smiles wearily at me, sighing.

"Thank you, Corinne. You have no idea how relieved I am to hear that. But still, I'm sorry. No hard feelings though, right?" I free a captured breath.

"Yeah, we're all good."

***

Morning sun forces its way between my eyelids and I sit up blearily, rubbing sleep out of my eyes. Despite resting most of the night and sleeping in late, I'm exhausted. My muscles ache and my head pounds. I groan, rolling on to my knees and stretching like a cat. The air is clean and fresh, and it clears away some of my drowsiness.

I slide down the roof and plop onto the balcony without a second thought. Strong arms slide up my thighs and around my waist before I hit the ground, and Rowan lowers me down. Eli's face plagues my thoughts.

"I could've gotten down by myself," I say, my voice weak.

"I know." He smiles, scanning my face. Then a small smile spreads across his face. "Hey, come see what Ben and Kara have prepared for breakfast." With that, he strides across the room and disappears into the hallway. I steel my nerves and trail behind him.

Rowan was right in his excitement for breakfast. Pastries and waffles and pancakes lay in heaps across the table, pitchers of juice and water stuffed in between. Bacon, eggs, and toast beckon to me and I slide into the seat next to Rowan, who is already wolfing down a plate of pancakes between bites of doughnut. I dish myself some apple turnovers and a few pieces of breakfast quiche. The food is rich and delicious, and I savor every bite, closing my eyes and sighing through my nose.

"Corinne!" a shrill voice shrieks. I open my eyes to see Gigi bound down the stairs and come barreling towards me. I set my fork down and rotate my chair just in time, and she leaps into my arms, snuggling into my shirt. I give her a hug and laugh. She's clad in old, pre-war pink pajamas with Pinkie Pie on the shirt saying, 'Party all night!'

"Hey you," says Rowan, mussing up her hair affectionately. "How'd you sleep?'"

"Good. Did Corinne go onto the roof again?" she asks, turning to look at me. I glance down and meet her gaze.

"Yes, yes I did."

"Huh," says Rowan. "I thought that's where you went. But I didn't come up because I heard you and River up there." He looks at me ruefully and I bite my lip.

"He just came up to apologize about what happened earlier," I say coolly. He mutters something under his breath and looks away. Gigi is looking back and forth between us frowning.

"Are you two mad at each other?" she inquires. Rowan looks back at her and smiles softly.

"No. It was just a misunderstanding," he says, ruffling her hair again. She crosses her arms and raises her chin.

"Well, I think you should apologize to make it better." My face ignites and I try in vain to mentally leech the color out of it. It doesn't work. Rowan is equally as flustered, but he's not red.

"Uh, that's okay Gigi, it's all fine," I say quickly.

"You sure?" He blinks over exaggeratedly, the beginnings of a smile making the corners of his mouth twitch. "Did I hurt your feelings?" I swallow, hoping it's not noticeable. He puts me in *very* pressured situations sometimes. I glance at Selena, but she, River and Breanna are wrapped up in a heated argument about who took the last chocolate doughnut.

I look at Gigi again and she gives me puppy eyes. "Pleeeeease? I wanna make sure you guys aren't mad at each other!" I laugh nervously, my mouth dry as the Sahara. I'm saved from the awkward moment when Ben and Kara hurry in. But from the looks on their faces, I kind of wish I had just made Rowan apologize for nothing instead.

"Alright, everyone up. Go to your rooms and pack some clothes. I'll get some food for you, but go now!" says Kara, her voice tight and frantic.

I stand up. "What's wrong?"

"They're here," says Ben gravely.

I'm almost afraid to ask my next question. "Who's here?"

There's a slight pause before Ben replies, "The Phantom Order." His tone is grave, and the name alone gives me chills. Kara, now at the window, yanks the drapes closed.

"They're outside," she hisses, her face pale and slick with sweat. "Everyone grab what you can and get to the basement. I've alerted backup."

Everyone stands up and races upstairs. I stuff a few shirts and some pants in a duffel bag from the closet, along with some extra underwear. Then from the bathroom, I grab a toothbrush, some toothpaste and a handful of tampons. Rowan, River, Selena, and Breanna are already out in the main room by the time I'm done. I'm about to ask what's next when a loud crash filters up from downstairs; a window breaking.

A second later, Kara bursts in through the door, carrying Dara, with Deezy, Duncan, and Gigi trailing behind her, clutching one another.

"Everyone, out onto the balcony. Get to the roof. Ben's holding them off," she says with a pinched, ghostly face.

"Is he going to be alright? What's he doing?" protests Selena. She's answered by someone yelling, then a loud bang and silence. Kara's lips tighten, and the children hold each other tighter. Breanna turns away and covers her mouth. River grimaces. I run to the balcony doors and fling them open, tossing my bag over and onto the roof. Kara hurries over and hands me Deezy while Rowan hauls himself up.

The small boy trembles in my arms and I give him my most reassuring smile saying, "It's alright. You're so brave, just hold on." He nods and Rowan pulls him up. We do the same with Duncan, Dara, and Gigi while River, Selena, and Breanna clamber up on their own. Then it's only me and Kara.

I realize it's been a good minute since what I can only assume was the gunshot. I mentally curse myself for stalling, and reach for Rowan's hand. Another shout echoes from the hallway, and this time I swear out loud.

"Go," hisses Kara. "Now, while you still can." Just then three people dressed in black come through the doorway; they're from the camp in the clearing the night of our attempted escape. They're the ones who attacked Kleka and killed Winny.

"I found some more!" shouts the one on the left; a man. Kara pushes me behind her, causing me to lose hold of Rowan's hand. She reaches into her sleeve, pulling out a knife and pressing it into my palm. I clutch the handle clumsily, having only used a knife for slicing vegetables, never as a weapon. Then she snaps the top button off her shirt cuff and pinches it between her thumb and index finger. Thin silver blades emerge from the sides and it becomes a throwing star.

She flicks the star expertly and nails the center person in the shoulder. They scream, skin smoking where the blades cut in. The other two advance, grabbing the guns off their belts and taking aim. One bullet ricochets off the doorframe right next to me, and I duck involuntarily, dropping the knife. It skids to the edge of the balcony, teetering precariously on the edge. I dive for it just as another shot rings out, shock turning my head and widening my eyes in time to see it hit Kara squarely in the forehead.

My mouth falls open as blood pours down her face and sprays the front of my shirt with a fine mist. She crumples into a bloody heap next to me. I shout her name but she doesn't move. Of course not, they shot her in the head; she's dead. I scramble again for the knife, grabbing a hold of it and shoving it clumsily through my belt, tearing a hole in my jeans and scratching the skin underneath.

"Corinne." I freeze. That voice, I know that voice. I turn

slowly back around. The man who had spoken before pulls his hood down. Oily, black hair spills out over his shoulders, his beaked Roman nose resting above a curled cruel smirk.

Pierre.

"Come now, darling. Can't we find an understanding here?" He tilts his head, his voice dripping with false sweetness, like sour honey. "I need your help my dear. Just tell me where your friends are and I promise you no harm will come to them."

I shake my head vehemently. "I don't want to help you and I never will. I'd rather die," I spit. He looks taken aback.

"Whatever have I done to warrant such hate against me? We were getting along so well I thought. I even threw a party for you," he mourns, feigning innocence.

"That place you run? It's a monstrosity. What are you even trying to accomplish?" I say savagely. Whether it was under direct orders of this man, or simply his men acting on their own, it's his fault that Winnie was killed, and Tarissa was driven insane until she the moment died, and my city was—well, I don't know.

Pierre doesn't answer. Instead he shakes his head saying, "I had hoped this would be a much more productive reunion. I apparently have no hope in you helping me of your own free will. You *did* sign a contract."

He nods at the person next to him. "Get her." He slinks out of the room and closes the door. The man lowers his hood as well, and I recognize the sunken beady eyes from that night at the café.

Buzz Cut.

He killed Winnie. A fire storm rages inside me, and I zoom in on the reflection in his eyes. I see myself, almost completely defenseless with eyes ablaze with fury.

"Where's your little friend?" I snarl, recalling the man with the green Mohawk.

He ignores my question and chuckles, stepping closer. "Such a pretty little thing. I think we have some time before Mr. Dolion needs to be on his way." I can see the hunger and greed in his eyes. Eli wore that same look the last time I was with him.

Suddenly, a hand drops down and I look up to see Rowan's face livid with anger and disgust. He glares at Buzz Cut—who looks at me in utter confusion—before grabbing my hand and pulling me up. But I can only get so far. Buzz Cut shouts a curse and fumbles with his pistol.

Then he raises his gun and fires.

Rowan's look of terror hits me just before the bullet does, pain lancing up my neck so violently that my body seizes, then goes limp. My shoulder burns and the impact tears our hands apart. I hear myself gasp in the silence, the sound echoing in my quiet brain, I hear Selena scream, and see Buzz Cut's look of triumph, just before I trip over the railing behind me and plummet to the ground.

Time slows and at first I just hear the wind howling around me. Through my pain-blurred vision I see River jump off the roof, slicing through the air like a knife through butter. He gains speed and laces his arms around my waist, holding me tight against his chest. My shoulder screams in protest but I ignore the pain, trying to focus my vision. Then he twists his body so I'm above him and we slam into the ground, the landing brutally jarring my shoulder. I scream through my clenched teeth, sobbing, and fall endlessly into the darkness of my mind.

***

When I surface again, my eyes feel gluey and I blink rapidly to clear them. I rub them hard and all of a sudden I can see again. I'm staring at a metal ceiling, and the ground is shuddering beneath me. I sit bolt upright and immediately regret it. Gritting my teeth, I look at my shoulder to find the sleeve of my T-shirt ripped off and clean, white bandages wrapped around it.

"What—happened?" I rasp. I see now that we're sitting in the back of a van, the small space full of tangible fear.

Selena answers. "You fell off the balcony and then River–" her voice catches. "jumped after you. He caught you and you both hit the ground. We—I thought you were both dead. But he just stood up and picked you up like you weighed nothing. A bunch of vans circled the house afterwards and the Phantom Order disappeared, like they were never there. The vehicles were owned by the Lotus Protection and they bandaged you up and put us in here to transport us to the next nearest safe house. Or so they said." She takes a deep breath and looks me in the eye. "How are you feeling?"

"Like shit," I mumble. I search the faces and realize something's off. My brain goes into panic mode when I realize the kids aren't here. "Where's Gigi? And the triplets?"

"They're safe. They're in a separate van on their way to the orphanage at headquarters. There's a special one for the kids whose parents died while in the service of Lotus Protection," says River from the back. I exhale in relief.

He's in the corner gazing at me. I nod in thanks, rewarded with a small smile. How on earth did he survive that jump without so much as a broken bone? Or wait—if Rowan's a Mute, it's not impossible that River has some ability as well. I'll have to ask him later, though; I don't have enough energy right now.

We ride in silence for probably another hour or so before the van rumbles to a stop and the doors in the back are thrown open. A group of people in dark gray, military-style gear hustle us out and up the front steps to a large yellow house, the dinged up red screen door slamming shut behind us as we enter.

Unlike where we stayed last time, this house is more rustic and run down, with shabby mismatched furniture and scuffed walls. The man who greets us is elderly, with graying hair and a sagging face. Deftly, he waves away the Lotus Protection and they reluctantly fall back, climbing into their vans and disappearing down the street.

Alone now, we look to the man, who silently brings us to the small kitchen, where ham sandwiches sit temptingly on the counter. He gestures at them, and we hurry forwards, gathering the food and seating ourselves on the stools around the counter.

"What's your name?" asks Selena through mouthfuls of bread.

The man shakes his head and opens his mouth wide. The purple scarred stump of a tongue wriggles at us, and I fight off a gagging fit. He smiles at us, the number of gaps from missing teeth noticeably more than the few that remain.

He proceeds to rummage around the kitchen until he unearths a collection of large knives, and doles them out to me and the rest of the group. They accept them silently; even Breanna takes one without a blink. While we devour the food—the breakfast with Ben and Kara had been burned through by adrenaline and fear—the older man scribbles rapidly on a piece of paper with some crayons.

Clapping his hands to snag our attention, he holds up his paper, which I can now tell has a drawing on it. The drawing holds a crude comic strip, depicting a stick figure in the first panel. The second one has a ball of orange behind the person, while the third showcases the figure engulfed in what appears to be flames. Then he points down at the floor with one finger, and walks to a door in the wall in the space under the stairs.

Reluctantly, we follow him, and upon opening it we reveal a set of rickety wooden steps covered with dust and cobwebs, presumably leading to a basement. Every horror movie I've ever watched screams at me not to go down, but I follow in the footsteps of the classic idiotic protagonist and descend.

The others are close behind. The old man is last, closing the door behind us. I shiver at the bottom as he brushes past, surprisingly nimble for his age. He pulls on a cord that resembles a discarded shoelace dangling from the ceiling and a single, bare bulb fizzes to life, illuminating the space.

We're in a stone room much like the room where the tunnel branched out from the camp. It's empty, save for a single rug in the center. With one sure flick, the old man shoves the square of fabric away, revealing a warped wooden trapdoor the size of a sled.

He waits until I tentatively step forward and pull up on the door handle, unearthing a crumbling stone staircase with old, yellowed skulls resting in niches about every ten feet.

My knees lock then turn to jelly in the same instant, and then I'm on the floor in the blink of an eye.

We're going back into the catacombs.

*Chapter 23*

# Selena

The trip underground is harder than it should be. Corinne is stepping gingerly from one step to the next, and tries to hide her shaking by pressing one hand against the wall. But I saw how she dropped next to the opening; something must have happened down here. But my question is, what could possibly shake my sister up enough for her to be so anxious about going underground again?

*Well,* a little voice in the back of my head says, *there are Souls running around down here, and probably countless traps covering the place.* I clutch the old man's illustration tighter against my chest; he had thrust it into my hands before he closed the door over our heads, pointing insistently at the little person and the fireball.

My thoughts clear for a second and I'm pulled back to the present by Corinne coming to a dead stop, staring straight ahead with a weary nervousness.

"Okay, something's not right. It's too easy," she says, her eyes flicking back to my paper. "Can I see that real quick?" I hand it over and she studies it, creasing her brow in concern.

"I'm not complaining," says River, raising his hands in a placating gesture.

"I'm not either, but it's strange. This place was loaded with traps earlier. We're bound to run into something at some point, and it's unsettling that we haven't yet," Corinne responds, handing the drawing back and moving her eyes to the dark tunnel before us. It's quiet for a moment before she shakes her head and keeps walking. "Never mind. It's probably nothing."

"Of course it's nothing, you're probably just trying to scare us into believing your unstable, underdeveloped abilities are actually useful so you can feel special," snipes Breanna. Corinne shoots her a razor-sharp glare, and I can barely see her hands clenching and unclenching, but she inhales deeply and forces her hands to relax before she keeps moving.

She's good at hiding things, keeping emotions at bay and for the most part in control, fooling others to believe nothing's wrong.

The thought turns over and over in my brain, making me feel sick. I lean against the wall just to feel something solid and real. But then the wall starts moving. I jerk back and see a small section of the wall where my shoulder was pressing against, sink backwards.

A button.

Corinne must have heard the rock moving, because she freezes again and whirls around, looking at the button. Then her head whips back around to the yawning darkness and she shouts, "Get to the side! Now!"

There's a small alcove on our right and we all lunge for it immediately. No sooner do we do that, than a deep rumbling shakes the tunnel and a whizzing ball of flame shoots past us, singeing my shirt. We're all pressing ourselves against the farthest point of the space to avoid getting char broiled.

"Holy shit," breathes River. No one has to say anything to know that we're all thinking the same.

"Is that what the old man's drawing was about?" whispers Rowan. Corinne slowly nods, but doesn't move from her spot.

"We should probably get to the surface as soon as possible, though," she adds, scraping herself from the wall and sticking her head around the corner to check for more threats. "We need to get to a new safe house and make a game plan there."

"A game plan for what?" asks Breanna.

"Oh, I wouldn't know. Maybe to *stay alive?*" Corinne hisses. "All we've got right now is that the Phantom Order wants us back, and we don't want to go where they want us to. In order for us to keep evading them, we need to go somewhere they can't get to us, and the Lotus Protection is our best bet. I'm willing to bet they've hidden lots of kids in similar situations as us before. We shouldn't be any different." She takes a deep breath. "Is that a good enough reason for you?" Breanna just sniffs and looks away.

"Well then," sighs Rowan, clapping his hands together, "shall we get a move on?"

In unison, we make a move towards the main tunnel again and walk for another ten minutes, which feels like hours. Maybe it *is* hours; my sense of time is muddled down here. I'm careful not to touch anything but the floor, and even then I'm paranoid that I'll trigger another trap by simply breathing. Then the energy in the space changes before anyone even says anything.

"Up ahead," says Corinne impatiently. "A ramp leading up. There's some sort of huge room in front of it, but it looks empty." She walks ahead and I feel rather than see the space open up. And there, just as Corinne said, is a small shaft of light disappearing up a ramp on the other side of the chamber. All thoughts seem to leave my brain because before I know it, I'm running towards the exit and the light and my sister is shouting my name behind me. I see the marked tiles on the floor a nanosecond too late. Before I can stop, I trip onto the first one.

Time slows as two slots in the walls on either side of me slide open soundlessly and two sharpened wooden stakes fly towards me. All of a sudden, I'm next to Corinne again, and the wood pieces slam into each other, splintering with the impact.

River's head whips towards me and there's just enough light to see that everyone else's eyes are as big as moons.

"How did you—how—what—" Corinne stutters.

"Oh perfect," grumbles Breanna. "Another freak show." I stare at my hands. How did I do that? Was it just adrenaline? I shake my head violently. The world seems to tip sideways and I then realize that it's me who's turning. I brace myself for the impact of the cold, unforgiving stone beneath me, but my arms seem to shoot out of their own accord and I catch myself before tucking and rolling to soften the fall. I pop up back onto my feet without even thinking about it, and with no hesitation. It felt almost graceful. I expect Corinne to be gaping at me with horror, but when I look up her eyes are full of tears instead. She tackles me with a hug.

"Oh my god Leenie! You have no idea how relieved I am," she cries, squeezing me so tight I feel as if my lungs are going to explode. She finally releases me and sniffles, looking me in the eye and giving me one more squeeze before taking my hand and taking a deep breath. I watch, awestruck, as she goes from relieved sister to determined soldier in a matter of seconds. It doesn't even look like she was crying. I wonder how long she's had to practice. "All right let's see here. The tile you stepped on has some sort of symbol on it, see?" she says, pointing to the spot I had jumped from.

She goes on for a little longer, but my mind is still spinning. Do I have an ability, too? Why wasn't it triggered until now?

"You got that Selena?" Corinne asks, pulling me back to the present. I shake my head sheepishly and she sighs. "Since we can't translate the symbols here, we have no choice but to guess. So we have to step on the crevice between two tiles because then neither will have enough weight to sink down. But you have to step *exactly in the center* otherwise one could be triggered." I nod, understanding dawning on me. "Great. Uh, I'll go first," she says nervously. I see Rowan clench his jaw on my left.

Cautiously, Corinne steps onto the floor in front of us, placing her foot where four tiles meet. When none of them sink, she exhales and looks back. "See? All good," she mutters, exhaling with a steady breath. "Now I just need to—" but as soon as she takes her other foot off of the solid part of the floor, all four tiles lower into the ground.

Four slots open in the walls, each flinging a different terror.

A knife.

An arrow.

A hatchet.

A dart.

All zinging towards Corinne.

And this time, I'm not fast enough.

*Chapter 24*

# Corinne

I hear the scraping of stone on stone as the slots slide into existence and immediately know it's over for me. There's no way I can move fast enough to get out of the way.

Rowan shouts something lost to the static in my ears. Then an arm wraps around my waist and pulls me backwards with such force that my breath leaves my body.

The four weapons clang harmlessly against the floor and I turn back to see River, not even out of breath. We're standing twenty feet away from the tiles. I'm about to say something when Rowan is by my side and taking me by the shoulders while River steps away.

"What the hell were you thinking?" he shouts. I blink in surprise.

"I—I don't know. I thought—"

"No, you didn't. You didn't think! You're always taking risks for the rest of us without considering the effects it might have on you! Let us take some risks for once. You need protection just as much as we do." His gaze is unwavering, his cornhusk eyes hardened in a way I've never seen before, and all I can do is nod, shivering. He releases me then, exhaling sharply through his nose and moving his eyes to stare at the floor.

It's quiet for thirteen seconds before I hear a slow clap

133

from behind me. I turn around and see Breanna with a bored expression on her face.

"Well," she yawns, "now that drama is behind us, can we please work on getting out of here?"

"You know what, I think I've had just about enough of you," growls Rowan.

"What are you gonna do about it, hmm?" Breanna retorts, eyes hard. "Maybe give me a sappy speech? What about threatening me with your little matchstick tricks?"

"Why you—" he snarls, starting to move towards her.

"Guys," Selena cuts in. "Stop it, both of you. This isn't getting us anywhere."

"She's right," smirks Breanna. "Go back to staring into Corinne's eyes and let the big kids handle this situation."

I feel the blood pounding in my ears before I lose my grip on reason, the world tilting to the side then sharpening. I'm not a damsel in distress who needs constant attention. I'm not just some lost little girl looking for a fairytale ending to her life. My face burns and my lips twist into a fierce scowl.

I stride swiftly over to Breanna and deliver a clean uppercut to her jaw. Her eyes roll back in her head and she crumples on the floor.

"Bitch," I spit. Looking back at the others I add, "Sorry. I've had enough of her attitude." None of them say anything, their eyes glued to the floor. "Well then? What's the plan?" I try to catch Rowan's eye to make sure he's okay, but he's lost in his own head, hands clenched at his sides.

"Well, I could run across the tiles to set them all off, and since I'm faster now I could get out of the way in time," Selena offers dubiously.

"Absolutely not," interjects River. "As it appears you and I have the same ability, and since you've had no practice, I'll do it."

"You—you mean you're —" she stutters, eyes wide.

River holds up a hand, cutting her off. "We all have a lot to discuss. But first, we have to get out of here. Selena's plan has no major flaws as far as I can tell, and it's the best idea we have." Selena blushes at the attention, pleased.

"Well then River, shouldn't you get to work on that?" Rowan asks gruffly. But before he's through with the sentence, River's gone and dozens of lethal weapons are being flung haphazardly through the air. He's back where he was standing before in about two seconds.

"Already done," he reports. Selena and I stare slack jawed while Rowan grumbles something in what I'm pretty sure is another language. "It should be safe to go across now, as long as we step only on the sunken tiles. Those are the ones that have been set off, and they shouldn't go off again. I'll carry our spirited Breanna, and you three go in front of me." And with that, we get into action. Selena in front, I follow her, stepping only on the lower areas of the floor. I hold my breath and wait to be shish kabobed by some airborne threat, but we make it to the other side without trouble and race up the ramp. It gradually turns into a zigzagging staircase, as if the builders couldn't decide which way it should go.

It spits us out in someone's basement, and we cautiously go upstairs to investigate. The woman reading in the living room takes one look at us and shakes her head. She has skin as dark as midnight, beautiful against the vivid orange sundress she wears.

"Come here everyone. We have much to discuss." She disappears into the next room and sits on the plush couch. "Sit. All of you." We all do so obediently, done without questioning these people. This is most likely the next safe house we were supposed to be transferred to, so we don't interrupt, her voice commanding attention and respect. "Now, tell me everything that happened, starting with the day the Phantom Order attacked Kleka."

So we do. We tell her about trying to escape the city, Winnie's death, Tarissa's warning, the safe house, the catacombs and everything in between. We don't leave out a single detail, filling in for one another if one of us forgets something or if we can't relive that moment. When we're done she nods.

"Alright. I still don't know where we need to put you, but first, there are some things you need to know that I'm surprised Ben and Kara didn't tell you," she says in her rich voice. But despite the kindness there, a sour image fills my head of Kara's body falling towards the ground, the bullet wound in her forehead oozing blood.

The feel of someone's hand on my shoulder clears the image for a moment. Rowan is sitting next to me, and he gives my shoulder one more squeeze before letting go. How can he tell when I need someone? Need him? I shake my head, because for a moment his eyes didn't look as pale as they usually do, but a darker, emerald green instead. I still harbor irritation from his—was it jealousy?—earlier, and it's hard to let go of.

"First off, my name is Sasha. And don't bother introducing yourselves because I know all about you. You've caused a lot of trouble for the Lotus Protection in a small amount of time." I worry she's mad until I see the sparkle of mischief in her eyes. "Do you know how to tell if someone's home is a safe house or the house of a civilian? I didn't think so. There are two steps to tell the difference. First of all, they must have something decorated with a lotus on the front of their house, in full view.

"Of course, some civilians might coincidentally have something of the sort; that is where the second step comes in. Go up to the front door and tell whoever answers these exact words: 'the rise of the lotus is near'. If you say anything other than those exact words, they will not let you in. If you get it right, they'll let you in if they're with us." Sasha takes a deep breath, giving me the opportunity to tuck all this new information away.

"Do you have any specific place you're trying to get to?" she adds as an afterthought. "You cannot stay here for long." My mind blanks; I hadn't thought of where we'd go after all of this blew over. If it ever did. But we're on the run now, so no place is safe.

"Where can we go where Pie—I mean the Phantom Order can't find us, and where we won't be endangering anyone?" I ask.

Sasha thinks a moment before answering. "There is nowhere truly safe from our enemies, but there is one place you can go. The Lotus Protection Headquarters is heavily guarded and almost impossible to find unless you know the right people. Even I am escorted there blindfolded and guarded. You never know who could betray you." Her eyes linger on everyone in our group for a few seconds, but she continues without missing a beat. "I believe if you can get to the main entry of HQ and explain your situation, they'll let you in to question you. If they deem you're telling the truth, they'll let you stay, possibly even begin training with a mentor. The one problem is that only a handful of people know where HQ is. I know one of them, but she travels a lot, so I can't be entirely sure where she is. There's a slight chance that she's here in Westol, and if she is, I know where she'll be. Are you up to the task?"

***

I'm the last one to come out of the shower, having mulled things over while the warm water cascaded down my body and washed the dirt away. I toweled dry and wrung my hair out before slipping on some cotton pajamas and brushing my teeth. Breanna had woken up shortly after we talked to Sasha and hasn't made eye contact with me since.

As soon as I walk into the room that Selena, Breanna and I are sharing, I notice the boys are here too. Rowan is pacing the floor and River is sitting on the edge of one of the beds. He stands up when I enter.

"Alright, I think it's time we talk," he says.

"I agree," says Selena, plunking down on one of the two queen sized beds. I slide on next to her, and hug one of the pillows to my chest, rapidly-cooling water dripping from my hair onto my arms and making me shiver.

"First," interrupts Rowan, "we need to clear things up about ourselves, and then we can talk through what else has been happening. Sound good?" We all nod and he, River and Breanna join us on the comforter, making a circle.

"Let me guess, you two are Mutes?" asks Breanna in a flat tone. Rowan looks thrown off, but River maintains his cool expression and plows on.

"That's right. Rowan and I are Mutes," he says. "Rowan has the ability to create and control fire, and I have speed and agility." Rowan flinches a bit at the word 'fire' but River keeps going. "It appears Selena, you have the same ability as I do, and obviously, Corinne's been trying to awaken her dormant abilities: elevated senses," he continues, looking at each of us individually.

"What about Breanna?" I ask, glancing at her out of the corner of my eye. She shoots me a glare.

"I'm not sure. She could be a late bloomer, or she could just be normal," River says, studying Breanna. She waves her hand as if dismissing a stupid thought.

"You're all so dense. Of course I'm a Mute. I just hate being one and never used my ability in front of you," she scowls.

Selena and I gape at her. "So, you acted like a bitch and harassed me about being a freak and made me feel like an attention-seeker while you had an ability this *entire fucking time?!*" I feel heat creeping up my neck and onto my face. My heart speeds up and I have to wrestle my breathing back under control in order to think straight.

"Yes; you aren't very bright are you? I just said this," she scoffs. I hurl the pillow I'm holding at her head, making her topple off the side of the bed then sit up on the floor, rubbing the back of her head and snarling at me.

I see Selena trying to hide her smile behind a hand to my left, while River looks away and Rowan stares at me.

"Anyone else want to say anything?" I grind out. River sighs.

"Let's just pick up this conversation another time. I think you and Breanna should talk things out before we do this again."

"No," we say simultaneously.

"Fine, but at least watch each other's backs okay? Don't let someone get killed just because of this dumb rivalry thing going on between you two."

Breanna shoots daggers at me and I try to set her on fire with my mind. No such luck.

With that, the boys depart to their own room and we switch off the lights. I think about how I'll never fall asleep with all the thoughts swirling through my mind, but as soon as my head hits the pillow, I blank out and sleep through the entire night.

✳✳✳

The streets of Westol remind me of the pictures of New York we saw in history class. Buildings that reach for the sky, and bustling foot traffic. The sounds of taxis and car horns mingle with the overload of people talking and shouting in the streets.

I clutch the paper with the scribbled address Sasha gave us before shoving us out the door after breakfast.

"Where are we going?" asks Breanna for the zillionth time. "We have an address, but we have no idea where this is, let alone if we're even anywhere close to it."

"Need help?" inquires a sly voice. I look to my right to see a slender girl with fair skin and dark copper hair that reaches her waist. She's studying the address in her hands and I start. When did she get the address? I look down at my empty hands and back up at her. I could've sworn I just had it. Did she take it? That was quick.

"Who are you?" asks River, not missing a beat.

"The name's Roxy, at your service," she says, dropping into an overly dramatic bow. "And I can get you where you need to go." She extends the address in her hand back to me, but before I can grab it, she draws her hand back again. "Ah ah ah! Not without a price!" she taunts. I grimace. She's a pain.

"What do you want?" sighs Selena. "We don't have a lot of money but—"

"These will do nicely!" she exclaims, holding all four of our lotus pendants up so that they glint in the sun. "They are real gold, right?"

"Hey!" I shout. Several people turn their heads but most ignore us. "Those are out of the question, give them back."

Then there's a blur of movement and Roxy stumbles backwards. River holds all four necklaces triumphantly in his hand while the girl brushes herself off, slight irritation peeking out in her face, but then she smiles.

"You're quick. Too bad those aren't the real ones though." She holds up a matching set in her hand and the ones in River's disappear like smoke blown away by the wind.

"What the hell?" Rowan mutters. River just stares expressionless at his empty fist, opening and closing his fingers in the relentless sunlight.

"She's a Mute. Her ability it seems is to create illusions. And good ones at that," he says at last, dropping his arm to his side. "We have other things we can trade. Those necklaces are family heirlooms and we would greatly appreciate it if you could hand them back over."

Roxy scoffs. "Family? All they do is get bored of you and throw you out. You're just setting yourself up for disappointment, so why hold on to these? I could use this gold to finally get out of this hellhole and it'll just go to waste if you're not even going to spend it."

"Look here Carrots, we need to find that address so we can get to our destination and—" starts Breanna, but Roxy interrupts.

"Where are you headed?" she purrs, grinning.

"You saw the address," answers River, grasping at her interest.

"You and I both know that's only a step towards your real destination," Roxy pushes.

River thinks for a moment. "Alright, we can't exactly tell you where we're going, because we don't know ourselves. If you help us out, we both get to know the place. And you mentioned wanting to get out of town. If you help us, we'll help you get out." She stares at the boy, looking him up and down suspiciously. "But, in return, you have to give us back the necklaces and help us find this address."

Breanna opens her mouth to protest but River holds up a hand.

"Deal," Roxy finally chuckles. She and River shake hands and she tosses us our necklaces. I secure it around my neck and narrow my eyes at her. The thief just smiles again and shrugs unapologetically.

"Alright, follow me; and please, try not to get lost."

*Chapter 25*

# Selena

Roxy weaves expertly through the crowd, dodging pedestrians and cars like a ninja. Several times her quick fingers slide a few wallets out of people's pockets, and more than a few earrings off of others. But I figure there's no way to get her to stop, and that she's probably done this many times before. It's fairly easy to keep track of her with her waist length hair floating behind her like a flag.

Soon enough, we reach a small apartment building sandwiched between two sparkling glass skyscrapers.

"We're here," announces Roxy. "Room 207 correct?" I nod and walk up to the front door. On the weathered keypad, I press the buzzer for the room number on the paper. We wait, but no one answers. I press it a few more times, but nothing.

"Maybe they're not home?" suggests Corinne. But the light in the plastic button is on, meaning the inhabitant is here. Whoever's inside simply doesn't want to see us. I sigh. That's not going to work.

"They're here all right," I say, watching the buzzer get declined again. "But since they won't come to us, we just have to go to them." I look around, but there's no way to actually get into the building through the door unless she lets us in.

"Wait here," orders River, looking around the streets before slipping around the back of the building. About a minute later he pushes open the front door from the inside.

"How'd you get in?" I ask, shocked.

"Went through a window in the back and walked through the lobby," he shrugs nonchalantly. I give up on being confused as we ascend the stairs to the second floor.

We're deposited into a narrow hallway with a worn carpeted floor. Room 207 is to our right and once we're all standing in front of it, I knock.

No answer. Not surprising.

"We know you're home, please open the door," I call through the wood. "We need your help to find the Rise of the Lotus. We talked to Sasha and she gave us this address." No sooner do I finish the sentence when the door cracks open, and I'm looking down into the single silver eye of a short old woman.

"Sasha?" she croaks. I nod slowly. I don't want her to close the door again. Instead she grabs my wrist, opening the door a little more and pulling me inside, shutting the simple hinged wood behind me. I can hear the others erupt in protest on the other side.

The apartment is small, with an olive-green couch and a small TV for the living room. A kitchenette lies to the left of that and on the right is a small hallway that I'm assuming leads to the bedrooms. I tentatively sit on the edge of the couch as she bustles around the kitchen, putting on a kettle to boil. I wait in silence until the pot starts to scream, watching her pour the tea. Handing me a cup, she sits next to me on the couch.

Finally fed up with the suspense, I say, "Do you know how to get to the Lotus Protection HQ?" She nods. "Can you tell us?" I add. She pauses, then shakes her head. I sigh, pinching the bridge of my nose. "So you know how to get there, but you won't tell us?"

She's quiet for a moment again. "I cannot tell. But I can

show," she rasps. Standing up, she then disappears down the hallway only to return seconds later with a map in her hands. Spreading it out on the low, wooden coffee table, she stares at me expectantly. I study the map and realize why it looks so strange. It's a map of America, what our country was called before the bombs from World War III messed with the genetic coding of the wildlife. These things are so rare now, not to mention illegal. How on earth does she have one?

She traces her finger south from where we are in Westol, stopping on a point marked Oklahoma. I wrack my brain trying to think of where that would be on a present day map; Vrasall, in Tenálin. We have to travel all the way to Vrasall without getting caught by the Souls or killed by any forests. Perfect. Why couldn't HQ just be down the street? Why all the way down there?

Then I remember the others out in the hallway. They quieted down once they realized the old woman wouldn't be opening the door again.

"Thank you, ma'am," I rush, setting my untouched teacup on the table. "I appreciate it. We've got to get going, but we are forever grateful." The old woman simply observes me as I return to the door. I give her one last glance before exiting into the hallway. The others are grouped expectantly right outside. And I talk on the way to the elevator.

"Did you figure out where we need to go?" asks Corinne hopefully.

"Yes," I sigh, rubbing my temples. "The entrance is in Vrasall." Corinne falters a bit but comes back up to my side quickly.

"What's in Vrasall?" asks Roxy, wrinkling her nose.

"Our destination," River says vaguely. She shoots him an icy glare but he doesn't seem to notice, or care for that matter. "It's a start at least," he says. "Did she say anything else?"

"She didn't *say* anything. Just took out a map of America

and pointed to a place called Oklahoma. It's in the exact spot where Vrasall is."

"She had a map of America?" asks Roxy incredulously. Her irritation evaporates instantly and she perks up, eyes glittering like jewels.

"If you even think about stealing it—" starts Corinne. Roxy sighs melodramatically and begins to pout again. She has some crazy mood swings.

"Alright then," interrupts Rowan. "If we're going to Vrasall, we'll need to pack some supplies, as we can't *steal a car,*" he says pointedly, raising his voice a bit when Roxy's face lights up for the hundredth time. She exhales dramatically once more. "So, we'll be going on foot, and to stay off the radar we shouldn't take any public transportation if we don't have to."

"So basically, you're saying we have to cut through the forests," finishes Breanna. "The forests that we were always warned about, never to enter, for as long as we can remember?" Rowan nods, undeterred. "Then tell us, O Fearless One, how will we avoid the shifters in the Shifting Woods? And since Vrasall is in Tenálin, what about the creatures in Drillwood? For example, its namesake, the Drillworms?" she sneers.

"That's what we need to figure out," Rowan explains, as if he were talking to a young child. I stifle my laughter with a hand. "This may sound crazy, but we all know about our matching necklaces right?"

I do a double take when Rowan pulls a necklace identical to ours out from under his shirt. Sure, Roxy had been holding four similar necklaces, but I didn't know they were the exact same. I free my pendant while River and Corinne take theirs out too.

"I thought you guys were just being cheesy and had four matching friendship necklaces." grimaces Breanna.

Rowan goes on as if he didn't hear Breanna's comment. "I think they mean something, like, more than them just being symbolic. Well obviously, since it can't just be a coincidence that we happen to have identical necklaces with, I might add, a lotus flower in the middle. Anyone notice the organization we're trying to get to?"

My eyes widen as I realize he's right. I never really thought to put them together that way. I guess it just never occurred to me that our heirlooms and a present-day community could be more than chance.

"Organization, hmm? Now we're getting somewhere," muses Roxy to herself; she goes unacknowledged by the rest of us.

"So you think these necklaces might be more than just decorative?" asks River skeptically, studying the unmarked backside of his pendant.

"I think," corrects Rowan. "that they have some sort of purpose, and we can figure out what it is at HQ, which is just another reason for us to get there as soon as possible. Maybe they can help us in some way."

"Help us how? It's not like we're going to try to take down Pierre and his creatures. That's not our job," Breanna argues.

"Just forget I said anything," says Rowan, rolling his eyes.

"Can someone *please* explain who the hell Pierre is and what we're even having a conversation about?" interjects Roxy. I had sort of forgotten she was there.

"Later," River promises.

"Rowan?" I ask thoughtfully, replaying the conversation in my mind as we stop in the lobby. He turns his attention to me. "As much as I hate to say it, you never answered Breanna's question." He raises an eyebrow. "How do you plan to avoid the dangers in the forests?"

"That's where I was going with the necklace idea, but I'll pick up on that later," he replies, waving the question away. "First, though, we need to pack some food and other necessities. We've got a long walk ahead of us."

## Chapter 26

# Corinne

The store Roxy takes us to is called Everyone's Something. It has everything from assault rifles to blueberry scones. It's about the size of my school back in Kleka, with four stories and just as many rooms. In other words, it's massive.

She takes us to a clothing store first, and when I ask how she plans to pay for all of this, she grins and surreptitiously snags a wallet from someone's purse. She opens it up to reveal several credit cards and a few twenties.

"Gotta admit Carrots," whistles River, stealing Breanna's nickname from earlier. "You're good." She smiles maliciously and closes the wallet again. In the corner of my eyes I see Selena's eyes narrow just a bit.

"Well then. What are we waiting for?" demands Breanna. "I need a new outfit, pronto."

I let myself smile, relaxing a bit. Roxy tosses me a credit card and one of the twenties. "Knock yourselves out. I'm going to go get us some hotel rooms for the night so we can pack and work out some details for the trip." I nod and we turn around. Roxy calls out one more thing before she leaves. "Make sure you get me a soft pretzel!"

"Will do," salutes River.

"Hey, Roxy!" Rowan calls. "One thing quick!" He runs

over and whispers something in her ear, and she nods, giving him a thumbs up.

I ignore the tightening in my chest and dole out instructions. "Alright. Everyone picks an outfit or two and a coat or something in case it gets cold. Don't forget durable shoes as well. Meet up in twenty minutes at the checkout then we'll move to the next store. Got it?" I ask. Everyone nods and we all head off in different directions, spreading out in the mini store. I head towards the women's section and gather two pale blue tanks, along with simple cargo pants and an insulated jacket. Then I pick out a stocking cap and go to the shoe's section for a new pair. The plain gray sneakers from the camp are still with me, and I want to trade them out.

I find a pair of thick-soled boots and twenty minutes later I'm standing next to a mannequin with River, Rowan, and Selena.

"Where on earth is Breanna?" Selena wonders aloud. As if her name summoned her, Breanna comes striding down the main aisle, proudly holding her black leggings, white cropped tank top, hot pink jacket, boots and headband. We all gawk at her.

"What? I got everything you demanded," she says defensively when she sees our faces. Selena rolls her eyes and I sigh. The boys just snicker as we move up in the line. I pay for our stuff with the stolen credit card and the cashier glances at us suspiciously, but rings our stuff up.

Selena went with a yellow shirt, pompom hat and combat boots, with a jean jacket and overalls decorated with embroidered sunflowers. The boys both went with gray sweatpants, black T's, hiking boots and thick, double lined fleeces. Rowan's is a deep green and River's is a navy blue.

Next, we go to the backpack store and we say ten minutes tops before we check out. I grab the first suitable backpack

I see: a camo backpack made of thick canvas with plenty of pockets. I want to hurry up and get to the next store because people are starting to look at us weird. I suppose a group of teens buying armloads of stuff with one credit card looks fairly strange. Everyone's at the counter within five minutes.

I put my bag next to River and Rowan's black knapsacks, Selena's light gray rucksack, and Breanna's magenta daypack.

"Really Breanna?" I ask, giving her a look. "We're not going to blend in very well with you looking like a living barbie doll."

She sniffs. "At least I have style."

I sigh, and we pay and move to the next store: hunting and wilderness survival; for weapons and other supplies. River rubs his hands together.

"This is our domain," says Rowan proudly. "We did a lot of camping growing up. We'll need rope, wire, and knives. Keep the stuff to the minimum, and compact kits if you can. First aid, too." With that, the boys dart into the store, jostling each other and grinning like little kids on their birthdays.

Selena shrugs and follows them. Breanna makes a face at the weapons on the far wall but slowly picks her way to them.

I wander around collecting the things Rowan suggested, and more. A Bowie knife, some hunting daggers, a thirty-foot length of coarse rope, some wires for making snares (which I'll leave for the boys to set up), a couple different first aid kits, a compact water filtration system, a thin sleeping bag that reflects body heat, and at the last minute, decide to take the machete I'd seen earlier as well.

The others have similar collections, minus the machete, plus a tent with space for six. But I'm startled when Rowan adds two rifles and a few cartridges of ammo to the pile. The cashier raises an eyebrow and smirks.

"Young man, what do you think you're doing with these? You could hurt yourself," he fusses, feigning concern.

"Don't worry sir, I'm a big boy, I'll be very careful," Rowan says soberly. All humor leaves the cashier, and his smile falls.

"Well, I'm sorry, you need a permit for these." He starts to take the guns off the counter but Rowan slaps a crumpled piece of paper down and shoves it at the man.

"I believe this is what you need. I've been shooting guns since I was old enough to hold one, and my father was an esteemed hunter. So I'd appreciate it if you could sell us the rifles," Rowan says, deadly calm. The cashier pales, but takes the permit, clearing his throat and sniffing.

"Fine," the man relents stiffly after a few minutes of examining the paper. He rings us up and I wince at the price, mentally apologizing to the woman who's paying for us. Arms laden with bags, the cashier says, "Now get out of my store."

Once in the main part of the mall, River smiles, punching Rowan on the shoulder. "That was awesome, he totally pissed himself." Rowan grins broadly and we all laugh, gaining more attention.

"Where'd you get that permit?" Selena asks. "I didn't know you had one."

"I don't," laughs Rowan, eyes glinting. We stare at him, waiting for the explanation. "I knew we would need one, so I asked Roxy to create an illusion for me before she left." Selena nods, impressed, and the knot of tension from earlier evaporates in my chest.

I drag my sister and Breanna to a store called Pretty Little Girls, cringing at the outdated name and telling the boys to wait outside. They look confused but agree.

"Us girls need some other stuff as well," I say when we approach the entrance.

"Oh right, I almost forgot," exclaims Selena. "Get enough

for two cycles just in case, okay girls?" Breanna and I nod and we make our purchase, the cashier a friendly talkative woman. We rejoin the boys a moment later.

"What did you need from there?" asks Rowan. Then it dawns on him. "Never mind."

"Well then, who wants lunch?" asks River, hands clasped. We all cheer and something seems to lessen inside of me. Stress? Fear? There certainly has been plenty of that in the last few days. I feel like I haven't laughed in ages; not for real anyway.

We set our numerous bags down at a table outside of the food court, and I feel like a normal teenager hanging out with her friends as River goes up to order our food, all of us talking and laughing. He comes back ten minutes later with five burgers, two large fries, sodas and a soft pretzel in a bag for Roxy. We eat ravenously, not saying a word until everything is gone. When all the trays are cleared away, we sit contentedly in silence until I feel a hand on my shoulder. My instincts kick in as panic seizes my heart and I drive my elbow back into the person's gut.

The girl behind me gasps and doubles over, and I recognize the head of long copper hair.

"Shit, Roxy I'm sorry I didn't know it was you!" I exclaim, getting up and letting her lean on me. Several people glance at our group, wary expressions on their faces.

"Jesus Christ, woman," she half laughs, half wheezes. "Where the hell did you grow up?" I apologize over and over again as she drops into the seat next to me, but she waves me off and snatches the bag with the pretzel in it from River. I notice their barely contained laughter and huff.

"You seem to have a habit of attacking people when they approach you from behind," observes Rowan.

"I thought she was one of them," I say weakly. That sets

them off. They all burst out laughing, and I join in after a moment. Even Breanna snickers a little.

"By the way, here you go," says Roxy, tossing something to River. "He reminded me of you." River lifts it up to the light. It's a rock with googly eyes glued to it and a shaky smile drawn on with a sharpie.

"Thanks," he says, rolling his eyes and stuffing the rock into his jacket pocket.

I smile as a thought settles over me. For better or worse, this is my family now. And it's pretty damn great.

***

The hotel Roxy found for us is plush and expensive looking, with violet velvet curtains edged with gold tassel trim and Persian rugs in the lobby. Soft music plays overhead near the cathedral style ceiling, and the desk clerk wears a starched shirt and slacks. He nods at Roxy and she points finger guns at him.

"Do you know him?" I ask.

"Oh yeah, Rupert and I go *wayyyyy* back," she assures. "I talked him down to half price for the rooms so that whoever's back account we're using doesn't end up *completely* empty. That would just be cruel."

I shrug, feeling a bit out of place in such a fancy environment. On the other hand, Breanna's practically glowing with excitement.

"Finally!" she says, bouncing on the balls of her feet. "Somewhere up to my standards." She dashes towards the elevator and beckons us over impatiently. "Hurry up! I want to see the rooms!"

Roxy hits the button for the sixth floor and up we go. She doles out key cards to each of us and keeps one for herself. "The boys' room number is 616, and we girls have

617. Everyone can get cleaned up and organized and we meet in our room in two hours. Chop, chop, let's go!"

We race to the rooms while Roxy unlocks the door for us. The place is huge. Probably the size of the lobby downstairs. The soft carpet is a deep crimson, and four queen-sized beds are pushed up against two of the walls. The other two are taken up by a kitchenette with a fully stocked mini fridge, snack bar, and a mini living room with a flat-screen TV.

"Holy shit," breathes Selena.

Breanna squeals in delight. "Roxy, you are now my new favorite person!" She gives Roxy the biggest hug I've ever seen, practically squeezing the living daylights out of her. She gasps for breath as Breanna lets go of her and rushes to one of the beds, leaping onto it and stroking the silk pillowcases, absolutely mesmerized.

"You've made her the happiest girl in the universe," laughs Selena, resting her hand on Roxy's shoulder, who's still massaging her rib cage. She gives a pained smile. My sister follows Breanna inside and flops on another bed, enchanted by the softness of the comforter. I'm soon to join them, and Roxy heads to the bathroom to shower and change. She had apparently done her own shopping—or stealing—while we were at the mall, because I see a few stacks of clothes on one of the beds and she comes out wearing silk pajamas, her long hair swaying around her hips.

"I picked up some pajamas for you guys," she says, gesturing to one of the piles on her bed. "Figured you wouldn't think of them when you were at the mall."

"Thanks Roxy," I say, grateful. "We got some pads and stuff too if you need any."

"I was hoping you'd get some," she replies, clearly relieved. "Corinne, you're up for shower. Just try not to scream when you see it." She winks at me and jumps onto her bed, flinging her clothes onto the floor.

I take a set of pajamas and open the door to the bathroom; my breath instantly catches in my throat. The bathroom is half the size of our room, with a ginormous bathtub, jets, two levels of water, and an array of salts and essential oils, as well as a dizzying amount of shampoos to choose from. The shower is an entire separate appliance, and has probably at *least* twenty different nozzles on one wall. Four sinks are inlaid in the marble countertop. Towels that look as soft as clouds are piled on a rack near the corner.

It takes me twice as long to shower as it normally would, because I spend probably ten minutes deciding which products to use, followed by another twenty minutes trying to figure out the shower before I actually get undressed. Almost an hour later, I emerge, confused but clean. Selena goes in next but it only takes her twenty minutes to do everything I did. Breanna's last and she *does* scream when she sees it.

"You can invite the boys over now, I'll be in here awhile!" she calls in a singsong voice. I can tell from the waterfall sound on the other side of the door that she's using the bathtub.

I head across the hallway and knock on their door, and Rowan opens it a second later, his damp, gold-brown hair hanging over his eyes.

"You guys can come over now." My voice is even and steady. He smiles and calls for River over his shoulder. A moment later we're seated in a circle on the floor, and I half expect Jax to pop out from under one of the nightstands.

"Alright first up, 'Roxy'," begins River, emphasizing her name. "What's your real name? Roxy isn't it is it?" She hesitates only for a moment before gathering her composure again.

"You're correct," she says simply, clearing her throat. "My real name is Victoria, and I'm only telling you this because we're going to be stuck with each other for a while it seems. As you said you'd help me get out, right?"

I stare, incredulous. How on earth did River sort that out? The others are as bewildered as I am because they don't say anything, just stare, dumbstruck. River allows a small, satisfied smile and a nod before moving on, completely unfazed.

"Next up, let us tell you a bit about ourselves. You know all of our names already, but here are some things that I think it's alright for you to know. We're from Kleka, and our city was raided. We were taken by the Phantom Order—their leader is Pierre—but obviously we got out and now we're looking for a safe place. Mostly, we've been traveling underground, and we, like you, all happen to be Mutes." Roxy—no, Victoria nods like this is completely normal.

"What are your abilities?" she asks.

"I have speed and agility, and so does Selena. Rowan can create and control fire, and Corinne has enhanced senses. We know Breanna has something as well, but she hasn't told us what yet. Rowan and I have known since we were kids, Selena and Corinne only just discovered theirs, and again, we're not really sure about Breanna," supplies River.

That makes me think, and a question bubbles up in my mind. "Why do you think you guys knew about your abilities before we did?" I ask.

Rowan coughs, pulling all the attention to himself. "You know those mandatory vitamins Kleka gave us that were actually the government's prototype gene switches?" he asks. "We were told not to take them, and we didn't know why until Pierre told you the real reason behind them. So, we developed our abilities at the average ages and were always super careful about who knew what we could do."

"The mayor, who told everyone to take the vitamins, also told his kids not to take them?" I ask, confused.

"Well, technically it wasn't him who told us. He didn't know," Rowan says softly, eyes downcast; I've hit a nerve.

"Anyone have anything else they need to know?" asks River. I shake my head, followed by the other three. "Well, in that case I say let's play a board game!" He stands up and goes to one of the numerous closets. Inside are dozens of different games. River selects a particularly colorful one and sets it in the middle of our little circle.

Just then Breanna emerges from a steaming bathroom, hair wrapped in a towel.

"Did I miss anything important?" she asks.

"Not really. We were mostly just filling Victoria in on what's been happening. Yes, Roxy was a lie; Victoria is her real name," River says in response to her confused expressions. She just shrugs and joins us on the floor. We set up the game and spend the rest of the evening playing different board games. My heart feels light for once, and I let myself lower my guard, relaxing and laughing more. I feel like I could take on anything and anyone with these people, because I know they all have my back. I'd almost forgotten what that felt like.

## Chapter 27

# Selena

I wake up tangled in my sheets and utterly exhausted, weak sunlight filtering down from the huge windows above our beds. I stand up somewhat groggily, yawning and stretching my arms above my head before looking around our room. Last night comes flying back like a cloud of warmth.

We had played board games for hours, laughing and getting really competitive. Finally, at about midnight, the boys had gone back to their room and we had all gone to bed. But last night will stay with me forever, I was so—happy. Just plain happy. No other word can describe it.

"Morning Leenie," Corinne yawns from the bed next to mine. I smile at her before heading to the bathroom to brush my teeth. On my way out, I swipe a tube of toothpaste and some of the extra toothbrushes for the trip.

"Here," I say, tossing one of them to Corinne.

Victoria is gone, her bed made, but Breanna is still snoring lightly, one hand thrown over her forehead. Corinne catches the toothbrush and disappears into the bathroom. When she returns she says, "We should probably start packing up and cleaning this place a bit." We stare at the floor, strewn with game pieces and cards. "You get your stuff together while I start on the games. When you're done we switch." I nod and while Corinne picks her way through the stuff on the floor, I get my stuff from where I had dropped it off by my nightstand.

I was incredibly proud when I found the rucksack with leather straps, so I take a moment now to admire it before getting to work organizing my other items on the bed. Setting aside my clothes for the trip, I take stock.

A second yellow tee, several changes of underwear we picked up from the feminine care store, two hunting daggers, a paring knife, a pocketknife, ten feet of rope, a first aid kit, a straw with a built-in filter, a canteen, a toothbrush plus toothpaste, my hat and jacket, a slim sleeping bag and the canary yellow combat boots with black laces.

Satisfied, I get dressed quickly, tugging on the boots and tying them tightly. I throw the pajamas on the foot of my bed and put the majority of my collection in the bag, leaving out a hunting dagger and the pocketknife while sliding the latter into the pocket of my overalls and securing the former to my waist. Lastly, I fold up the jean jacket and place both it and the hat near the opening of the bag, in case it gets cold and I want to get them out quickly.

"I'm finished," I state, setting my bag up on the bed. Corinne nods and stands up. While I was packing, she had finished picking up the games. So, instead I perch next to her pile of things and study the collection. She systematically adds her supplies to her camo backpack. She zips it up once it's filled, setting it next to her sleeping bag.

Then she attaches the second hunting dagger to her thigh, and straps that deadly looking machete to her back. It came with a sheath, so hopefully she won't cut herself. And it will be mostly obscured with her backpack, covering the majority of its shape.

Our door clicks open and Victoria enters, arms laden with muffins and bagels, along with some bottles of orange juice.

"Where'd you get all that?" Corinne asks.

"There's a breakfast buffet downstairs. It's complimentary with our stay," she says around the cookie in her mouth. She sets the pile down on the table in the kitchenette and plops into one of the chairs. "Is everyone packed? We should also stop quickly at a store to get a few more non-perishables."

Corinne and I point simultaneously at Breanna, still dead to the world in her bed, hair fanned out around her head like a fairytale princess. Victoria starts to say something but is interrupted by soft knocking on our door. Corinne goes to open it and River saunters in, knapsack, the tent, and sleeping bag slung over his shoulder. Rowan follows, carrying the two shotguns.

"You guys want something to eat?" I hear Corinne ask. They all rejoin us at the table and we eat just a bit, saving some for Breanna and some for the trip.

"Someone better go wake up sleeping beauty over there," Victoria comments.

When no one volunteers, I sigh. "I'll do it."

***

Forty-five minutes later, we're out the door and back into the streets. Breanna's sour face and the painful bruise on my arm tells me she was not happy to be rushed out of her comfort zone. But we have to get moving so we can make some headway during the day.

Victoria leads us to the edge to town where an electric fence surrounds the city. Unlike Kleka's fence, this one is made out of thick, vertical metal bars that are twice the height and have triple the electrical charge. We avoided it on the way in by going underground, but now we can exit on the surface. The southern gate is open. People are streaming in and out of the city. Guards holding assault rifles stare expressionless at the crowd, and we join the throng of people on their way out. But instead of heading to the platform to board the train, we slip off unnoticed into the foliage of the Shifting Wood off to the side. One man with a peculiar hat for a day with hardly any sun eyes us, and tries to make his way through the crowd. Before long however, he's lost in the sea of faces and we're gone. Safe from sight of the public, we ease into a steady pace.

"Well, that went much smoother than I had hoped for," says Victoria, swiveling her head to look at the tops of the trees far, far above us. "So now we just keep moving south until we find the entrance? Do you guys know what it looks like?"

"No idea," admits River. "Our goal right now is to make it to Vrasall and dig around to see if anyone there will spill the location."

"Wonderful," she mutters.

"Why are you so anxious to get there?" I ask, genuinely curious. "Do you have someone waiting for you?" She stands up straighter and just shakes her head, lips pressed tight. There's something else she's not telling us, but we let her keep her secrets for now.

Rowan pulls out a compass from one of the pockets on his bag and lays it flat on his palm, rotating his position slightly and walking in a new direction. "We'll have to adjust our direction frequently; these trees are already starting to mess with us, to get us lost," he says. Corinne moves to his side and they exchange a few words. He nods.

We walk, and we walk, and we walk. Every few minutes, Rowan checks the compass and changes our course again. At one point the forest had us heading back to Westol in the north. I try to track the trees as we move, but they look like normal, still trees. It infuriates me, and yet I'm distracted by their beauty, enthralled with their fluid swaying and peaceful auras. Several times, Corinne has to lead me away from a lovely bloom or an unfurling fern.

And yet we keep walking. No one talks much. All of us are too busy avoiding the forest's subtle attempts to slow us down. Roots snake out and try to wrap around our ankles, the trees thicken and thin, attempting to split us up. We even had to cut Victoria loose from a branch that lifted her into the air at one point.

Finally, my legs shaking from exhaustion, the sky begins to darken subtly and the boys tell us we should set up camp.

"We need to set up the tents and snares," they explain.

We hunt for a clearing, but before we can find one, Corinne stops in her tracks, cocking her head and paling. "Get your weapons out," she whispers, still gaunt. "Someone's coming. Lots of someones. From all directions." Without any hesitation, we all drop our bags and make a circle facing outwards, everyone with some sort of weapon drawn. We're like a well-oiled machine, the way we work together without communicating our next move. I still hear nothing, and wonder if Corinne was just being paranoid.

"Well, well, well," a husky voice snarls. "Look at who we've found."

## Chapter 28

# Corinne

A man dressed in full hunting gear emerges from behind a nearby tree, the brim of his hat shading his eyes. Silently, about a dozen others emerge from the growing darkness, forming a tight circle around our little group. What unnerves me the most are their masks. Each and every one of them sports a white mold of a generic human face, but twisted in agony and despair. They resemble the masks that symbolize theater, only these characters are tortured.

"A friend of mine—he works the register at a wilderness survival shop—mentioned he witnessed your little permit stunt. Such a strange collection of items for such a young group of kids. I've come out here to investigate, then saw y'all traipsing into the woods off the platform, and well, that pretty much speaks for itself," says the lead man. "Y'all aren't human are ya? Or at least, not completely. You've all got somethin' wrong with your coding."

"That's absurd, you must be mistaken," pushes River, completely deadpan. "We're all one-hundred percent human, just as I assume you fine people are."

The man's lips twist into a humorless snarl of a grin, and he unslings his gun from his back, making sure we hear him click the safety off. At that signal, all of his companions tense up, dropping slightly lower for a more even stance.

"You kids are gonna come with me now, ya hear? Put your hands up and walk over here nice and slow."

"We're not going with you. But if you like, you can leave now, and you can keep your submissive lives," presses River, completely calm. The people around us howl with laughter, but he remains unfazed.

"You think you can hurt us? You're children with a few play knives, not a threat," spits the man. My eyes pick out a spot in the air that seems–different somehow, blurred, like a glitch almost, and nearly indiscernible. I can most likely see it only because of my enhanced vision, which I use to follow it as it drifts towards a stocky man.

"Not just any children," cackles Breanna. She appears out of the blemish in the air, and drags a knife across the man's throat in a quick, clean slice. He drops to the ground, dead. Everyone watches, rooted to the spot as she picks up his revolver and twirls it in her fingers. "Anyone else?"

Absolute chaos erupts from the dead silence, everything happening at once. Breanna throws herself at men and women alike with a wrath I've never seen in her before. River and Selena turn into blurs of movement, tackling two more people to the ground as round after round of bullets are unleashed in the air. Rowan uses the confusion to get close enough to punch one of the masked men in the face, the plastic cracking as he staggers backwards.

Gunshots puncture the heavy air, whizzing back and forth, but all I can do is watch, my heart contracting and my brain screaming at me to move. Two people move in my direction, having avoided the brunt of the melee. Someone grabs my wrists, and I come back to myself enough to twist free and deliver a solid punch to someone's gut. They grunt, but the second person slaps my face hard enough that I fall to my knees, earning a kick to my ribs and a scream from me. Stars dance in my line of sight as I try and fail to get back on my feet.

They lower their face to mine and whisper, terrifyingly calm, "Usually the government would pay an extremely handsome price for the lot of you, but someone else has agreed to pay double."

I instantly put together that this client must be Pierre and the Phantom Order as a whole, since no one else would pay that much for a random group of Mutes.

Out of absolutely nowhere, a blur of gold and brown rockets from the underbrush on my right and cuts off the person's gloating instantly, blood pouring from the new hole in their neck.

I turn my attention dizzily to see others grappling with a lynx, the beast's snarling maw snapping at every opening. It latches onto someone's forearm and they scream, thrashing under the creature's weight. A knife flashes in the fading light as it's driven it into the lynx's front left shoulder. The animal yowls in pain, but doesn't let go. Instead it sinks its teeth deeper.

The person is finally able to shake the creature off, only to get their throat torn open a moment later, screams dissolving. The last man standing is the leader of the group, whom Tori currently has in an impressive headlock. A steady stream of curses spews from his mouth, but this doesn't faze Breanna as she happily ties his wrists and ankles with a length of our rope.

I return my distorted attention back to the lynx, who currently sits on its haunches, growling and licking its wound. Then before my very eyes, the animal begins to stretch and morph, growing in size until there's a person standing in its place. It's a girl with wispy blond hair thrown into a messy bun sitting atop her head. She's wearing a black hoodie and gray cargo pants, along with shiny black boots.

"Damn it," the girl mutters. "That hurt."

She turns around, realizing for the first time that she has

an audience. But then her eyes meet mine, and memories shed their shadows, emerging into the forefront of my mind. I would know those mottled, two-toned eyes anywhere. A lynx cub, part of my adopted shifter family that raised me until I was five.

Jinx.

"Corinne?" she whispers, eyes as big as full moons. "Oh my god you're fucking joking!" she cries, crashing into me and crushing me with a hug. "When those hunters took you away I thought I'd never see you again!" At a complete loss for words, I hug her back tightly, tears sliding down my face as my brain does a full one-eighty in an attempt to process this. Jinx is crying hysterically, letting go to hold me at arm's length, studying my face.

"Anyone mind explaining anything?" Selena asks, her tone icy. Jinx's arms drop to her sides and she faces my sister, stunned.

"Selena," I say, biting my lip. My sister's gaze is unwavering. "This is Jinx. Uh, it's kind of a long story." *And I don't want to talk about it.*

"Well," says Rowan, his expression equally as cold. Why is *he* upset? "Let's set up a camp and then we have plenty of time to hear the story."

***

The tent is up in ten minutes, and sleeping bags laid out in another two. The boys roll some fallen logs over for benches and get a fairly strong fire going. By the time everything's ready however, it's pretty much completely black out.

Everyone sits down and looks at me expectantly as River passes around some of the food from the hotel. I can distantly hear Roland—the leader of the white-masked people—struggling against his bonds a ways out in the forest.

"I—" The words get stuck in my throat, blocking my airways. I don't want to tell the story. It hurts because it was all my fault.

"I've got you," Jinx whispers to me. Then she proceeds to tell the story I had buried deep inside of me for so long. About living in the Shifting Woods for the first hazy years of my life, no parents in sight, let alone a sister. No one knew or knows now what caused my sister and I to be separated. She recalls playing with squirrels and hunting rabbits, wrestling with the lynx cubs. As she talks, I can almost feel the dappled sunshine on my skin from those distant memories. She talks about how we lived together, her shifter family and I, in a small den a little ways away from a hunter's house. We were always careful, and avoided them at all costs. The hunter had two little boys and a wife, and they were always ignorantly killing animals without knowing they were really shifters.

One day when I was a few weeks over five years old, I wandered close to their house and the father saw me. I tried to get away, but he followed me back to the den and saw me with the lynxes. He thought they were going to hurt me, so he attacked. My family fought to protect me, but they were no match for the man's shotgun. They died trying to protect me, and Jinx was the only survivor.

The man brought me to the local orphanage immediately, which then realized they had my sister in their care through our uncanny resemblance and matching birthmarks, followed by a DNA test. Jinx had watched from a bush, hidden from view as I was reunited with my blood sibling. And then she had simply faded into the forest, surviving on her own since.

"I can't believe you never told me any of this," Selena breathes. "It's like you lived a whole different life before you even knew I existed."

"I'm sorry I never said anything," I mumble, twisting my hand in the hem of my shirt. "It was just too painful to think about, and I didn't want you to feel like I wasn't glad I had found my blood sister, because that was one of the happiest days of my life."

Selena looks deflated. No longer angry, just weary. "I'm going to sleep on it. We can talk more in the morning." With that, she disappears into the tent. I want to talk to her now, tell her how sorry I am. But she's gone. I'm too late.

"I'm off to bed as well," River announces. "Who else?" Breanna stands up, and Victoria gives me a small sympathetic smile before following them. The only sound now is the crackling of the fire.

"I can tell you two need to talk," says Jinx, a little awkwardly. "I'll be back in a few hours." She gives me another quick hug, whispering, "I'm so glad I found you again. I've missed you." Then she slinks off into the forest, a lynx once more. It's just Rowan and I now.

"Why?" he asks, staring at the flames. "Why didn't you fight back?"

"Why didn't you use your fire?" I counter. His jaw tightens.

"Answer the question, Corinne. Why did you let them hurt you and get away with it? The girl I know is stronger than that. She fights back."

"I don't know!" I say, frustrated and frankly a little hurt. I pick up some pebbles and toss them at the fire. More silence. I stare at the sharp stone in my hand, clenching my fist around it. The skin of my palm splits, but I ignore the stinging and squeeze it harder. The pain releases some of my frustration. Why didn't I fight back? Why did I just stand there like a frightened child?

"Corinne, enough," says Rowan. All of a sudden he's taking a hold of my wrist gently but firmly. "You're bleeding."

I distantly notice the blood coating my hand. My palm

is throbbing, but I don't care. "I couldn't move," I breathe, haunted by the memory. "It was like I was being controlled." Rowan digs around in his bag for one of the first aid kits. He wipes the skin around the wounds with some hydrogen peroxide and once clean, wraps my hand tightly in sterile white gauze.

"Then you need to practice," he says, securing the bandage and looking me in the eyes. The intensity draws me back to reality and the dull throbbing of my hands. "I'll help you work on it, but you have to *promise me* that you won't just let people beat you down like that again. Swear it."

"I—I promise," I say, having to drop my gaze. He relaxes a bit, but doesn't let go of my hand. "Will you answer my question now?"

His head whips up again.

"Why didn't you use your fire when they attacked? And you used a lighter to start the campfire. Why?"

"Because fire shouldn't be allowed to be wielded by a human. It only ends in death," he whispers, distraught. "Nothing good comes of it." When he doesn't continue, I watch the dancing flames eat away at the wood.

"Do you really think that the necklaces mean anything?" I ask quietly, keeping my gaze on the flickering heat.

"Wholeheartedly," he admits. "We just need to figure out what it is." I nod, exhaustion clouding my mind. My eyelids droop and I fall against him, not able to catch myself. He smells good. Like spiced chai and campfires; I don't move. I feel him tense, then rest a hand on my head. "Get some sleep." There's a note of fondness in his voice, but I push myself to stand up, staggering to the tent. Once inside, I collapse on the ground.

***

"Corinne. Corinne, wake up." Jinx is shaking my shoulder. I sit up instantly, disoriented. I'm laying on my sleeping bag inside the tent and we're the only ones in it. Did I walk here last night? "We're leaving soon."

"We?" I ask, surprised.

"Yeah. Rowan invited me to tag along. Your sister didn't seem too happy about it, but I promise I'll stay out of the way," she assures.

"That's great," I smile. "I was hoping you'd come with us. I think you and Selena could become friends." She shrugs, tugging me to my feet and pulling me outside. I squint in the brightness and look around. Pretty much everything is packed up, the fire doused and the tent the only thing left.

"Here," says Victoria, tossing me a bagel. "I saved it from our new friend this morning. She can eat."

"Thanks, Victoria."

"Please, call me Tori," she says, smiling painfully.

Selena is sitting on the dirt, munching thoughtfully on a handful of Cheetos. "Leenie, I'm sorry I didn't tell you about all of this before," I blurt out suddenly.

She looks at me as if she's seeing me for the first time. "No, I'm sorry Corinne. It was your business and you would've told me when you were ready to. I shouldn't have been so dramatic." She gives me a small smile, then notices my hand. "Oh, god, what happened?" She stuffs the rest of the Cheetos into her mouth and wipes her hands on her overalls, then takes my hands to examine them.

"I got a little too attached to a rock," I say in a resigned voice.

She stares at me. "You're not kidding?" I shake my head and she starts laughing, pulling me in for a hug. "Why on earth did that seem like a good idea?"

Relieved, I hug her back, the knot in my stomach loosening a bit. But with the absence of exhaustion, I'm acutely aware of the stabbing pain at the base of my skull.

"What are we going to do about our friend tied to the tree?" I ask, rubbing my neck in the spot where the headache stems from.

River joins in the conversation, stating, "We'll let him go, but not until we've given him a little reminder to stay out of our way."

Just then, Tori and Breanna drag a howling Roland over to the center of our group, dropping him unceremoniously on the ground. Realizing he's severely outnumbered, he doesn't attempt an escape.

"What are you gonna do to me, eh?" he chuckles. "You gonna lecture me? You gonna make me pinkie promise to stop hunting you fucked up freaks, huh?"

River nods to Jinx, who rolls up her sleeves excitedly, the nails on her right hand stretch themselves into claws. Roland goes sheet-white, swallowing his next words.

"Oh, Roland. Can I call you Rolly? Yeah? Well Rolly, one thing's for sure. You will definitely be leaving us alone, as well as any other Mutes you may come across. It's not that I don't trust you, which actually, I don't, but that we need a way to recognize you no matter what."

"Please, don't kill me," Roland squeaks, backing up until he reaches Rowan, who shoves him back into the middle.

"Oh, I won't kill you, I promise. You don't deserve that easy of an end." Jinx titters. In one clean movement, she brings her hand up and then down onto Roland's face, leaving several trenches in the skin there. The man screams in shock or agony, possibly both, and crumples to the ground. Jinx retracts the claws and wipes her hands aggressively on her pants.

"You're free to go, Roland. But if any of us ever see you hunting Mutes ever again, that mark will be across your neck next time," promises Jinx. Roland merely whimpers on the ground, his face cradled in his hands.

"Alright, we're done here, so let's clear out!" calls River, loading the last bag onto his shoulder. A few minutes later, we're on our way again, beginning the endless trek once more and leaving our attacker in the very spot Jinx slashed him. River calculated that it would take roughly three weeks to get there.

Over the next few hours, I mull that over. Three weeks of grueling hiking, and—the creaking of buried rope sounds to my right.

"Everybody stop!" I shout, going stone still myself.

"Why?" asks Jinx, taking a step towards me. I see it happen in slow motion. The net snaps up under her feet and then I'm there, shoving her off. But my luck only lasts as long as that. In a split second I'm catapulted upwards, the net closing over my head and completely enclosing my body.

"Why the hell'd you do that!" hollers Jinx. "I could have just clawed my way out!"

"I don't know!" I shout back sourly. "But if you can get me down, maybe I can think of a good excuse!"

"Corinne, try cutting it with one of your knives!" calls Victoria, cupping a hand around her mouth. I mentally facepalm myself and maneuver my body so that I can reach the hunting dagger on my thigh. I use it to saw back and forth on the net, but the knife just sparks off and nicks my thumb.

"Godammit," I mutter, sucking on the wound. Then louder, I say, "It doesn't work. This net's made of something other than regular rope. You think a Mute set it?"

"Clever girl," purrs a voice next to me. I whirl to my right and come face to face with another person. Letting out an undignified squeak, I back away as far as the net will allow. The person backs up, allowing me to make out some features. He's crouched on the thick tree branch next to the net, grinning. Deeply tanned skin is stretched over toned, lean muscles. Inky black tattoos cover him with complex and captivating patterns of lines. He wears nothing but a pair of dark gray sweatpants. Mischievous gold eyes glint at me through the mess of black curls falling over his forehead, elongated canines bared over his lower lip.

"Who are you?" I ask, struggling to regain composure.

"The name's Jotaro," he says, standing up and bending at the waist in a mock bow. "And you will do perfectly for tonight's entertainment."

## Chapter 29

# Selena

I notice the strange boy creep up before Corinne does. I can't see him clearly from so far below, but it looks like he has snaking black tattoos all over his chest and arms. Corinne jumps when he speaks, and they exchange a few words; my sister appears horrified.

Then the boy pulls out a large knife from his waistband, and slashes through the ropes holding Corinne suspended in the air. She cries out, freefalling, before landing hard on the ground. Rowan sprints to her side as she rolls over, coughing up blood and clutching her left wrist. The boy drops from his branch and lands nimbly on all fours in a crouch.

"Jotaro!" a sharp voice exclaims. "You're damaging the catch!" A group of people emerge from the shadows, dressed in baggy clothes and no weapons save for a few knives from what I can tell.

"Oops," muses Jotaro, peering at Corinne as if he's just noticed she didn't land on her feet. "I didn't think it was that far of a drop." Corinne sits up slowly, glaring at Jotaro and wiping blood from her lips.

The woman who had spoken before comes forward, shaking her head. She has raven black hair cut in a jagged line at her shoulders and snow-white skin. "What's your name?" she asks, turning to Corinne and acting as if the rest of us aren't there.

"Why should I tell you anything?" Corinne spits while Rowan helps her struggle to her feet.

"Because we like to know the names of our catch before we send them to their deaths." the woman says, her voice measured as if she's said this many times before. My sister pales a bit, but then she looks to Rowan then back to the woman, and she seems a bit sturdier.

"Would you care to elaborate?" snips Corinne. She's going for a cocky and confident defense.

"Certainly. We shifters don't get much entertainment around here. So every so often we like to catch some stupid humans who think they can just waltz right through our territory and make them fight each other until one of them dies!" There's a spark of excitement in her black eyes, and it sends shivers running down my spice. Those are the eyes of a psychopath.

"Right," Corinne agrees, changing course. Using her most diplomatic voice, she continues. "I'm very sorry for your unfortunate circumstances but we really must not be delayed. My group and I are on a very important mission to get to the headquarters of the Lotus Protection. We are currently being hunted by some very unpleasant people, and if we dwell in your custody for too long, I worry that we might draw them to you."

The woman laughs. "Oh, I like you! Let's make a deal shall we? I'm in a good mood today. If you fight our seventeen-time champion and win, we will let you *and* all of your friends go on, undisturbed. We'll even give you a lift as far as our territory extends. I really am feeling generous. But, if you lose, and die, we will force your companions to fight *each other* until only one is left and then leave the winner to the pack, and hand your corpses over to your pursuers for them to do as they wish, as I am assuming they don't necessarily need you to be alive."

Corinne swallows, and I see Rowan's hand tighten around her waist, making my sister tense. Then she steps forward, away from Rowan, away from us, and sticks out her right hand.

"Deal."

The woman claps her hands, then shakes Corinne's. "Wonderful! Now that that's behind us, come along. We must get you dressed!"

Corinne drops her hand and we all begin to silently file after them. Jotaro gives my sister a smirk and a once over with his eyes, but she stoically ignores him.

We walk for about another hour, without even stopping once. Our company seems to have endless stamina, and I can see no way to avoid this, even with all our abilities combined. Finally though, we come to a stop at a wall of vines. A stocky man with salt and pepper hair steps forward and parts them to reveal a cave. A den by the looks of it. We crowd into the small space and the woman—who seems to be the one in charge—moves to the back. She places her hand on a particular stone with five indentations and grips it, twisting it counterclockwise ninety degrees. The back wall of the den splits down the middle and disappears into slots on both sides. A gaping tunnel stretches on behind the door, and I flick my eyes to Corinne, knowing she can see perfectly.

"Let our guests go first," she says, addressing Jotaro. He stops where he was pushing forwards and bows his head. Corinne leads the way, and one by one, we're swallowed by the darkness. How I don't trip over my own two feet, I'll never know. But after a little while the passage spits us out in a huge underground cavern, reminding me of the catacombs. I shiver, realizing we must be inside a section of them.

The entire place is lit up with fluorescent lights, and

everything is enforced by exposed metal structures, giving the cavern a grungy, mechanical, steampunk look. We're standing on a large platform with a railing blocking the hundred foot drop off the end. On either side, stairs are carved into the stone, and there are animals everywhere. They're almost all predators, but they bound and saunter in between humans and no one even gives them so much as a second glance. The woman shoos us in the direction of the steps.

"Hurry! We're a bit behind schedule and we must get you prepared and explain some of the rules! We can't have you looking like that for such a grand event," she orders. We follow her down the steps on the left and along some decently wide but unprotected paths shaped out of the walls. We descend until we reach the bottom of the room, and she stops again. "Alright. Jotaro, take our guests to the premium seating. "Corinne, follow me dear."

River is by my side in an instant.

"How are you putting up with this?" he mutters. "I don't trust them. What's stopping them from going back on their half of the deal? Corinne might *die,* Selena."

I clench my jaw and keep my cool. "I am very aware of that fact, thank you. But I don't see any other option. We just have to trust Corinne. She's probably trying to figure out a plan as we speak, so just try to stay alert."

"No problem there," he says, patting my shoulder and moving away again. My face heats up with irritation but I force my mind to focus on Corinne. I see Rowan give her shoulder a quick tight squeeze before she's whisked away in a flurry of women who seemingly appeared out of a murder of crows. Understanding hits me like a brick to the face.

The animals I'm seeing are all shifters in their animal form. I'm willing to bet that the humans I saw are as well, just in their original shape. Corinne gives me one last desperate look before she's swallowed by the chattering women and rounds a corner.

"Come on," growls Jotaro impatiently. "I have important… places to be, and I don't need some witless freaks eating up my time." He sort of resembles River, if River had tattoos and anger management issues.

He leads us down a series of halls and into a room only slightly smaller than the one we just came from. A rowdy crowd of people and forest creatures alike are packed on bleachers that go all around the circular space. In the center and dominating the majority of the room is what looks similar to where gladiators would fight. A sandy pit with ten-foot-high concrete walls surrounding it save for two doors on either side of the circle. Jotaro sits us down in a blocked off section called 'premium seating'. Only three other people are there, and we're placed in the row right on the edge of the pit.

"Enjoy the show," whispers Jotaro, grinning like a shark.

## Chapter 30

# Corinne

The gaggle of girls won't stop their high-pitched laughing and giggling. They whisper to each other, giving me looks of contempt and making each other snicker with rude comments they don't think I can hear.

It's not until I take notice of my surroundings that we stop. There is a smooth, stone room about the size of a classroom that reminds me of a pop star's dressing room. Racks of identical outfits of various sizes dominate most of the floor, but beside that there's a counter littered with tubes of lipstick and other beauty items. A shower and a stack of towels is set into one corner; and there is a second door with a ruckus emanating from the other side of it on the far wall.

I calm my nerves by asking the woman some more questions. "I told you my name, so it's only fair if you tell me yours," I say, almost collapsing with relief when my voice comes out steady and defiant. The girls all gasp in horror, but my captor just grins.

"My name is Kaylee. I run this place that so many shifters call home." She raises her arms as if she's unveiling a statue. "Ladies, get her dressed please."

The girls voice their consent and I'm rushed over to one of the racks. They begin stripping me and I'm shoved into the shower. Hot water pours down my skin and they scrub at the dirt on my skin vigorously. Once satisfied, they haul me back out and dry me with a rough towel. I wince as they examine my wrist and hands, still sore from my fall out of the tree and my episode with the rock. My shoulder is also still sore thanks to Buzzcut's bullet. The skin has healed, but not the inner wound.

One of them drips a few drops of liquid from a jade bottle onto my injuries and instantly the pain subsides. I flex my hands in wonder, marveling at the healed joints and skin.

"What is this?" I ask distantly as another girl maybe a few years older than me holds up different sizes to my body, muttering to herself.

"One of our proudest reputations around here is our healers. They infuse herbal pain killers with their healing essence, making it the strongest healing agent in all of Shesta," Kaylee boasts, puffing out her chest.

Once the older girl locates a set that fits, she and the one who healed my wrist wrap the bits of clothing around me, tightening here and loosening there. Finally, they push me in front of a full-length mirror to let me see how I look.

I gawk at how little coverage there is, including the *full* exposure of my birthmark. The outfit is themed a rich indigo color with silver accents. A silky strip of cloth holds my breasts in place, iridescent ribbons wrapped around my torso. They clasp onto the waistband of the simple, flowy miniskirt that starts right below my navel and ends halfway down my thighs. There's a sort of underwear attachment underneath, so I don't have to worry about flashing anyone if my skirt flies up, but still. I feel like I'm wearing lingerie, never mind how flattering it might be. Translucent gauzy sleeves hang loosely around my arms, and end tightly around my wrists. Everything is trimmed with braided, silver cords. Lastly, they clip thick, silver bracelets around my ankles and wrists, and wind purple ribbons around my thighs, securing them at my knees with perfect, practiced bows. Apparently I'm also fighting barefoot.

"Oh, you look absolutely gorgeous!" squeals Kaylee, clapping her hands and jumping up and down excitedly. "Wonderful job girls. We're on in ten minutes!"

She and the giggling girls leave me alone in the room and I sit down to think. But then the door opens and Jotaro walks in, sending me shooting to my feet again.

"You look—exquisite," he breathes, his dark gold eyes raking up and down my exposed body as he prowls closer. I step back, but one of the racks is in my way and I can't move any farther. "The girls did well fixing you up. There's something I want from you, but we don't have a lot of time." He reaches out a hand, brushing my collarbone with his fingertips. When the door swings open again, he jerks back suddenly. I nearly cry when I see Rowan. He takes in the scene and narrows his eyes at Jotaro, who clears his throat and edges around the former, nodding stiffly at my dear friend and giving me a strained smile. Once Jotaro's gone, Rowan rushes towards me, stopping short a foot away.

"I'm sorry," whispers Rowan. "They wouldn't let me see you until Kylee got back. Are you alright?"

I nod petulantly, keeping my back carefully turned away from him. "Yeah. They healed my wrist and hands. My shoulder, too. But that didn't help with the nerves. I'll be fine, though." His eyes are unfocused, apparently noticing what I'm wearing—or rather, what I'm not wearing—for the first time. I shiver, thinking of Buzzcut, and more importantly, Eli.

"Have—have you got a plan yet?" he swallows, returning his eyes to my face and taking extra care to keep them there. I shake my head gloomily. I have no idea what I'm going to do. I have no idea who I'm even up against. He notices my indecision and says, "Hey, remember your promise? Just keep calm and don't let them intimidate you. You have the upper hand here; they don't know you have abilities, let alone what they are."

"But what good are advanced senses in a fight to the death?" I fret, twisting the clasps on my wrists. I glance down at my top. "Maybe I'll scare them badly enough when my boobs fall out that they'll surrender." Rowan laughs, covering his smile with a hand. Then he gets serious again.

"I wonder if you could pick up on any hints their movements might give. Like, sort of predict their next move in a way. For instance, if you notice them getting ready to throw a punch you might be able to avoid it easier. That coupled with your extensive martial arts skills, well, your competition is as good as done for." He gives me a halfhearted smile, but I can see the fear behind his green eyes.

"Rowan," I murmur fearfully, a new thought occurring to me. "I've never killed someone before. I've only ever knocked someone unconscious, not actually killed them."

"Just imagine you're—knocking them out. Permanently. If they hit you, you hit them harder. They can't be allowed to get back up again. Just, just try to imagine Pierre."

"Alright, okay," I nod, not trusting myself to say more than that. He doesn't mention that if I fail to end this person's life, we will all be killed by each other, afterwards to be given to Pierre, as if death wasn't enough leverage.

The door opens a third time, and Kylee pokes her head in. "Showtime!"

Rowan looks back to me, clearly distressed. He takes my hand, causing me to jump, and nods confidently in my direction before leaving. Kaylee steers me towards the second door; the loud door.

"This is going to be so much fun! We haven't had a competition in months," she chatters. Then she gets serious for a moment, looking me dead in the eyes. "And Corinne? I sincerely hope you do win. I really do like you; you've got spunk." She gives me a warm smile and twists the knob, the deafening roar of a full stadium blasting my eardrums as the door swings open. My legs turn to jelly as I see the packed bleacher-style seats, every one of them occupied with almost every occupant holding a sign supporting "The Mimic". Kaylee gives me an encouraging push into the pit. People cheer, and I hear catcalls and whistles, but I stand tall, wrestling my fear under control.

The spill of red skin crawls, feeling like actual flames where the flares lick my shoulders.

It escapes again though when the gate across the ring slides open with the grind of metal on stone. A hush falls over the crowd, my heart pumping ice water. The boy who emerges can only be described as disturbing, and he stares at me stonily, taking in my presence with bloodshot eyes. He's tall, at least six feet, which is already eight inches taller than me, and a brute of a person, with pasty, white skin and a close cropped head of ashy blond hair. A lumpy scar creates the illusion of a haunting smile across his throat, and he bares his teeth at me in a gruesome snarl.

I wait for my heart to restart and search the crowd for my friends while The Mimic raises his fists in the air, causing the crowd to erupt in applause. I finally spot my group in the front row ten feet above the ground, a little ways and to my right, their anxious faces studying my every move. Even Breanna appears worried. Jotaro is seated near them cheering wildly for my opponent, who grins at the shifter and salutes him. Jotaro returns the gesture. They must be friends of some sort.

The Mimic roars, bringing my attention back to him as he throws his floor length champions cape to the ground, kicking up a cloud of dust. He's wearing a silk vest, showing off his heavily muscled chest, and billowy indigo shorts that come to his knees. He has the same silver bracelets and anklets that I do. He stalks towards me, laying a rough, heavy hand on my shoulder.

"Beg a little and maybe I'll grant you a painless death," he whispers, his voice gravelly. I tense, taking note of his every movement, every betrayal of his next play. He takes three huge steps away again, and we face each other in the center of the ring. A whistle blows from somewhere far above, sending the electric lanterns flickering ominously. The fight has begun.

The Mimic immediately sprints to the wall, where he rips one of the support beams from the concrete before sauntering over, the rough metal scraping against the sand as he drags it behind him. Panic starts to fog up my mind as I try to build a plan to get out of this. How on earth do I stand even the slightest chance against someone twice my size, wielding a metal beam as thick as my leg? Panic threatens to take control, but Rowan's advice rings inside my head. I have to prognosticate his moves before he executes them. So, I hone my vision in on the arm holding the metal, concentrating as hard as I can without physically bursting my skull. I see his muscles twitch a second before he swings, then leap backwards, landing in a crouch as his weapon swings through empty air. The crowd isn't sure how to react; The Mimic must not usually miss his target.

I smile to myself, confident now. He may be bigger and stronger than me, but I have more tactical experience. He snarls at me as I rise to my feet, giving him a sweet smile.

"What's wrong, Mimic?" I taunt. "Too slow?"

"You're faster than me," he notes.

"Mentally? Or physically?" I ask, trying to lure him into a rage. It works. Mostly. His expression darkens and he charges at me again. This time when he swings, he adds an extra lunge. But I duck this time, instead of jumping back. He yells in livid rage, disproportionate features contorting further.

"Why do they call you The Mimic anyway?" I ask, wrinkling my nose. "Sounds kind of silly don't you think?" Apparently that was the wrong thing to say because instead of getting more upset he smiles maliciously.

"This is why:" He jumps at me again and I fly to the side. But just before the exact moment he could possibly see me move, he changes his direction. He's still not as fast as me, but he's fast enough that the bar connects with my shoulder. The same shoulder that is newly healed from the gunshot wound. I scream in pain, toppling to the ground and wincing as I roll my shoulder to assess the damage. It'll be bruised, and the surface wound seems to have reopened. Blood dribbles down my arm, thickening into a stream and staining my outfit as The Mimic turns to the crowd and raises his arms like he's unveiling a magic trick.

So can he mimic movements or—no.

He mimics abilities.

While he's distracted, I lunge, ignoring the roughness of the sand and the blinding pain in my shoulder, flying across the dirt and tackling the back of his knees.

He crumples almost robotically, and it's enough for me to tear the ribbon off of one of my legs and wrap it twice around his throat. He chokes, scrambling for purchase on the fabric, but it's thin and flat, and pulled tight.

"Who should be begging now?" I pant. "Oh, sorry, guess you're not really in a position to speak at the moment." He gurgles, his face beginning to swell and pale, then turn red, then blue. He somehow struggles to his feet with me hanging on his back. My feet dangle a few inches above the ground, my nose picking up on his sweat and strain mixed with the scent of my own blood.

He stumbles backwards, and at first I think he's falling, but then he rams me into the wall and the crowd cringes audibly. The air is crushed from my lungs and he steps forward, slamming me into the wall again. I gag, feeling something splinter in my chest. The next time he moves away from the barrier, I let go, dropping to the dusty floor to crawl between his legs.

*I have to get up. I can't be on the ground. This is the worst place to be in a fight.* There's no way to shield yourself from kicks if you're on the floor. I force myself to my feet and stagger around almost blindly. The Mimic is still trying to regain his breath from his near-death experience. The crowd is near silent, the entire stadium on the edge of their seats. No fight has gone on this long.

*Time to finish this.* But The Mimic has the same thought.

"I can promise you that I won't hold back anymore," he warns menacingly.

"Good," I spit. "I wouldn't want you to get soft in front of your fans."

He grins at me and we lunge at the same time. I make countless attacks and dodges but he mirrors every one of them, forcing me to retreat.

He's mimicking my ability.

My ability to guess his next move based off of the slightest twitch of an eyelash. He can now do the exact same thing.

Dread settles in my stomach as I wrap my mind around that. I can't beat someone who's copying my every move. The stabbing pain in my chest is starting to mess with my movements as well; I'm stumbling, and it hurts to breathe.

While I'm trying to catch my breath, The Mimic comes at me full force, barely bruised. He roars, bringing his fist back and aiming at my ruined shoulder. The force behind the blow would be enough to dislocate it. Suddenly, a move Master Jeen showed me plays out like a slow-motion movie in my head. He helped me to develop a personalized move if I was ever in a situation with someone hopelessly stronger than me. I lower myself into a wide stance, and start an entirely different move than what I have in mind, acting as if I'm going to try and duck the punch. The stadium is buzzing with anticipation as I get far enough into the move that the Mimic can't possibly think I'll back out.

As soon as his fist is about a foot away from me, I switch my footing and reach out quick as a flash. Wrapping my fingers around his wrist, I rotate on my feet so that he's behind me, using his forward momentum to roll him off my shoulder and slam him face up onto the packed dirt. Before he gets the chance to get back up, I keep hold of his hand and swing myself around his head, simultaneously wrapping my free arm around his neck. This ends up with me straddling his chest and holding him in a headlock. His arms are pinned beneath him. I can end this here and now. Just one quick jerk of his head, and I win. But then I see fear in his dirt-stained face. Such a human expression.

So I hesitate.

In that one crucial moment of fate, I hesitate. The Mimic uses my mistake to roll over, completely turning the tables. I'm pinned beneath his massive weight as his fist flies towards my face. I dodge his first few blows, but he connects once with my nose, and I hear something crack as a cutting wave of pain washes through my face. A spurt of hot, red blood dribbles into my mouth, cutting off my only other airway and I choke, coughing violently and swallowing more blood. He grins maniacally, wrapping his massive hands around my throat and squeezing.

I try to remain calm through the haze of pain from my ribs and the lack of oxygen in my blood. But logic melts into desperation as my vision begins to blur, little explosions of color blooming behind my eyelids. The pulsing pressure at the base of my skull is ever so prominent, building hotter with each second, growing and spreading until my head feels like it's about to explode. I can't die here. I promised Rowan I wouldn't be beaten down.

A deep rage I didn't know I possessed erupts in my chest and I let loose a bone-numbing scream. My vision goes white as I feel The Mimic's hands release me, his limp body listing to the side before sliding off of mine. The pain in my head lessens, as if it's being let out slowly, but steadily. I stand up unsteadily, my sight still tinted white. I see The Mimic writhing on the ground, clawing at his throat. I realize there's an invisible string stretching between the churning in my head and his body.

An impossible amount of glee washes over me, compelling me to tighten my hand into a fist. The Mimic twitches, then goes still. My eyesight returns to normal as the rush of excitement evaporates instantly. I'm left standing there in abject horror, staring at the lifeless eyes of the seventeen time champion.

I won.

The stadium is deathly silent. What do I do now? Four more seconds pass before the crowd erupts in applause and cheering. People bounce around, some even jumping into the pit to race over and clap me on the back, sending me to my knees in pain. I take it all in as static in my ears, hardly registering my friends, Kaylee, and Jotaro approaching. The vicious stabbing jolts in my chest and shoulder finally overwhelm my battered body.

Dimly, I hear someone shouting to get out of the way before gentle arms hoist me up, and I cry out when they touch my ribs.

A quiet voice whispers in my ear. "You kept your promise, Corinne. Just hold on a little longer now."

## Chapter 31

# Selena

We rush Corinne back into the dressing room, muting the crowd when we shut the door. Kaylee unfolds a cot that was leaning against the wall, and Rowan lays Corinne on it. Her head lolls to one side, and her eyes are shut. No sign of the silver light that emanated from them earlier. I shake my head to clear the image away and focus on my sister's unmoving body.

Kaylee removes a jade bottle from one of her pockets and soaks a cloth with the entirety of its contents, wearing a stoic expression the entire time.

"She has three broken ribs. Two are slightly fractured and one is a little more seriously injured. She has a rotator cuff tear in her left shoulder, along with a reopened gunshot wound, plus a broken nose and quite a few bruises. She'll be sore for a few days, but this should fix her up quickly," she says distractedly.

"What is that stuff?" asks Breanna, wrinkling her nose. It has the distinct smell of bug spray.

"A little concoction my healers whipped up. It can heal most non life-threatening injuries faster than your body can, and it can reduce the pain. I can send some along with you. As a congratulations of sorts."

"Along with us?" asks Victoria, her mind taking more than a minute to process Kaylee's words.

Kaylee looks up from where she was laying the cloth on Corinne's ribs. "Yes. Corinne won, fair and square. She also provided the best game in months, so you all will be sent along your way first thing tomorrow. I am a woman of my word. Jotaro and I will escort you personally to the edge of our territory in respect of this young lady's victory."

Jotaro looks as if he wants to protest, but says nothing, jaw clenched tightly. Something sinister roils in his eyes.

"Are we all just going to ignore the fact that Corinne went completely psycho and then The Mimic just—died?" Breanna finally blurts, exasperated. I wanted to ask the same thing.

River is the one to answer. "I believe our Corinne has a new ability, one that is powerful enough to get Pierre to send trained mercenaries after her. Remember Tarissa?" Rowan and I share a disturbed glance, met with confused looks from the rest of our group. River continues. "She said the attackers were coming for Corinne. It was as if we didn't even exist. And when our personal stalkers showed up in the woods, they tried to take Corinne with them, trying to simply discard the rest of us." His explanation is very logical, and I can't think of a better answer. At least not one that would make sense, anyway.

"Okay," starts Rowan, a barely controlled look of calm on his face. "But what power would be so powerful that Pierre wants her alive?"

"That," sighs River, studying Corinne's face, "is something we're going to have to help Corinne figure out. For the good of all of us."

My sister makes a noise somewhere between a gasp and a whimper just before her eyes flick open. She sits up and whips her head around. We all stumble back a bit as she looks around. Her eyes are desperate, searching for something. Or someone. When her frantic gaze lands on me, her eyes widen and she lurches forwards.

"Leenie!" she whispers. Wrapping her arms around my shoulders and hugging me tightly. Concerned, I hug her back gingerly. "I don't know what happened—everything hurt, everything went white and The Mimic—he—he just died. I swear I didn't mean to. I felt so happy, for no reason at all, and then I felt guilty, and—and—"

"Hey, it's okay, slow down," I whisper, stroking her hair as she takes a deep breath. She pulls away and I watch as her expression shuts down; she smiles apologetically at me, back in control of her emotions. I only see what she wants me to see.

"Sorry, I just need to think this through. I didn't mean to worry you all. I'm alright now." I stare bewildered at her as she sits on her knees and brushes herself off as if she wasn't just freaking out ten seconds ago. Kaylee looks her up and down, then shakes her head to herself.

"Let's get you changed," she says, standing up and offering Corinne her hands. My sister doesn't take them, but follows Kaylee's lead and she trails her to a curtained-off portion of the room. A few awkward minutes later, they reemerge with Corinne dressed in her old clothes, but they're all clean now. Her eyes are downcast, and she avoids eye contact with everyone.

Kaylee waves us all up, and silently directs us to the door. "Jotaro? Bring them to the guest accommodations and get them settled," she commands, barely glancing at the boy. He nods stiffly and we follow him through the halls and underground rooms.

"Here we are," Jotaro announces flatly, stepping into a space with cots lined up neatly along two walls. We throw our stuff down, all of us fall asleep instantly.

***

The next morning, we enter the room next to the one we slept in. In it are weapons and a large opening that lets in the uneven light from the forest.

We're back at the surface.

"Wait here. Your rides will arrive momentarily." Jotaro yawns, stretching leisurely and leaning against the wall next to Corinne, trying to talk to her and getting closer with every sentence. She politely—but firmly—pushes him away, offering up short, to the point sentences about needing some space; he's absolutely oblivious.

I notice our bags against one wall the same time Breanna does, and we both move to collect our own. The rest of the group follows our lead. I see Rowan glance at Corinne, who almost imperceptibly moves away from anyone who gets within a foot of her.

My attention is caught by Kaylee entering the room, followed by five other people. "Alright, time to go. I've packed a few vials of our healing mixture in here," she says, handing a small bag to River. "Use it sparingly, and only a few drops at a time for minor injuries. It's quite potent and you won't need much." River nods and tucks the pouch into his bag.

"How are we being transported?" inquires Victoria, very clearly puzzled. As if that was their cue, all but Kaylee and Jotaro shimmer and shrink, a pack of wolves appearing in their places.

"This is how," laughs Kaylee.

"I can follow along just fine; I don't need a ride," Jinx states. Kaylee raises her eyebrows, but snaps her fingers. The smallest of the wolves disappears through the door, leaving us with four others.

"Anything else?" she asks, glancing around the room. No one says anything. "Great. Then we leave now. Ready for departure!" She signals to the wolves and they trot over to us. A large, brown canine stands next to me and bows his head, an invitation for me to climb on. Hesitantly, I swing one leg over his broad shoulders and dig my knees into his flanks as he stands up. The others follow my lead, and I notice Corinne standing without a ride.

Jotaro slinks up to her and rests a hand on her arm, leaning in close with a coy expression on his face. He whispers something quietly to my sister, but is met with no reaction. Corinne scrunches her eyes shut and powers through whatever mental battle she's fighting.

Rowan is still as a stone on his huge, tar black wolf, his eyes never leaving Corinne's face. Jotaro glows brightly and fluidly shrinks into the lean muscled form of a jaguar. Corinne slowly mounts him, and if looks could kill, Jotaro would have died the most painful death imaginable from the look Rowan was shooting at him. I see his arms quivering in restraint as he clenches the fur on his ride's back. The wolf growls in warning and Rowan starts, letting go of the fur but not taking his eyes off of my sister and Jotaro.

The others pick up on his tenseness as well, and Kaylee lets out one sharp whistle. The wolves take off at a sprint, Kaylee melting into a petite gray timber wolf and leading the pack with Jotaro and his rider at her side. Jinx appears in lynx form at the back, and suddenly we're racing through the forest.

The trees blur by, a watercolor painting of greens and browns, the rich scent of dirt and rain and growing things filling my lungs and easing my tight posture. I hear Victoria whooping to my left, arms raised and only holding on with her legs. Breanna joins, followed by River. Corinne smiles and closes her eyes, lifting her head high, and even Rowan relaxes a bit. I smile to myself, closing my eyes and feeling the whipping wind dancing across my skin, as if I was in the middle of a hurricane. My short hair flies away from my face, and I turn up to the sunlight, streaming in broken beams across the forest floor.

And I feel free.

*Chapter 32*

# Corinne

We ride for hours non-stop. My legs are beginning to feel sore from gripping Jotaro's sides. I look around our group, and everyone seems just as exhausted as me. Out of nowhere, my stomach tightens and a sharp lash of pain goes through my abdomen. I nearly let go of Jotaro with the force of it, cursing. I had hoped my period would hold off until we got to Tenálin, but no such luck.

Kaylee lets out two loud yips and the wolves stop. She grows, becoming a human again.

"Let's stop for a break!" she shouts, stretching and sitting against a tree. I sigh in relief and slide off of Jotaro's back. He smiles at me but his words from earlier refuse to vacate my mind. *You'll get what's coming for you.* I don't miss the poisonous glare Rowan gives him before disappearing into the forest.

Jotaro follows me a short ways into the trees, trying to elicit some sort of reaction from me. I politely ignore him until he drops a human hand on my shoulder and turns me around. I instinctively drop, sweeping my leg out and sending him to the ground, keeping him down with a firm foot on his chest.

"I would greatly appreciate it if you could leave me alone. I have no interest in you or whatever you're looking for, so

I will be taking my leave now. Don't follow me," I warn. With that I shoulder my bag and weave between the trees, searching, and leaving a rather pissed-off Jotaro behind me.

Finally, I find what I'm looking for: a clear shallow pond maybe twenty-thirty feet in diameter, with a point blocking the view of another section of water. It's sheltered by the thick pines growing all around it. I slide down the bank and set my bag down at the shore, rooting around until I find my supplies from the mall. Setting those aside, I scan the tree line again, just to make sure Jotaro really did go back. Then I begin stripping, folding my clothes into a neat pile next to me. Once I rid myself of all my clothing, I wade into the chilly water, shivering as I sink to my shoulders.

I swim out to the middle, feeling the cool water closing over my head as I wash away the dirt and memories from the fight. I scrub at the bit of blood still crusted on my upper lip and shoulder, then dunk my head under again, letting the cool clean water soak into my skin. When I surface again I push my hair away from my face and try to keep myself from thinking too much. If I think, I'll get lost in the past and I'm not sure I'll be able to come back to the present.

I freeze with the echo of a small splash coming from around the point. I listen closely, but even with better than average hearing I can't tell what it is. Slowly, I turn to face the point and paddle towards it. There's probably a good bit of water that I can't see from my spot.

I've almost reached the spit of land when a head of pale gold, brown hair pops into view and I realize my mistake. I try to paddle backwards but at that point Rowan has already heard me and is turning around. All I can do is stare in shock at him. He's standing in the pond with the water reaching just above his hips. Against my will, my eyes drift down his bare, shining chest, slick with the water from the pond. He turns around fully then and his eyes get bigger than I thought humanly possible when he processes my presence. I jerk my eyes away and glue them to his face, which doesn't help. I'm met with shocked green eyes and very red ears.

"C-Corinne?" he stutters.

My voice comes back to me then, words spilling forth like a tsunami and I cover my face in shame. Holy thoughts Corinne, holy thoughts. "Oh my god, Rowan I am so sorry. I didn't know you were here. I heard something so I came over to investigate but then you were here—oh my god."

I peek between my fingers to see him now chest deep in the water, floating like a cork. He's not facing me, so I turn around and float, worried he thinks I was stalking him.

"It's okay, Corinne," he assures weakly, his voice an octave higher than usual. I try to play it off by giving him my own laugh, but it comes out as more of a mouse being stepped on than anything, so I just wait for him to reply.

"Corinne?" he asks.

"Yeah?"

"If you want, we can forget about this."

I nod vigorously before remembering he can't see me. "Yeah, definitely," I amend. I swim furiously towards my belongings and double check to make sure he's not in view before climbing out and redressing. I finish up with my stuff and shove everything back into my bag before sinking to the ground, the last few minutes having sapped my energy. Hanging my head between my knees, I wait for my fluttering heartbeat to return to normal and try to force the heat to recede from my face.

A warm presence draws me away from my self-pity and I lift my head to see Rowan sitting next to me. How did I not hear him approaching? I start to panic. I can't deal with this right now.

He exhales, and gives me a look. Not a sexual or

judgmental look, but rather a genuinely curious look, perhaps even fond.

"Thank you," he says gently, catching my eyes and holding me there. "Thank you for keeping your promise."

I suck in a breath, memories flooding back where there had once been blank spots in my memory. "Rowan, how can you look at me like that?" I ask accusingly. He seems taken aback. "I'm too unpredictable! You said you don't use your fire because no human should be able to have that much control. What I did back there, whatever that was, no one should be able to do that, either." My breathing is getting out of control for the second time in the last ten minutes as I remember the exhilaration I felt as I stopped the oxygen from reaching The Mimic's lungs. The glee when he exhaled for the last time, and the anger that jump started the whole operation.

"That doesn't make you inhuman. You have a power that nobody knows about, but that doesn't mean you're not you—you're still Corinne."

I keep my eyes fixed on the rippling water, refusing to meet his gaze. He keeps talking.

"I think this new ability took a while to mature, and that's why we didn't know about it at the same time Pierre discovered your senses. And I was doing some thinking while we were riding, and I think this is the power that he was after in the first place," he contemplates. "Ever wonder why he didn't just knock you unconscious and take what he needed? I think he has some agenda other than simply 'curing' you."

"But what is it?" I mutter, remembering my unnerving first encounter with the man.

"This attribute was still unknown to you, and even he didn't know exactly what the ability would be, only that it was insanely powerful."

I think about his logic for a minute. Pieces click together and I stare at him in abject horror. "So this entire thing is my fault," I mutter.

"No! That's not what I was saying!" he says quickly, trying to backtrack.

"It's the truth," I murmur, guilt and sadness quickly forming a tangled knot in my stomach. "It's my fault. All of it. If it weren't for me, Winnie and Tarissa would still be alive. So would Lilac. Gigi and the triplets wouldn't be orphans, and Ben and Kara would get to see their kids grow up. Everything that has happened, is my fault. We don't even know what happened to Kleka! For all we know, it could be a pile of rubble and ashes."

Rowan is moving faster than I can register, his face ablaze with anger only a few inches away from mine, which he has firmly between his hands; his grip is too strong for me to pull away. "Enough with the self-pity, Corinne. Maybe they all died because of you. Maybe it is all your fault. But we can't do anything about the past. We didn't have enough information, and we had no idea what was happening. You want to waste away moping about how terrible of a person you are, be my guest. But when we get to headquarters, I'm going back to take out Pierre," he says, his voice very quiet. It would have been less scary if he were yelling. I wish he would just scream at me instead of this cold, dead quiet.

"I'm going to put a stop to his entire operation and obliterate any trace of his existence. I'm going to expose the whole thing and take it apart brick by brick if that's what I have to do. I want your help. Help me save the people in his labs, and all the Mutes that are in danger of falling into his traps. What else can we do? Just sit around and watch? We won't be safe at HQ, no matter how many people assure us. Pierre is smart, and he'll find some way to get to us. The only way we'll get out of this nightmare is to get rid of that man. Will you help me? Please?" I stand up, twisting away from his hands and shoving him back.

"What happened to, "Oh, they're only the greatest MAA to ever exist! I want to join them and protect all the Mutations!" huh? You were ecstatic when we met Ben and Kara! Practically kissing the ground they walked on! What changed?"

"What changed is that I saw the fear in Gigi's face when her mom was killed right in front of her. I realized that they might be the best MAA, but that they weren't everything I thought. I saw how easily they killed Kara and with absolutely no emotion just to get what they needed. However strong Lotus is or was, the Phantom Order is much more powerful, and they need to go."

He searches my eyes, desperately searching for a part of me that will help him without hesitation. A part that is brave and fearless, and won't let anyone beat me down. But that part isn't here right now. She died along with the Mimic and the discovery of this horrible power.

"I don't know Rowan. Maybe we really can be safe at HQ. We won't know until we get there," I say, throwing my hands up in the air. He clenches his fist by his side, grimacing.

"If that's what you believe," he censures. I watch him walk away with his bag over one shoulder. I exhale sharply, picking up a stone and hurling it at the water, watching the placid surface shatter like glass.

*Suck it up Corinne.* I scold myself, swiping at my eyes. *You're better than this. Rowan can do what he wants. He's wrong. We'll be safe at HQ.*

I grab my backpack and head after Rowan, making sure to stay an even distance behind him. Through the trees I see him sit down at the sizable campfire the others had apparently set up. I guess we're waiting until morning to keep going, which is fine by me. The tents are up as well and I quietly join the rest of the group, sitting on an unoccupied log.

The conversation continues undisrupted but I tune it out, replaying and trying to analyze the conversation between me and Rowan.

Soon though, people start filing into tents to rest up. I get déjà vu when Rowan and I are the only ones left, but he gets up and leaves without giving me a second glance. Feeling depressed and useless, I walk back to the pond in the dark, letting my night vision guide me. I sit on the bank and throw rocks at the water, watching the ripples travel across the glass-like surface. Since when did Rowan want to get back at Pierre? He never mentioned anything of the sort before, save for his outburst after discovering I would probably die during the operation.

Frustrated, I get back onto my feet and start to pace back and forth. I walk the same path for so long that a shallow depression is worn into the dirt by my restless feet. I have to let off some steam; this is too much to try and think about right now, but I can't go back to the camp, so I decide to spend the night here under the stars.

I wash off my hands in the pond and curl up on the dirt, alone, but not entirely lonely.

✳✳✳

"Wake up sleeping beauty," someone whispers. I reluctantly crack open an eye to Jinx smiling sadly down at me.

"I—"

"Hurry up. I'm going to go catch something for breakfast, then we're out of here," she says, helping me up to my feet. "Get back to the camp and get ready to leave; we have a long day of riding ahead of us." I nod and she shifts to lynx form, bounding off into the trees as I trudge back to camp and wordlessly start packing up.

Before long, Jinx trots into view, a rabbit in her maw. In

the blink of an eye she's human again, the rabbit now in her hand.

"Breakfast!" she beams. She goes to snap the rabbit's neck, but before she can, the rabbit morphs, growing and stretching. Pale beige fur becomes dark clothes, and ears shrink and melt into the skull. Suddenly, there's a girl in Jinx's arms. The unexpected weight topples them both, and Jinx lands on top of the newcomer with a gasp, the two of them staring at each other for a moment.

The new girl has platinum blond hair and big black eyes. She is dressed in black leggings, a white t-shirt, and a baggy camo jacket. She's small, and looks to be about thirteen. Jinx scrambles to her feet and away from the rabbit girl.

"Who the hell are you?" she asks, clearly shaken.

The girl stands up, brushing off her torn pants. "My name's Naomi," she says carefully. "Who are *you?*" Jinx looks her up and down, not saying a word.

"Where are your parents?" asks Selena nervously.

"Stuck in a hellhole as lab rats for being who they are. And I'm sixteen; I can take care of myself," Naomi assures. I blink in surprise, taken aback. She looks more like twelve than sixteen. "What was all that for?"

"You were going to be our breakfast," grumbles Jinx, kicking at the dirt. "We can't have you for breakfast can we?"

"I'm afraid not," says Naomi, a small nervous smile playing at the corners of her mouth. It's deafeningly quiet; no one knows what to do now.

"Well, sorry for—for catching you—I guess," says Jinx awkwardly. "I owe you one?"

"Sounds good," agrees Naomi. "Do you happen to know where I can find the Phantom Order?" Everyone goes dead still, staring at Naomi uneasily. Is she working with them? She seems to pick up on the change of atmosphere. "Did I say something wrong?"

"How do you know the Phantom Order?" asks Selena quietly. River surreptitiously thumbs a pocket knife, and Rowan slowly reaches for the rifle on his back. Naomi shifts her weight, realizing their intentions immediately.

"Drop your knife," she pleads to River, before turning her attention to Rowan. "And please don't shoot me. I'm not with them if that's what you're worried about." Both boys freeze, clearly surprised that she noticed them.

"Then how do you know them?" persists Selena.

"They're the ones who took my family. I'm trying to find them so I can get them out of his camp," she says soothingly. Rowan's head snaps up at this.

"Then you should come with us," he suggests hopefully. "We're on our way to the Lotus Protection HQ right now."

Naomi laughs, sounding like silver bells in a spring breeze. "Oh, thank you, but that won't be necessary. I have my own destination and that is actually in the exact opposite direction you're going."

"Well, then, I apologize on behalf of Jinx for almost break-ing your neck," sighs River. "And good luck."

"You too." She smiles warmly.

"Alright, time to go," announces Kaylee, a bemused look on her face. "Everyone ready?" Her pack shifts, becoming their animal counterparts once more, and I mount Jotaro. Jinx waves sadly to Naomi—who whirls into a small rabbit and darts off into the trees—before returning to lynx form herself. Kaylee looks over the group and nods to herself. "Ride out!" She shifts mid leap and we're off again.

The forest tumbles by and I close my eyes to try and block out the world. Especially the disappointed look on Rowan's face whenever he turns his cornhusk eyes on me.

We reach the tracks by sunset, and dismount, utterly drained, having only stopped twice the entire day to stretch and relieve ourselves. I look around at our surroundings and nearly have my breath stolen from me. We're perched atop a large grassy hill, the train tracks that weave between and around other similar protrusions glinting in the setting sun. The grass we stand on is a deep, pine green and the last rays of sunlight bathe them in its golden glory. A sharp, biting wind races past, rustling the trees of the Shifting Woods behind us. It causes me to pull my jacket tighter around me; Autumn is around the corner.

A thought occurs to me then: before we left, River had estimated it would take just over three weeks to walk to Vrasall. The addition of the train to come would cut the trip in half, and riding would cut time off as well, but we've only been traveling for two days. How did we get here so fast?

As if Kaylee can read my thoughts, she comes to stand by my side, looking out over the endless, undulating grass to the horizon smeared with crimson reds and royal purples. "Along with shifting, I possess one other attribute. One that allows me a small amount of control over time and distance for a short time. It saps my strength quickly, but it can come in very handy. I used it today and yesterday to slow time around our little group and shorten the distance between us and here. To us, we appeared to be traveling at a normal pace. To anyone outside of the bubble, we would have been a rustle in the foliage and then gone."

"Wow, Kaylee, that's really impressive," I say, astounded. "You must be exhausted." She shrugs, and I take note of her pale face and the very prominent bruises under her eyes. "Why don't you get some rest. Tell the others to do the same. I'll keep watch for a bit in case Pierre or his goons are anywhere nearby. You and your pack need it," I add when she begins to protest. Kaylee looks at me for a long time before nodding, then walks back to her people. They all shift and curl up next to each other for warmth.

I smile at the trust they share, then turn to see the rest

of my group huddled together, talking in hushed tones. So, I swallow my feelings and call out to them. "You guys get some sleep. I'm going to keep watch."

"Corinne, you need sleep just as much as we do. You can't—" begins Selena. I hold up a hand to halt her.

"If I get tired, I'll wake one of you to take my place. Just get some sleep guys," I say, annoyance creeping into my voice; I try to tamp it down. Selena nods reluctantly and they stretch out their sleeping bags, most of them out within minutes.

I sigh and sit down on the soft grass, watching as the last inch of sun disappear behind a rise. The world is plunged into twilight and I watch in wonder as the stars begin to pop out, one by one. They burn brightly, pinpoints of fire in a galaxy of complete blackness.

I'm not sure how much time passes, but I hear River approaching a few seconds before I see him. His footsteps are even and sure. I've been dozing off, so I pull myself back to the present as he sits himself next to me.

"Get some sleep, Corinne. You're the one who needs it most," he whispers, resting a hand on my shoulder. I try to resent him for being so sure of himself, and what he thinks. But he hasn't done anything to deserve that. Truthfully, I just resent myself.

"Thanks, River," I yawn, giving his hand a pat. He doesn't say anything, so I go curl up between Victoria and Selena. I expect to be welcomed by warm sleep, but instead I'm sucked into the cold world of nightmares.

## *Chapter 33*

# Jinx

I twitch awake, something breaking through my haze of sleep. Perking up, I see Corinne wandering towards the train tracks in a zigzagging pattern, the light of the moon guiding my sight. River is dead asleep where he was "keeping watch" and doesn't appear to hear anything himself.

*What is she doing?* I wonder to myself. A sound pierces the air: a train horn. Rowan and River both jump awake, on their feet in an instant. The rest are too deep asleep to have heard it, and Corinne keeps walking.

"What the hell is she doing?" asks Rowan, voicing my exact thoughts.

"I don't know, but if she keeps going she'll get hit!" River realizes, stunned.

"We have to get down there; I don't think she knows what she's doing," I say in a low voice, dread settling in my stomach. I close my eyes and reach out to the warm glow deep within. My body warms as my vision sharpens, and I feel my skin stretch, my bones lengthen and my muscles thicken, becoming sleek and powerful. Now a lynx, I sprint down the hill towards Corinne, a race between me and the train. It barrels down the track full speed and Corinne now stands in the middle of its path, unmoving. What the hell is she thinking?

I race across the grass so fast that I'm practically hovering above the ground. Corinne is just a few yards away, but the train is closing in fast. Ten feet. Five feet. Two feet.

I close my jaws around…nothing. Corinne's just beyond my reach. I misjudged the distance, tripping over a rock instead and returning to human form, a ragged scream tearing from my throat, arm flung wide as the train reaches her.

At the last possible second, a small form darts out of the grass, shifting midair to haul Corinne off the tracks *just* as the train screeches by, grazing her shoulder. Her jacket catches and she jerks backwards before it rips, then they're both safely out of the way.

Corinne's eyes shoot open and she screams, drenched in sweat. Tears stain her face and her breath is coming in short gasping bursts.

Naomi is holding my sister by the shoulders, shaking her to keep her awake while simultaneously talking to her and trying to get her to calm down. But Corinne is in no mood to cooperate, being in too much of a frenzy that Naomi abandons her attempts and edges away.

The boys arrive and skid to a stop then, Corinne collapsing without Naomi's support, now. Instead, Rowan catches her before she hits the ground and she goes stone still in his arms.

"No!" she yells suddenly, regaining full consciousness and launching herself away from him. "Don't fucking touch me! You're just like him, you're just like Eli and I *knew* it! It was too good to be true." Her eyes are shining like two huge moons reflected in a pool, but not sadly. They're ablaze with anger, and more prominently, fear.

Rowan looks shocked, his eyes just as wide and puts his hands up. "What did I do?" he looks to Naomi, then to me for an explanation, but I have no answer.

"You know exactly what you fucking did!" she snarls,

backing away. "I thought maybe you were different, but you're all the same. I'm just a plaything in your eyes until you get bored of the word 'no.'" Her voice feels like venom, even though it's not aimed at me. I can tell Rowan is confused and worried. I know because I'm feeling the same way.

Naomi is just standing next to me, looking lost. She just popped out of the sky and rescued my sister. Had she been following us?

"I—Corinne—I have no idea what you're talking about. I would never—I don't see you that way," he whispers, barely audible. "Look, maybe it was just a dream—"

"No," she spits before turning her gaze on me, her brown eyes stricken. "Jinx, Naomi, get away from him. He's a fucking traitor!"

Rowan shoots to his feet. "What the hell, Corinne? Tell me what I did, because last time I checked, it was you who let everyone down, not me!"

Corinne stops moving altogether, and her expression sends goosebumps erupting along my skin. She slowly raises her eyes to Rowan's face and when I see them, they're pure silver, not the warm cocoa brown I love to see.

"Wait, Corinne," I start, attempting to bring her back before the situation inevitably spirals out of control.

She doesn't say anything, her breath uneven and her eyes distant as she raises a hand to examine it closely. "I sort of figured that out by now." She clenches her hand into a fist and Rowan drops to his knees, choking on nothing. It's a repeat of the arena.

"Corinne!" I scream. She doesn't seem to hear me, her feet hovering an inch above the ground, the soles of her shoes brushing the ends of the plush grass. "Corinne, stop! You're killing him! Naomi go get the others!"

Naomi shifts, and sprints up the hill as a brown streak among the green.

Rowan is on the ground now, his face turning blue, his struggling form barely moving.

"Corinne!" I bellow, pulling the glow from my chest and lunging at my sister in full lynx form. I knock her from the air and she tumbles onto the tracks, her head slamming into the wooden planks. The silver fades from her eyes, leaving her unconscious and limp.

Rowan gasps, swallowing huge gulps of air and coughing violently. He rolls away from Corinne, still panting, and looks frantically between me and her.

"Go, now," I order sternly. He staggers up the hill, the others meeting him a third of the way there. They keep a safe distance while I tentatively step over the gravel and onto the tracks. Kneeling on a wooden plank, I brush Corinne's hair away from her face. Her skin is pale, and her breathing shallow and inconsistent. There's blood pooling around her head from a large gash right by her hairline, the wound glistening in the moonlight and grinning at me with torn skin and blood turned black in the night.

"Hey, wake up," I whisper, patting her cheek. She groans, wincing as she tries to sit up. Her hand flutters to her forehead, and she pauses as she processes the blood, the past few minutes seeming to come back to her only just now.

"Did I kill him?" she asks, her voice neither concerned nor hopeful. I can't tell which answer she wants to hear.

"Almost. He's fine now," I reply slowly, trying to gauge her feelings. She doesn't show any hint as to what she thinks on the matter. After another stretch of silence, she continues.

"He never actually did anything to me did he?"

I shake my head and she goes quiet again.

"Go back to bed, Jinx. I'll be okay, I just need to clear my mind," she whispers, studying her hand in the pale, wispy light. I don't move. "Go," she repeats, louder this time.

I sigh and push myself up to standing before striding over to the others in our little group.

I notice Victoria grimacing a little ways off, and I turn to her.

"Do you know anything about what happened?" I ask suspiciously. Victoria hesitates, as if deciding she should tell us, before closing her eyes.

"Dream Reapers," she forces out. She says it quietly and then glances around as if to check for anyone listening.

"What are Dream Reapers?" Selena asks.

"Shh!" She lowers her voice, so that we have to lean close to hear her. "Dream Reapers are entities that invade the mind when it's recharging. In other words, when the person is asleep. They show you your worst fear in a dream, and make it worse. The one so terrible that it makes you want to kill yourself. Corinne was *extraordinarily* lucky to have survived an encounter with one. Only a rare few do."

"Hey, slow down a second," interrupts River. "How do you know so much about these things?"

"The people in Westol talk. I wasn't sure if they were real or if they just made it up to explain suicides. Guess they're an actual thing," she says without skipping a beat.

"Fine," he sighs. "And Naomi?"

The girl perks up when she hears her name, eyes wide and guilty, almost solid black in the poor light.

"I'm sorry—I was intrigued, so I followed you. I was planning to stay at a distance for a while longer but then your friend just stepped on the tracks and I couldn't stay put. She seems very special to all of you," Naomi confesses, coming clean and fiddling with a brown, woven bracelet on her wrist.

"Thank you," is all River says. "Since you're all this way from where we first met you, we can give you a lift until our destination, where you can probably find help with getting back on track."

"That would be a huge help," Naomi admits, sighing with relief. "Thank you, too."

We walk back up the hill while we talk, leaving Corinne to her thoughts. I don't want to leave her by herself in case the Dream Reaper comes back, but she made it clear that she didn't want to be around anybody right now. Breanna is still asleep when we return, and Kaylee and her pack are nowhere to be seen.

The former yawns and stretches upon our approach. "What's all that noise? Did Corinne discover yet another amazing ability and throw a fit over it?"

Rowan cringes.

"Go back to sleep, Breanna. We'll wake you up if anything important happens," says Selena, resigned. But Breanna's already snoring again and the former rolls her eyes. "We should probably all get a little more sleep before dawn. We've got a long couple of days ahead of us."

I throw one last glance back at my childhood soul sister, nothing but a silhouette on the tracks, dark and alone against the midnight blue backdrop of the sky.

*Chapter 34*

# Corinne

I sleep next to the tracks, and wake up the next morning with blood setting the knots in my hair, coupled with stiff muscles. I groan as I sit up, the rocks that had been cutting into my arms all night sticking to my skin for a few seconds before falling off and landing with their brethren with soft clicks.

There's movement at the top of the hill, but I don't bother going up to help. I need to keep my distance now, especially after last night.

Last night—.

All I remember are Rowans' jagged words, cutting straight through my chest and into the very marrow of my bones. I felt a cold, cutting, seething anger that couldn't be contained in a body of flesh and blood. Everything went white, then black. Then Jinx's face was there, the disappointment and fear poorly hidden behind her features. But I know from past experience that the stretch of time where everything was coated in that silvery sheen, I was killing Rowan. And I wasn't bothered by it. That's what scares me the most.

The dream last night was so vivid, and I was absolutely convinced it had happened. In the dream, I was back with Eli, his blond hair curling perfectly behind his ears, his smile so warm and soothing, his green eyes sparkling perfectly in the sunlight. We ran through a corn maze, out onto the hill, his contagious laughter breaking me down into my own fit of giggles.

I could see the train tracks below us, and I felt his lips against my skin, warm and filled with desire. Then his body was blocking off the light emanating from the last shred of sunset, his eyes getting lighter, his hair darker, and before long Eli was Rowan, and he pressed close, telling me this was forever, it was meant to be. I told him no. He kept promising, promising I could say no. I did. He wouldn't listen. I screamed, but we were alone, no one to hear me cry for help.

I took off running, straight onto the train tracks. I could feel his breath against the back of my neck, promising I could say no, that it was my choice. I stood in front of the train, wanting it all to end, to be free from him. But as the train reached me, I was pulled sideways, my shoulder feeling as if it was being freed from the socket entirely.

I opened my eyes and Jinx was there. She and River were standing next to Rowan, and that's when I must have woken up without realizing it. Naomi was there, too; how strange.

I sigh at the memory, massaging my temples then wincing when I graze my head wound. They really do bleed a lot.

I catch movement again, and look up to see the group starting to make their way back down to the tracks. So I hold my breath and force myself to stand, finger combing my hair out so that there are at least fewer snarls.

Kaylee is the first to reach me. She comes to stand by me with a solemn expression and I try to act as if nothing happened last night. Jotaro is nowhere to be seen, and it scratches something at the back of my mind.

"So how do we get on when it comes by?" I ask, arms akimbo.

"You jump," replies Kaylee bluntly. I bark out a laugh and then look at her placid face, registering her seriousness.

"Jump? Onto a moving train?" Breanna questions shrilly. "Are you kidding me?"

"I'm being one hundred percent genuine here. Do you see a station anywhere? It's the only way to board. Just run alongside it, open one of the cargo doors and swing yourself in. Easy-peasy," Kaylee assures. Breanna looks horrified. "Ah, here it comes now. This is where we say goodbye."

I turn my head to see a sleek, black engine racing at breakneck speed towards us, hauling several dozen cargo cars in its wake. Looking back at Kaylee and her pack, I'm at a loss for words.

"Thank you so much. For everything. Even if you did capture me to have me fight to the death against a madman, thank you. We would be walking for weeks without your help," I say. "We're eternally grateful."

Kaylee smiles small, a warm satisfied smile. "Anytime. I hope to see you again someday." I nod, and turn my attention back to the train.

We get ready to run, although Breanna still looks a bit queasy. The engine roars by and I break into a full sprint, grabbing the first latch I can and letting the door slide open. Keeping a grip on the handle, I haul myself up and land with a sharp gasp on my stomach inside the car. Someone climbs up behind me, quick and easy. When I turn around I see it's Rowan.

"Where are the others?" I ask nervously.

"They're all in the cars behind us. No need to worry," he promises, his expression blank. That's not what I was nervous about, but I settle on the floor. The car we're in is filled with wooden crates, giving us minimal space to move about.

*Get a grip Corinne. You're way more worried about this than you should be.* I grit my teeth.

"What happened last night, Corinne? From your

perspective," asks Rowan, forehead creased in that way of his as he stares out the door. I sit as still as is possible on a moving train and glue my gaze to a spot above his head; I can't bring myself to look at him.

"I didn't mean what I said. About you being like—like him," I say softly. "I had a nightmare, but not like one I've experienced before. It was so vivid, so real, and it transitioned into reality so fluidly that I couldn't tell the difference." I can't bring myself to go into any more detail, so I zip my lips and wait for his response. My excuse is shitty and poorly constructed, but it's the truth and it's the best I have.

Below my gaze I can vaguely see him frown, a little downturn of the corners of his lips. "Victoria said you were probably possessed by a Dream Reaper. They find your biggest fear and use it against you, until they put you back into your real life and you kill yourself, not knowing it's actually happening."

I blink. The explanation raises more questions than it answers.

"And I want to apologize," he says, eyes downcast. "What I said was horrible, especially in the state you were in."

"Please," I stop him, chewing on the inside of my cheek. "Don't apologize for anything. I got so out of control and I don't know what happened. I'll stay out of your way, and from now on I won't let my emotions get the better of me. I'm sorry."

Rowan mulls this information over and opens his mouth to say something, but closes it again with a look of pain. I can't tell if he's wanting to apologize again, or if it's something else lurking below the surface of his own feelings.

I spend the next few bumpy hours shoving crates around until we have a much larger open space, with our sleeping bags laid out in opposite corners. There's also a small part sectioned off near the door with a bucket serving as a bathroom. I shiver at the thought of having to use it.

By the time I'm finished rearranging, sweat is running down the side of my face and I wipe my brow gingerly, grimacing at the pain from my head wound.

"Come here, let me take a look at that," exhales Rowan. I eye his face suspiciously, debating whether I should let him or not. Finally I sit delicately on the edge of the crate next to him. He sighs. "You're gonna have to sit closer than that."

When I don't move he scoots closer until our knees are touching. He rests his hand gently on the side of my head. I keep my breathing shallow, and my eyes fastened to the flaking red letters stamped onto the flimsy boxes.

Rowan pulls away and rummages through his bag until he finds some alcohol, a piece of gauze, and a bandage. He soaks the gauze in the alcohol and cleans around the wound, then secures the bandage over the wound with some Vaseline underneath.

"That should do it until we can get some of Kaylee's solution from River," he mutters, almost to himself. "What should we do to pass the time? I'm guessing we'll be stuck on here for a good three or four days."

I cringe at the notion, nothing occurring to me. We sit in utter silence, moving lethargically around the car until Rowan checks outside and proclaims it night. I lay stiffly on my sleeping bag and stare at the rocking ceiling, the chugging of the train lulling my body to sleep. But my mind is awake as ever, and racing.

Rowan flinches across from me in his sleep, and I turn to face him. Despite the distance between us, he looks scared and sad, reaching out for someone in his dream. With no warning, he stands up, eyes still closed, and goes to stand near the wall. With a slight start, I realize he must be sleepwalking.

I watch as he rests his forehead against the wall of the car and starts muttering to himself. Shattered moonlight streaming in from the rusted-out holes in the walls illuminates the thin sheen of sweat glinting on his forehead.

"No," he mumbles, reaching out tentatively. "No, please." The train jerks, knocking him backwards as he stumbles over his own feet. I lunge, ears ringing with nervous energy, catching him before he falls into the pile of crates. He's shocked awake as we sprawl across the floor. I'm holding his head tight against my chest, chin in his hair.

I release him, moving away.

"You were sleepwalking. Then you fell," I explain flatly. He nods, lips pursed.

After a few minutes he returns to his sleeping bag, the last few moments churning in my mind until I drift off into my own fitful, nightmare-ridden sleep.

Days are long and dull, time spent practicing martial arts to keep my body in shape. I'm only able to review some basic moves with the minimal space and complete absence of food; we ran out the day we hit the tracks so we're all holding out until we can reach HQ. Rowan watches me practice with poorly disguised fascination.

The next two nights pass similarly as the first one, both of us twitching in our sleep while nightmares terrorize us in our minds.

The fourth night I'm not awake in order to steer clear of Rowan's sleepwalking. He moves to my side and I wake up with his arm cinched around my waist, drawing me close. I go stone still as he buries his face in my hair, mumbling something indiscernible. I pinch my lips together and close my eyes tightly, feeling the forbidden memories churning just below the surface of my conscious mind.

Rowan doesn't let go of me for at least another half hour, so I power through it and almost sigh in relief when he turns away, his arm going with him. I didn't have the heart or the energy to wake him, but this is dangerous. For him and for me.

*Chapter 35*

# Jinx

The train vibrates hypnotically as it plows along, oblivious to any happenings around it. It's the fifth morning on the train, and based on River's estimations, we should arrive around mid-afternoon. I got stuck with him, Victoria, and Naomi, meaning Selena, Breanna, Rowan, and Corinne are somewhere else on the train. I sigh melodramatically and slump against the crates surrounding us. At first, I was paranoid they would fall on us with their constant shifting and creaking, but now I wish they would. It has been four whole days with nothing to do, and I'm slowly but very surely going insane.

"We'll be there soon," placates Naomi. "You just have to be patient."

"I've been patient for days," I whine, drawing my knees up to my chest.

"Would you rather we walk for three weeks?" sighs Victoria.

"She has a point," River concurs, lounging atop one of the boxes and tossing one of his shoes up into the air, catching it as it plummets towards his face.

I watch as the boot rises and falls hypnotically, and we lapse back into silence.

"How—" begins Victoria. But she doesn't get the chance to finish. The train car rocks violently to the side, and it teeters on one wheel before overturning, sending us all flying around the car. I'm so in shock that I can barely process the situation as I bang my arm against the edge of a crate, my head connecting with the wall as the train rolls down an incline. It creaks and groans, the metal bending and snapping.

We slow to an uneasy stop at what I can only assume is the bottom of a hill, and I can't bring myself to sit up, my head pounding and spinning; River groans somewhere to my left.

"What—the hell just happened?" grumbles Victoria. She gets her answer when the top of our roof begins to dent and screech, three huge claws puncturing the seam where it joins with the wall. The claws peel back the top of our car like a sardine can, and the gruesome face of some sickly creature abuses our eyes. I'm paralyzed; both in fear and in pain. My arms and legs feel as if they were stuck into a washing machine and spent hours tumbling around.

"Soul!" hollers River, eyes wide.

"Jinx, watch out!" screams Naomi. My eyes focus again on the Soul, now reaching down into the train towards my immovable body. I will myself to move, my brain breaking down and scattering into a million pieces while my heart pitter-patters faintly inside my rib cage. But I can't. I can't move even one of my muscles as the sharp, slicing claws slide around my waist and hoist me up into the air.

*This is a pathetic way to die,* I think sourly.

Then I'm falling. River had drawn a knife and had severed the Soul's hand clean off. It howls in anger or pain or both, clutching its newly made stump of a wrist.

I land hard again on the floor, but it jolts me back from my stillness, and I crawl away, fear biting at my nerves. Naomi hauls me out of the car through the door, which had slid open in the havoc. Rowan and Corinne are just climbing out of a different car, maybe three cars ahead in the procession, while Selena and Breanna jump out from the car behind us.

"Jinx!" Corinne cries, sliding onto her knees next to me. "Are you alright? What happened?" She's holding her left arm gingerly, which seems to be a little bent in the wrong places.

"I'm fine," I manage, finding my voice again. "What happened to your arm?"

"Oh, nothing, it's alright," she assures. But I can see she's in a lot of pain the way her eyes are glinting in the sunlight. "We've got to get out of here."

The hand of a Soul shoots out of nowhere, missing her by mere inches.

"Go!" she shouts, hooking an arm under my shoulder and grunting with the effort it takes to get me back on my feet. Naomi takes my other side and together we make slow progress towards the shelter of the forest, only a hundred yards away.

Corinne ducks out and raises her machete in her good arm, barely scratching the next claw that attacks us. The creatures converge on us, too many to count, everyone scattering while Corinne and Selena haul my disobedient body over to the protection of one of the cars for temporary safety.

"Aim for the chest!" screams Breanna.

Corinne hefts her machete and attacks one of the Souls, shouting in rage. I watch her in wonder as she hacks through the leg of one monster, crippling it. Once it's on the ground she thrusts the blade through the blue glowing orb in the center. It cracks and shatters like a crystal ball, and the light vanishes. So does the sheen in the white eyes. It collapses completely, and a translucent form appears, hovering above. It's the shape of a small girl, probably only seven or eight years old. She nods at Corinne, smiles, then fades with a relieved sigh.

Everyone stares for a minute, and the other monsters give pause. I wonder if anyone's ever taken down a Soul before.

Then all hell breaks loose; Souls begin attacking left and right, and Corinne can't do anything but impair them and move onto the next one. For every one that we take down, three more seem to materialize in its place. The others are following Corinne's lead and attempting to break the orb in the monster's chest cavities.

I force myself to my feet and try to help, but I'm overcome with vertigo and run headlong into the ground, dazing myself even more.

Through the ringing in my ears, I hear one Soul—apparently the leader—scream at the top of its lungs and the last four Souls dash forward, scooping up Naomi, Selena, Rowan and me in their gnarled hands.

River gets to Rowan while Corinne sprints after Selena. Breanna comes after me and Victoria attempts to free Naomi.

Only River succeeds in freeing his brother.

The Soul clutching my useless body returns to the leader's side, grumbling happily and stroking my hair. I struggle in vain, kicking at the claws digging into my flesh, then cry out as one of the points pierces through my thin, human skin, injecting some sort of poison into my bloodstream. Drowsiness floods my mind and I kick feebly, barely even shifting the hand holding me. Corinne screams as the other Souls do the same to Selena and Naomi. They both still, and through my hazy vision, I see my friends shrinking into the distance.

I realize that they're running towards us, but the Souls are running in the opposite direction, and they're faster by a landslide. They gallop over the hill, and I lose sight of Corinne.

Perhaps for the last time ever.

*Chapter 36*

# Corinne

I slowly sink to the grass, staring after my sisters and our newest team member as they disappear over the hill. Taking a deep breath, trying to hold together my shredded nerves. But letting it out releases everything else that's been pent up, and I sob openly, a sound so contorted with sadness and anger that I barely recognize it as my own. It feels as if my heart was torn from my chest.

I had just gotten Jinx back, and now she's gone. And Selena, my home, my family is gone, too. My cries deteriorate to sniveling whimpers as the sun reaches its peak and begins to go down in the west.

I'm aware of the others standing a ways behind me, but I don't care. I failed them. How could I let them get taken away from me so easily? Every time I think the tears have dried, more flow. I don't know what to do. I want to run after them, I want to curl up and stay here forever, I want to find Pierre and kill him. I can't do *any* of it though.

The wind tries to comfort me, or maybe it's another facet of this cursed mutation. She swirls around me, drying my tears and tugging at my hair, which glints through the dust in the setting sunlight. She pushes the grass to dance, swaying and leaning every which way. My shivering body stills, entranced by this small moment until the wind sighs and then fades.

I let myself humor a few more shaky breaths before I steel my nerves and stand back up, wiping my eyes which I imagine are red and puffy.

"We can't do anything for them standing here," I whisper. "We need to get help from HQ. We need to get to Tenálin and find the Lotus Protection." The others nod solemnly. "How do we get there now?"

River speaks up, steady and reliable as ever. "We should be close now. If we just follow the train tracks, I think we can make it around dark." I watch my breath puff out in front of me in the chilling air.

"Then let's go."

We trudge back to the overturned train and then up a hill to the tracks, keeping a steady, silent pace until we reach the colorful frontier of the forest. I grit my teeth as I wrap up my arm tightly to keep it from moving, mourning the loss of Kaylee's solution. The precious vials, along with the tents, River's rifle, the sleeping bags, and all but two backpacks got crushed in the train wreck, the latter belonging to me and Breanna.

I'm not entirely sure what happened to my arm, but I had forgotten about the pain until just recently.

"Anyone ever been into Drillwood before?" asks Victoria. I shake my head. I've never even been beyond the fences of Kleka until just under a month ago.

The pink hues of the leaves reflect in Breanna's eyes and she reaches out to touch the bark: a smooth, playful, pale yellow. River clamps his hand around her wrist before she makes contact.

"Don't touch anything. Everything in this forest is designed to kill you," he mutters when she begins to protest, keeping one eye on the innocent looking woods before releasing her. Breanna pouts, stealing another glance at the pink trees before dropping her gaze.

"Who wants to go first?" asks Rowan, prodding the soft soil at the base of the trees with his boot. "I volunteer River."

His brother shrugs and steps nonchalantly between the trees. Standing there, he looks at us expectantly until Victoria tromps up next to him, followed by Rowan, Breanna, and finally me.

"How do we get to Vrasall from here?" I inquire.

"We just walk in from here, and we'll run into it in maybe an hour or two, based on what Selena said she saw on the map," replies River, voice faltering on my sister's name as he gazes around the place. My heart twinges with renewed grief, and my body aches in sympathy with my emotions, feeling weighed down and useless. To distract myself, I follow Rivers' glances around the forest.

It's as if we stepped into an alternate universe when we entered the shelter of the trees. The rosy leaves of the tall, graceful trees penetrate the light with their color, giving it a warm quality. The whole forest is warm, in fact. Not humid like the Shifting Woods sometimes gets, but warm like a winter night spent swaddled in blankets and curled in bed.

The floor is blanketed with soft, spongy moss the color of shining emeralds. As we walk along, I watch humming-birds float by, their vibrant, ruby throats glinting in the comforting light. Flowers of every single color imaginable spring forth from the loamy ground and permeate the air with dozens of rich, exotic scents, while a pond glitters with blue ripples made by koi fish gently gliding through its turquoise waters. Pristine white water lilies float gently on the surface.

I feel my eyelids get heavy, and I want nothing more than to lay down on the cushiony ground and sleep. Maybe submerge myself in the warm water. It would feel so nice to let the water close over my head, or let the flowers coax me into a never-ending sleep.

I blink. *Water close over my head? Never-ending sleep? Pull it together, Corinne. This forest is playing tricks with your mind; remember what River said.*

Looking through clearer eyes now, I see how long and sharp the beaks of the birds are; perfect for skewering someone's neck. The ground would envelop you if you fell into its trap and the bathtub-like waters would soon make you forget your troubles before pulling you into your watery grave.

I notice Breanna and Rowan staring wide-eyed at the beautiful foliage, while River continually pulls Victoria back from something potentially lethal. She almost fell into one of the numerous crystal-clear ponds, but River had snagged the back of her flannel just in time.

I swear I see a jaguar slink through the tree trunks at several points during our walk, keeping perfect pace with us, glittering eyes on me. Who was it that could turn into a jaguar? It was someone in Kaylee's safe haven, I think, but I can't quite place them.

As distracting as everything is, my mind can't shake the images of my sister, Jinx and Naomi being whisked away. I clench my jaw tightly as her terrified face fills my vision, the pleading in her eyes. What's happening to them now I wonder. Are they being questioned? Tortured? Manipulated? Are they being sent down to the lower levels to work? Or are they being pampered and buttered up by Pierre? I press a hand to my mouth to keep from screaming, and blink back the tears taunting me from just behind my eyes.

Rowan comes up by my side, looking confused and nervous. "Am I the only one thinking strangely?" he asks in a hushed tone, wincing as a bird calls out. It sings a sweet little melody that makes me want to stop and sway with the tune.

"No," I whisper. "It's this forest messing with us." He nods, but still looks fidgety.

"Can I—can I just stick near you in case I can't tell what's real?" he stammers, eyes darting around frantically; he's struggling to hold onto reality.

"Yeah, of course," I say. He walks so close that our shoulders are pressed together, and I try not to think about it too much. All of a sudden Rowan sucks in a breath and grabs my hand. I nearly stop breathing, feeling a pressure starting to build in the back of my mind. "What's wrong?"

"Sorry, just— sorry," he rushes, almost crushing the bones in my hand. I guide him along, giving him sidelong glances to make sure he's still tethered.

I'm fighting off the temptation to go lay by the roots of the tree when I spot it. A lone building, standing out in the forest with its brown and white colors while also blending in with its rustic cottage-style theme.

"Everyone see that?" I ask, hoping it's not just a hallucination.

"Yeah," they chorus, silently making our way to the front of the house. Up close, it's not as nice as it appeared from a distance. The wood and siding are etched with mold, thin cracks spider-webbing along the foundation. The creamy white of the siding is tinged yellow with age, and the pavement leading to the front door is overgrown with weeds poking their way between the slabs.

I lift the old brass knocker, shaped like—a lotus.

"I think this is a safe house," I murmur, staring at the tarnished metal.

"Well, there's only one way to find out," River responds, reaching past me and lifting the knocker. It falls with a resounding boom that rattles the door and echoes throughout the house.

A minute passes by before the door creaks open, only an inch; a chain on the inside prevents it from opening farther. And a single eye glitters at us from the gloom inside. The iris is a stark, ice blue, seeming to penetrate my very soul.

"I don't want any, thank you. Have a good day," the man says in a growling voice.

"The rise of the lotus is near!" I interject before he can close the door. He stares at me, sizing me up. Then the door slams shut.

I open my mouth, but close it again when I hear a scraping followed by a clunk from the other side. The door then flies open and I'm jerked inside, a rough hand clamping over my mouth as I open my eyes wide in surprise.

"Not a word," he warns. I nod my head and he hauls the others inside one by one. Rowan glares at the man, who I now have a full look at. He's tall, with a shock of blond hair, and a pale beard. He's wearing a thick, felt coat and blue jeans, with sturdy work boots on his feet. The wild look in his pale eyes searches our faces suspiciously. "Who are you all?" he asks contemptuously.

"We're looking for the Lotus Protection Headquarters," informs River. "The Phantom—"

"Not another word!" the man hisses. "Don't you say that name here!"

"What is happening?" cries Breanna, clearly distressed. "Isn't this a safe house?"

The man goes quiet. When he speaks again his voice is softer. "It was."

***

In the next few hours, we learn so many things. The man's name is Eric, and his wife and children were taken by Pierre just weeks ago. That's why he's so skittish and disconnected. He used to work as a weapons blacksmith for Lotus's new trainees, creating intricate, personalized inventions suited to every persons' needs. His backstory took much coaxing to be revealed, and many oaths of secrecy after that.

He ignored our numerous questions about where we might find HQ, which means he either doesn't know or won't tell us. Finally, I get tired of him evading the point.

"Eric, look. Do you know where HQ is or not? We really need to find it so we can get our friends back," I press. Eric sucks in a breath and stares at the wall. He's silent for so long, that I sigh and stand up from his beaten leather couch. "Let's go. We need to find someone who will tell us," I say solemnly. The others rise to their feet and we all start for the door.

"Wait," says Eric hoarsely. "I'll tell you." I pause by the opening to the kitchen and look back over my shoulder at the hunched figure on the couch. The lines on his face are deep from grief, and he seems so sad and haggard. I sigh through my nose and slowly make my way back to the couch opposite him, sitting down and leaning forward on my knees expectantly.

"I'll tell you where the headquarters are, but you mustn't tell them I was the one who revealed the coordinates. They'll shoot me for it if they find out," he says miserably. He looks up and meets my gaze, icy, blue eyes melted by a sorrow so deep they look more like oceans. My own sadness weighs down my heart as I look into those portals to who he is. He speaks again.

"When you leave this house, go out the back door. Head straight south from there until you reach a tree bigger than all the others. It's also one of the only trees in this forest free of Drillworms. This is the only entrance I know of, but I am sure there are others. I was never told how to get in, only where the door was. And I didn't want to tell you because—Lucy and I spent our entire lives working to keep it hidden." He drops his head back into his hands and squinches his eyes shut, taking a shuddering breath.

Understanding the pain he's feeling, however far back

it might have been, I rest a hand on his shoulder, causing him to look up in surprise.

"I know how it is to lose someone, and I thank you for telling us what you know despite your losses. When we get to HQ, I'll make sure they know what happened to your family."

His eyes water and he clasps my hands, a look of hope spreading across his face. "Thank you girl. Thank you." I nod, smiling slightly, then back away.

"Let's get moving," I say softly, leading the others away from the glassy-eyed blacksmith and to the back door across the house. I open the door and gratefully gulp down the sweet, fresh air. I hadn't noticed how stuffy it was in the house until I was back outside.

"Corinne, that was incredible," declares Rowan. River nods in agreement. I give them a halfhearted smile and push back at the fresh wave of tears trying to make their way to freedom. I can't think for too long, not right now, while we need our wits about us. So I take one, two, three deep breaths, revisiting the techniques taught to me by school counselors during their trips to classrooms, then pull out my compass. I watch transfixed as the little red needle swings around, then align it with the big letter N. I'm facing the house. South must be straight out from his door, just like he said.

"Alright crew, time for another hike," I announce, keeping my voice steady and my eyes on the ground in front of me. One step at a time; left, right, left, right, left.

*Are you okay?* I nearly jump out of my socks when Rowan's voice echoes in my head. I whirl around and stare at him blankly. Was I just imagining things? Out of the corner of my eye, I see Rowan frown a little. The slight downturn of his mouth and the way his eyebrows knit together brings me back to that first day we spoke.

*Rowan?*

His frown deepens, and he throws a look my way. I'm about to try again but he shakes his head. I stare for a moment longer, then turn my attention back to the trees ahead of us. Whatever it is can wait until we get to HQ.

It's gotten dark in the hours we were inside Eric's house, and the visibility is decreasing quickly. I don't want to have to camp another night outside. Or any night in this particular forest for that matter.

I quicken my pace, impatience souring my thoughts as I wonder what might be happening to my sister, Jinx, and Naomi. Thinking about them stirs a force inside me that I'm not sure should be known to humans. A rage so hot it could burn down the earth. I clench my fists by my sides as a twisted smile creeps along my lips. We shouldn't be able to do these things, but we can. I'm going to have to get used to it, because whether I like it or not, I'm going to need it. This is reality, and it is what it is.

I'm torn from my train of thoughts by someone talking.

"Hey, up ahead," points Victoria with one slender, pale hand. I follow her line of sight to an enormous tree in the distance. The thick trunk seems to have been twisted around, listing to the side and giving it a graceful stance. The gnarled branches reach for the sky as if yearning to leave their deceiving prison, and the leaves are dozens of pink and orange hues.

"It's beautiful," I breathe. I can only imagine how much Selena would love it, too.

"Where's this door?" demands Breanna, approaching the tree and circling the base with her hands on her hips. "I don't see how we're supposed to get in." River inspects the roots spidering over the ground surrounding the trunk. They dive above and below the surface of the earth, making it difficult to pick your way through to the tree itself.

I distantly hear twigs snapping a ways behind us, then frustrated hiss or growl or something, but I put it to exhaustion and lack of food for the past few days.

"Hey, Rowan," River says absentmindedly. "Come take a look at this." Both Rowan and I go to where his brother is standing, while Victoria walks carefully to Breanna's side. River gestures to one of the protruding roots, but I don't see anything out of place.

"What?" asks Rowan, voicing my thoughts.

River glances at us and then back at the root. "You don't see anything?" I shake my head. "Look closer, here." He traces his index finger along the bark, and I begin to see a rectangular outline nearly invisible to the eye. He moves his hand away and I press my finger against a swirl on the bark. It reminds me of a fingerprint. No sooner do I make contact, the rectangle piece presses in like a huge button and slides out of the way under a layer of bark. I suck in a breath at the metal plate beneath. In the very center of the plate is the small indentation of a circle, with a simple lotus design giving it texture.

"What do you think it means?" asks Victoria. She and Breanna had noticed us all over here and came to inspect our discovery. Rowan smiles.

"Remember what I was saying about our necklaces helping us along the way?" he says, struggling to contain his pride and pulling his necklace out from beneath his shirt. "I think this is where it comes in handy." He unclasps the chain and presses the pendant face down into the indentation in the metal; it's a perfect fit. I hear clicking and gears shifting before a slot opens up in the apex between two huge roots, maybe two feet by three feet. It opens into a metal ladder leading down into a tunnel, fluorescent lights highlighting the whitewashed walls and concrete floor far below.

My heart beats rapidly in my chest, anxious and buzzing

with apprehension. Before I can change my mind, I descend, not really caring if the others follow or not. The tunnel at the bottom of the rungs is short, and there's a steel door at the end. A sleek security camera is suspended above it, and I stare into the blinking red light, remembering similar cameras in Pierre's camp. I can sense the others directly behind me as I rap on the door, three hard knocks. The door swings open on well-oiled hinges and I step through, choking as I come face to face with the barrels of two assault rifles. I stare down the gaping hole where it's leveled between my eyes.

"State your names and your business," says a mechanically chirpy voice.

"Corinne Loralar," I say immediately. I mentally congratulate myself on keeping my voice steady and confident, even though my brain is still trying to catch up to my mouth. "We're seeking asylum with the Lotus Protection Corporation."

It's quiet for ten seconds before the guns lower and then retract into the ceiling. "Proceed," intones the voice. I shoot a glance back at the others, who are still a little jumpy. Then I steel myself and step through the door.

*Chapter 37*

# Corinne

I notice three things when I enter the room. First, that it's very bright, and I have to shield my eyes for them to adjust. Second, there's a person standing in front of me, blocking my view of the rest of the room. And third, that person is Jax.

"Jax?" I sputter, reeling back and staring wide-eyed at the slender boy. He grins like a shark and meets my gaze.

"The one and only," he confirms. "It's good to see you all again. But—where's Selena?" He falters a bit as he does a head count, and finds my sister to be missing.

"She and a few other companions got—taken. By Pierre," I manage. A fleeting look of rage dominates his soft features for a second, and he stands straighter. Does he know something we don't? But then his eyes land on Breanna and their gazes lock.

"Oh—" is all he says. Breanna stares coldly at him, then flicks her gaze back to the floor.

"What?" asks Rowan, glancing between the two. "What happened?"

Jax looks surprised. "She didn't tell you?" Breanna's eyes widen and she whips her head back to Jax. His lips curl in a smug smile. "Breanna is—" before he can finish his sentence, Breanna lunges at him, covering his mouth and tackling him to the ground. I jump in surprise before helping Victoria and River to pry them apart.

"Not a word!" yowls Breanna, struggling against River's arms, which are keeping her from attacking Jax again. The latter massages his jaw and scowls at her.

"Why? They should know. They *need* to know. Everything," he says shortly. Breanna pales but seems to deflate, going limp and hanging her head.

"What the hell is happening right now?" I ask finally, confused as ever. Jax gives Breanna another withering look before speaking.

"Breanna is my cousin," he says, meeting my gaze head on. I stand there. It doesn't make any sense. My head pounds, and the world seems to tilt on its access. I lean against the wall hard, trying to get a grip on reality. Did he say what I thought he said?

"But that would make you—" I sputter.

"Pierre's son. Jax Dolion, at your service." Jax shifts irritatedly. The rest of my group stares slack jawed at him. "It was quite rude of you to leave without saying goodbye."

"I can't believe you. You're the one who told me the notes I saw were outdated. You lied and I believed you," I accuse, crossing my arms tightly across my chest.

"I'm sorry. I panicked, knowing that if you tried to get out and failed, you'd die anyway. Sure, you probably would've died during the operations, but at least you would have had a *chance* that way." His shoulders drop and he drags a hand over his face.

"I prefer to make my own chances, thank you very much."

Rowan steps in, eyes narrowed. "What's Pierre's son doing all the way out here inside of the *Lotus Protection headquarters* of all places?"

"I'm what they call a double-crosser." He says, splaying his hands placatingly.

"How do we know you aren't lying? You seemed pretty devoted at the facility."

"I'm a good actor. But, if you want proof, you can ask the founder of LPC herself. We're pretty close. I've been working with her for some time now. Recently, we've been working on how to contain and treat Rotlings, maybe reverse my dad's treatments."

"I think I heard Pierre mention those at some point," I say. I can't remember when, but the name rings a bell. But he never did talk about them. It was one of the few other words I caught out of context on his note sheet. "What are they?"

"I'll let Breanna tell you. She knows more."

Breanna sits a little straighter and inhales deeply, holding it for a couple seconds before letting it out in a whoosh.

"Rotlings are sort of like humans and vultures combined. They're the size of humans but have a vulture's body, with black feathers all over them. And instead of a normal vulture's head, they have the head of a vulture's skull. No eyes, no skin. Just the bone. One scratch and you begin to rot from the inside out." She stares numbly at her hands, reciting the information as if it were a line in a play.

"How come we never saw any at the facility like we saw the Souls?" I ask, bewildered.

"Only a few people can see them. The ones gifted with The Sight. I have it, and so does Pierre. They're incredibly unpredictable, whereas the Souls can be trained and mellowed. He keeps them in a separate containment area," Breanna responds. "My mom always rants about them because Pierre was only supposed to have one type of mutation, and instead he made two. He also created the Dream Reapers, but she ended up taking over that one and refining the results." I soak in the details, trying to connect some dots and understand anything at all.

"Where in Linaria is her facility? Are they the only two?" I ask, racking my brain.

Breanna thinks for a moment, before a look of disbelief spreads across her face. "I—I don't know," she marvels. "I've lived there as long as I can remember. But I've never—I've never asked where we were, let alone been told." She looks so confused and so lost I almost feel sorry for her.

Jax fills the silence. "My dad went to get you in the morning when you didn't show up for training, and when you weren't there, he freaked. You know him, he's always so—calm. But this was something else. He was screaming and he looked mad. Like the crazy kind of mad. He started pointing fingers, and I was the first to blame. I had to disappear for a while so he'd forget about me."

"I'm sorry we didn't tell you," I sigh.

"No, it was for the best. I lied before, I'm not a great actor. He would have seen right through me. As much as I hate what he does, I can't let go of the person he was before his work got out of hand. He used to be so sweet, so invested in his family, the kind of dad who would have tea parties with me and Breanna as kids." Jax looks like all the fight's flown out of him. Pallid skin and dull eyes.

"Maybe we can knock some sense into him," I say flatly. Except the image in my head shows a man who manipulates the people around him to push his agenda forward, not a man who pours imaginary tea into little porcelain cups.

I'm still stuck on the unknown location of Arcane's camp. And if the Dream Reapers were manufactured by Pierre, then why did Tori tell us that they were made up by people looking for explanations? Was she simply ignorant to the fact?

"Will Lotus be able to get Selena, Jinx, and Naomi out of the labs?" I ask distractedly.

"I'm not entirely sure. They've only ever performed six

successful extractions," replies Jax, scratching the back of his head.

"And how many total have they attempted?"

"Fifty-three."

The silence that follows is thick. Despair drags its dead fingers across my skin, beckoning to me. Out of that many extractions, only six succeeded. What chance does that leave for us?

"You should all probably sleep on this. And fill me in on the last few days. Maybe I can help figure something out," Jax says. But his voice tells me he's not sure what to do either.

"Will we be safe here?" asks Rowan. The question is for Jax, but he keeps his eyes on me the entire time.

"Safer, but there's never a guarantee."

I feel his gaze burning on my skin, but I purse my lips and refuse to look at him. Now though, with Selena and Jinx taken, really what's stopping me from going back? Without them, I feel lost. And now I have a motive. If either of them are hurt, Pierre will have to pay.

I nod absentmindedly at Jax, my head pounding. I catch Tori glancing between me and Rowan, suspicion behind her face.

"Well, Jane has been wanting to meet you for a while, so let's get a move on before she wonders where I've gone," sighs Jax. "Follow me."

Victoria assists Breanna to her feet and the latter, ashamed, skulks behind the rest of us, shuffling her feet and keeping her eyes glued to the floor. We let Jax guide us along a corridor, unadorned steel doors spaced at even intervals along the way. Finally, at a cross section, Jax takes a right turn up a metal staircase, much like the one we descended from the tree, and through some sort of mess hall.

About a dozen people laze around the space, playing cards or prepping for a meal of some sort. Everyone stops what they're doing to stare at us, covered in dirt and red and black blood alike. I must look especially bad, with my blood crusted hair and face, and a mud-streaked, makeshift cast on one arm.

Jax enters some code into a keypad next to what I can only assume is an elevator door and hits the button for the floor labeled seven.

I notice that instead of the bottom button being the first floor and the highest one being the seventh floor, they're labeled in the opposite order. I'm about to ask about why when the elevator jerks down. So there must be levels down and not up. I suppose that would make sense.

A single door lies outside the elevator, the only wooden door I've seen in this place. It's embossed with *Jane Heffling, founder and protector of the Lotus Protection Corporation MAA,* in glittering gold letters that swoop and curl along the dark shiny wood.

Jax raps two times against the solid door, and it opens before his fist makes contact with it a third time.

"Jax!" gasps the woman standing in the door frame. She's tall and willowy, with thin brown hair cut sharply below her ears. "You're back? Why didn't you stop by sooner?" She hustles us inside the room and over to a varnished, mahogany desk at the far end. The windowless room is small in size, but very cozy. She has a lamp illuminating the desktop, and candles to light the rest of the room. A thick, ancient looking rug occupies the floor while two small couches and a coffee table rest opposite the desk. The room smells like vanilla and well-worn books.

"Sit down, sit down," she breathes, gazing at us with reverent eyes. We squish together on one of the couches while she and Jax sit themselves down across from us. "Tell me your names," she demands. "Many of the recent reports have mentioned several children with your descriptions, each interaction ending with disaster. I've done some digging into your backgrounds and you all have very interesting stories. I probably know more about you all than you do," she laughs. It unsettles me, the glinting in her viridian green eyes.

"Well, I'm River, and you must be Jane," observes River.

"Yes. I'm assuming then that this is your brother Rowan?" inquires Jane with a nod in Rowan's direction. He smiles tightly at her, knee brushing mine.

"And you're Corinne, yes?" she asks me. I nod. "Meaning you must be Selena." Her gaze is on Breanna now, whose eyes widen as she shakes her head. Jane frowns, leaning forward on her knees quizzically.

I clear my throat. "Selena, as well as two of our other friends were just taken by the Phantom Order. We were hoping you could get them out."

"Oh, I'm so sorry Corinne. I truly wish we could, but all operations are suspended right now. We've had some rocky weeks recently, and we're lying low. With all your activity being tied to us, we can't act out directly against the Phantom Order until this blows over and they get off your trail."

Panic builds in my lungs. They can't leave them in the labs. They can't.

"Please, you have to. They'll die in there. They won't stop following us, either. I was tricked into signing a contract, but we got *out*. We've spent the last week and a half trying to get here because we were told you could help us get away. There has to be something you can do."

"You got out through pure, unfiltered luck. It was a fluke, a one in a million chance. It doesn't mean we can replicate it. You had their trust on your side. There is nothing we can do, I'm sorry." Jane's voice sounds distant, clinical. The vanilla-scented air of the room turns sour, clogging my throat and poisoning my lungs.

"Corinne, come on, let's get you some air." Rowan speaks

quietly next to my ear, taking my hand gently and leading me from the room. The vanilla fades in the hallway.

"You were right," I murmur. "They're not everything they claim. I should've listened. If I had, we wouldn't have gotten on that train. The Souls wouldn't have attacked. Selena would still be here."

"Stop. It doesn't matter. It happened and we can't change that. But we can figure out how to fix it, we don't need Lotus's help." He tilts my chin up until my eyes focus and lock on his. "If you give up now, we go back to square one."

*You have to keep your head.*

I blink. His voice again, but his lips didn't move.

"Rowan what was that?" I breathe.

"So, it does work," he mutters, dropping his hand. "Breanna said something while you were talking to Eric. "You two don't need to speak to talk to each other, or something like that. She wouldn't answer me after, but I guess this is what she meant."

"That we—what? Have a telepathic connection? Rowan, that's absurd. I've never heard of that happening."

"Well obviously you haven't. If anyone ever said anything of the sort they would have been sold off to the government labs for testing. Is it really that unbelievable?"

"I guess not, but why? Why specifically us?"

"Like I said, she wouldn't answer any other questions, only told me to try it."

I feel exposed and vulnerable, having Rowan inside my head like this. I try to visualize words in my head and put them in his, but the blank stare from him tells me it didn't work.

"Why can't I do it? I did it earlier, right?"

"You did," he says, eyebrows drawn together. "We probably need to practice or something. I'll try asking Breanna for more information. And how she knows in the first place."

"Okay."

Through the quiet, I can vaguely hear Jane going on and on about the Lotus building and how it works. I focus on that to avoid Rowan's attention. But he's not oblivious, and he waits until I look at him to continue speaking.

"Corinne, we're going to get them back."

I nod. If I try to speak I'll break. Rowan leans in a fraction, but opens the door and we rejoin the group where Jane is just wrapping up.

"I have taken the liberty to arrange dormitories for you all," she says finally. "We'll get the chance to speak again tomorrow, but I can tell you need some rest. Jax, show them to the rooms please." Jax stands up, sighing, and smiles tiredly at us.

Another game of follow the leader ensues, and Jax brings us back to the elevator, Jane smiling warmly at me before we leave. I could have sworn that just before the door shut, her green eyes glittered with a malicious excitement, but I put it to the lighting and exhaustion. On floor two, Jax brings us to the med bay to get patched up. They properly bandage the cut on my forehead, and set my arm, which they say has a hairline fracture based on their x-rays.

Then on floor three, he leads us into another unlabeled hallway lined with door after door, and one by one, Jax pushes us into the rooms. When he closes the door behind me, I look around to see a plain, simple room with a bed and a dresser, nothing more.

It hardly takes more than a few minutes for sleep to find me.

*Chapter 38*

# **Selena**

Through a haze and a raging headache, I vaguely process the length of time that passes as Pierre's Souls gallop through the valleys and back into the Shifting Woods. I must be drifting in and out of consciousness because all of a sudden we're in one of the service elevators, heading down into the depths of Lake Superior. Back to the place I hoped I'd never have to see again.

The Soul sets me down in the loading dock entrance with a pat on my head. I look up slowly to see Pierre, hands clasped behind his back. He looks disappointed and the angriest I've seen him. The expression doesn't fit his face.

"So, Corinne is still out there?" he inquires, voice rather even.

"She is," I say. Unlike his, I can't keep the tremor from my words.

"How *inconvenient*. I suppose now I at least have some— leverage." He flicks a hand at two men in white security uniforms. They each curl a hand under my arms and start hauling me into the depths of the facility. Pierre watches silently as I stumble along, panic seizing my gut.

I sob and struggle feebly, but I'm still too numb. I crane my head to look behind me, watching Jinx and Naomi as they're given the same treatment. The former is still out, but Naomi is awake and walking mostly on her own, face deathly still.

We pass the corridor that leads to the rooms we stayed in before we escaped, as well as the entertainment hall that held the masquerade Corinne attended.

The facility is the same as I remember it, but it seems busier, as if there are more people. More security, specifically. How many more cities have been raided? How many more kids just like us have been forced on the run? I need to move, need to get out, but I'm immobile thanks to whatever venom these recovery Souls were charged with.

Eventually, we reach an all too familiar hallway. Blank, whitewashed halls. Bleach and citrus poisoning the air. And room eight-seven-eight. The same one they kept me in before.

The security slams the door behind me. One look around the room gives me déjà vu. Pressed sheets, clean floors, and a new pair of gray sweats folded crisply on the end of the bed. The sight drains me, the lifeless mechanics of it all.

I grab the clothes off the bed and shower slowly, letting my salty tears mix with the frigid water, wondering what everyone else is doing right now. Are they coming after us right now? Have they reached Lotus Protection? Are they organizing a rescue team at this very moment?

Or are they giving up on us?

No, Corinne is my *sister*. She wouldn't just leave me here. Would she?

Out in the main cell, I sit down on the bed. Something snaps beneath me, and I whirl around, staring with wide eyes.

A single wilted sunflower. The stem is broken where I crushed it, and the once perky yellow leaves are faded and scarred. It wasn't here when I got in. I know Pierre put it here, or at least he had someone else do it. It's a reminder, a threat.

I hold the dying flower against my chest, willing it to bring me away from here.

A knock on the door. It swings open. Pierre.

"Follow me, we're going to have a little chat." He smiles with his too many teeth. From hardly thirty minutes ago, he's in a worrisomely good mood. But still I stand. He continues speaking as we walk.

"I'm awfully sorry for my coldness when you returned, I've missed you all dearly. Your two friends are new to me, but I'm sure I'll grow fond of them with time. You see, Corinne promised to help me. I thought we stood on common ground. But then she took advantage of my kindness and used it against me, and for that I hope you see my frustration. Without her genes, the entire agenda is stalled. That is where you come in, my darling Selena."

We've reached our destination, a small medical room that reminds me of a dentist's office. There's a gray, reclining seat in the middle of the room, a pale, bright light pointed at it. The implications stand my hair on end and I shiver.

"Have a seat. I know it's not very welcoming, but it's simply for convenience," assures Pierre. Strangely enough, I receive no comfort from those words. I sit anyway, leaning stiffly against the backrest.

"I'd like you to meet a close friend of mine."

Said friend enters the room and nears, leaning down close to my level. I don't recognize him, but he has the look of someone used to causing other people pain. His eyes are a clear, watery blue, and his pupils are contracted, as if he spends his time staring into lights. A few days worth of beard growth crowds his lower face, paired with his black hair streaked with white. It's rugged and eccentric. He smiles blandly at me, the joy not quite making it all the way to his eyes before disappearing altogether when I don't return the favor.

"My name is Herssal," he introduces, standing straight again before sticking out a hand. I don't take it, so he pulls up a chair and goes on. "You can call me Sal. I will be your main—caretaker. I'm going to ask you a few questions, and I truly hope you answer them honestly, otherwise I'll have to incorporate other, hmm, methods." He smiles again, but this time it's a cold, dead smile.

"I'm sure you'll come to find that Sal here is quite a thorough interrogator," advocates Pierre. "You and he will be doing most of the talking, but rest assured I'll be here as well."

Again, no comfort there.

"Let's begin," says Sal. As soon as he does, shiny metal clamps snap around my wrists and ankles. I blink in alarm, my fight or flight instinct kicking in; it's all flight.

"Again, just a precaution," Pierre assuages, resting a fleeting hand on my shoulder. Sal clears his throat and Pierre retreats to the shadows.

"Do you know the location of the Lotus Protection Corporation headquarters?" Sal inquires.

*Vrasall.*

He meets my panicked gaze with easy inquiry, but the bands are tight and they dig into my wrists. Do they not know? Or are they just toying with me to see how much I'll reveal?

How much do I say, if anything at all? If I answer one question and stay silent the next, they'll assume I was either lying or withholding information on one or the other.

I sigh in frustration, moving my eyes to the wall behind Sal's head.

"Let's try it again," he says gently. This is the calm before the storm. "Do you know the location of the Lotus Protection headquarters?" He puts an extra emphasis on *location.* I stare down, hoping my eyes aren't betraying my heartbeat pounding out terror on a drum. When I don't answer for a second time, he purses his lips. Before I can react, his hand flies towards my face. My cheek stings, and I slowly blink against the pain of the bruised skin, Sal putting on another venomous smile.

"We can circle back to this question, yeah?" he suggests complacently. "Let's try a different question. Has your sister's ability fully matured? Maybe—a second ability has shown up?" I startle a bit.

*She killed the Mimic.*

But is it worth denying? It'll just show that I was holding something back on the last question. So I remain silent, giving him the iciest glare I can muster, which isn't very cold. Another slap, this time a backhanded blow, and I feel my lip split. Another smile.

"Come on now," Sal coos. "We can help each other out pretty easily, just answer the questions. Here's another one: where are Jax and Breanna?" I stare at him, bewildered.

"J—Jax?" I stutter. "I didn't know he was gone." I clamp my lips shut, mentally scolding myself.

*Don't say anything. That sentence alone just told them Breanna was with us.*

I wait for another blow, but his hand never flies. His smile just broadens, stretching nearly ear to ear, giving him the disturbing look of a shark that has found its next meal.

"Was that so hard?" he chuckles, maneuvering one ankle over his opposite knee. "It's as easy as pie. Were you and Jax close? What of he and your sister?"

*Close. We were all close. Friends? Maybe not. An ally.*

I can't bring myself to respond out loud. Sal's expression visibly darkens and I flinch as he raises his hand for a third time. He stops just before he makes contact with my face, relishing my cringing and squirming.

"Where are they?" he purrs, attempting a soft voice. Needless to say, he fails miserably.

"I don't know," I say sternly, sitting up straight and piecing together my resolve. He shouldn't intimidate me. I should be stronger than this. I think of my sunflower, dropped on the floor as Pierre retrieved me.

"You do."

"No."

"Fine," he sighs, leaning back in his chair. I blink.

"Fine?"

He jerks his head at Pierre, who hands him a shiny, black baton. He looks sad, but when his eyes land on mine, there's glee behind them. Sal takes the baton and hefts it, pushing his chair back.

"Fine."

I have never known fear like this in my life. It's cold, and I can't breathe, and I'm already crying. I have information they want, but if I give it up, we'll *all* die. I want to crawl under something, anything and tuck myself away from this world and all the seeking hands and prying voices that plague it.

"Answer one question, any question, and we'll put the baton away," Sal growls. He is becoming noticeably more hostile, but I can't give him anything. I can't.

"I don't know any of the *answers,*" I whimper, desperation poisoning into my voice. Sal's lips purse together into a thin line and he snaps. He raises the stick and brings it down hard on my left, tethered hand. I sob and scream through clenched teeth, pain rocketing along my nerves. I squeeze my eyes shut, too scared to look at the damage. I'm sure my fingers are broken, if not my hand in general.

"Any question," he repeats calmly, hostility gone and replaced with something worse: an unfeeling cold.

"No," I cry through my teeth. Hot tears are rolling fast

down my face. I haven't cried this violently since I was young. It hurts. It hurts so bad. I can feel it everywhere, burning, cutting, eating away at my consciousness. The baton flies again, landing on the same spot as before. This time I hear the fragile bones snap and crack, and I scream.

The two men wait patiently until I'm reduced to quiet tears, hopeless tears, broken tears.

"I think this is enough for today, Sal," says Pierre. Sal nods and drops the baton on the counter with a clatter.

"Same time tomorrow?" he asks me, patting my shattered hand. I clench my jaw so hard I fear I'll break a tooth. Wave after wave of pulsing pain washes up my arm and shoulder. He leaves, the click of the door confirming it.

"I must say I am impressed," admits Pierre. The clamps release with a hiss and go limp, but I don't have the strength to move. My eyes feel swollen and my face hot.

"I won't tell you anything," I mutter. A broad smile crosses his face, his eyes glinting.

"Why darling, you told me everything."

*Chapter 39*

# Corinne

When I wake up, I don't get out of bed, even though it's already nine in the morning. No one needs me. I'm no help to anyone. No one comes for me either, but it's just as well. Rowan tries to check in with me through mental messages, but I don't answer. Maybe he'll think I'm still asleep. Selena's absence feels ironically like a tangible presence.

After another hour though, Rowan knocks on my door and drags me out of bed to come eat something. I protest the whole time, making excuses about not being hungry even though I very much am. He just silently pushes a plate of toaster waffles in front of me in the mess hall and stays until I've eaten all of it.

"You're worse than Linc," I grumble when he tells me to shower by pushing me into the communal girls' bathroom and shutting the door. I finally give in, washing off dirt and scraping the crusted blood from my skin and hair. He's standing outside my room when I'm done, waiting expectantly.

"What?" I mutter.

"You need to keep moving," he states, looking me in the eye. I shrink away from his penetrating gaze. It feels like he's trying to read my mind. "We can't help Selena or the others if you stay in bed all day." I rub my eyes, letting him usher me back to Jane's cottage-like office. Everyone except Breanna is already there—she's most likely still asleep—talking animatedly and looking refreshed from a good night's sleep. I wish I could say the same; I feel like I've been hit by a truck and then run through one of Pierre's labs.

Jane does a double take when we enter, shooting to her feet and clapping excitedly.

"So glad you could join us, Corinne! I hope you had a restful night. We're just waiting on Bre then we'll discuss training." I whirl to Rowan. He only shrugs and leads me to the couches. I can't sit still, though, and at that point I just stand up and pace around. I probably look more than a little unhinged, with hyper thoughts racing in the reflections of my eyes and the uneven pattern of my footsteps on the thick rug.

Jane makes small talk while we wait for Pierre's niece, but River eyes me suspiciously before turning his attention to his brother, then back to me again.

I'm about to ask him if he needs anything, when Breanna shuffles through the door looking bleary eyed. She didn't get a wink of sleep. I almost feel a little sorry for her, knowing we're in the same boat. Except for Jax with all his not so little secrets. I glare at the side of his head, stewing in the silence.

"Wonderful, everyone is here," sighs Jane, smoothing out the wrinkles in her dark brown skirt. Distractedly, I note how well it goes with the indicolite and brown sweater vest she's wearing and the corresponding clips keeping the hair out of her face. There are two on either side of her head. She smiles when she notices me watching and pats the spot next to her. Awkwardly, I sit down, letting her put an arm around my shoulders, a caring yet unfamiliar gesture. Then, she begins her speech.

"There are a few options for you. You could remain here at headquarters in our residence halls and live out the rest of your lives in peace under our protection. Or, you could opt into our training programs. If that were to be the case, we could initiate you into a group of your chosen specialty. These include maintaining a safe house, extracting compromised members or Changed, working as security here at headquarters, etcetera. Lastly, you do have the choice to leave and try to survive on your own. If that is what you ultimately decide, one of our staff would have to wipe several of your memories to keep our location hidden. I'm sure you understand."

She meets each of our gazes expectantly, the room silent except for the steady ticking of yet another infernal clock on the wall behind Jane's desk.

"I'm in," Rowan declares. He looks around as if daring anyone to doubt him. No one does.

"Guess I am too then," sighs River.

"So am I," states Victoria hurriedly.

"Breanna and I are a given," Jax says. When Breanna begins to protest, he gives her a harsh look and she settles down again with a depressed look on her face. That's everyone. I'm the only one left. I let go of my last hope of returning to normal life, whatever that may be.

"I'm in," I whisper. Something inside me resolves itself, and I feel a little more at peace. The twisted, gnarled knot in my stomach unties itself somewhat, and it's like a small bit of weight has been lifted from my shoulders, because after this I'll have a better chance at getting my sister back. Rowan looks visibly relieved as well.

"It's settled then." Jane smiles. "We have a member and his family out in the woods that can help train you. He's a master weapons blacksmith and his name is—"

"Eric," I finish for her, sitting up straighter. I'd nearly forgotten about the sad, old man, alone in his dilapidated house with only the ghosts of his family for company.

"Yes, how did you know?" Jane blinks, appearing bewildered.

"We met him on our way here. His wife and children were taken by the Phantom Order only a few weeks ago," I say, his watery blue eyes sharpening into focus in my mind. Jane raises a hand to her mouth and gasps softly. Then she turns her head to Jax.

"Add Lucy, Jule and Claire to the list and we'll see if we can pull a status update," she says gently. Jax stands up and exits the room silently. I want to ask what "list" they're referring to, but I keep quiet. Once he's gone, Jane lets out a rattling breath.

"Eric is highly revered here at Lotus Protection, and his weapons are magnificent and genius. I hope he will train you, as he turns out some of our best mission members. I will personally go to him this afternoon to offer my condolences and request he train you. Thank you for your time." She seems rushed, hustling us out of her office and locking the door.

Just then, Jax returns, a pale look on his face. "You guys are going to want to see this." A sinking feeling settles in my stomach as we take hallway after hallway before reaching another office, this one empty. Nestled between flowerpots is a large screen TV on the mantle of a huge stone fireplace—electric, of course. And on the TV, the familiar face of Matthew, our local newscaster in Kleka, is speaking darkly.

> *Police are still in shock by the attack on Kleka, and now several other cities as well, including Glenston, Quadale, and Reni. They have no leads whatsoever. Dozens of buildings and other structures are either unrecognizable or completely abolished. Survivors are still being pulled from the wreckage after weeks of searches, but they're becoming rarer. Rescuers have been working 24/7*

*to get people out. The death toll has risen to three
thousand and seventy-two as of today in Kleka
alone, and is expected to continue ascending as
rescuers uncover bodies of those who didn't make
it out.*

The footage shown is an aerial view of my hometown, and I breathe in sharply through my nose. Swaths of land once bursting with protruding buildings and colorful businesses have been leveled, leaving only destruction and grief behind. I search for Bubble's Café among the wreckage and nearly choke on tears when the corner of Winny's bright sign shows up, poking out from the rubble like a drowning plea for help. I wonder if they've found his body yet, or if they've figured out that he was killed by a bullet, before any of the mayhem began.

Then the camera view switches to witnesses and survivors sharing their stories. I have to sit down on one of the overly stuffed chairs when a pale face appears.

Ella.

*There was no warning,* She whispers into the microphone. *The people dressed in black, they were everywhere, blending in with all the other civilians. My friend, her name is Corinne. She went off to dinner with her sister and the mayor's kids, but I haven't seen her since then. The people who attacked left for a little while, but a week or so later they came back. They kept asking where she was, they were beating people. They took others hostage, too. So many people have disappeared. Corinne.*

She looks directly into the camera, her brown eyes tired and scared. Her blond hair with the purple ends is straggly and limp, and she looks thin.

*Corinne, if you're watching this, don't come back.* She lowers her voice even more to a conspiratorial tone. *They still have people here. They're waiting, watching. Don't come back, Rin, stay away.* The footage turns to static and then a disturbed looking Matthew is back on screen.

I sit in disbelief, staring at the newscaster's cropped salt and pepper hair as he talks about the unsolved disappearances of dozens of people in the city. But Ella's alive. She's okay. She's not dead. I drop my head into my hands and take a shaking breath in, and out. A hand on my shoulder makes me jump, and Rowan steers me out into the hallway while the others start talking all at once.

"What is it?" I ask sluggishly. My mind needs time to process everything that's happened today, and I'm not sure if I can take any more new information. But Rowan doesn't say anything. Instead he just pulls me to him and bundles me up in his arms, resting his chin on my head. I gasp slightly; my body and mind are in disagreement whether I should pull away or not.

"You just looked like you needed a hug," he mumbles, holding me tight.

I swallow my nerves. "I did, Rowan. I really did," I breathe, letting myself accept the comfort. I reposition my arms around his waist and press my cheek to his chest. He reminds me so much of Eli before he—lost it—got too possessive, too forceful.

We stay like that for a bit, Rowan slowly swaying back and forth. My heart eventually starts to beat normally again, and I pull myself back from the verge of a mental breakdown.

"You okay?" he murmurs. I nod and he lets go, searching my eyes for something. "If you need anything, come to me." I bob my head again. He leans down and presses a quick kiss to my forehead, huge hands on either side of my face. Despite the surprise, it feels familiar. "Ready to go back in?" he prompts.

We enter the room to our friends talking over one another,

trying to get their opinion out. They see us and instantly pull us into the conversation.

"We have to help the people in Kleka if there really are agents from the Phantom Order hanging around there," pushes River, his voice urgent.

"Were you even listening to the girl on screen? She spoke directly to Corinne, telling her not to come back. The Phantom Order will snatch you like bugs in a Venus flytrap," scoffs Jax.

"Her name is Ella," I break in. They all look at me. I meet each of their gazes defiantly. "We will help Kleka, but to do that we need to take down Pierre. The Order first, then our city." I hold my breath as they glance at each other; Rowan looks absolutely thrilled.

"Fine," relents River.

"Jax, can we trust you not to give us up to your father?" I inquire, trying to keep any emotion out of my voice. Jax contemplates his answer before responding.

"Yes, I think so. He is part of my family, so naturally I have even a small desire to protect him, but I don't agree with him and what he does. It's wrong and inhuman, and it needs to be shut down. I know he has some sort of grand scheme, but he hasn't divulged any pieces of information to me whatsoever," he admits, somewhat hesitantly. I massage my temples, trying to clear my thoughts. How are we going to do this?

"All right. Let's just focus on getting Eric to train us and then we can come up with something, okay?" I ask with resignation. They all nod, their own thoughts and battles raging in their minds.

We spend the rest of the day in that room, keeping an eye on the news and trying to brainstorm ideas for some sort of plan.

Four o'clock rolls around much later than it feels, but the

clock's hands point to four and twelve. About ten minutes later, Jane strides into the room with a huge smile, making her delicate features stretch and showing off her perfectly white teeth.

"He has agreed after some—convincing," she announces. "You will depart in the next hour, so get your things and let's go." My brain is slow to process and Tori has to pull me along to get me moving. We're going already? Then I'm alone, standing in the middle of my room feeling lost. I have my backpack over one shoulder, but what else is there? Nothing. I'm about to leave when the lights flicker ominously, plunging the room in and out of darkness.

*No. No, no, no, no, no,* my mind mutters. I'm almost to the door, stumbling over nothing. *Not here, not now.* But the flashbacks have a mind of their own, and I've been resisting memories for too long. I collapse as they take over my mind, needing to be re-lived against my will.

*The close-walled closet Eli pushed us into was plunging in and out of darkness, the naked bulbs swaying close to our heads as they flicker in and out of life. We were laughing quietly as the security strode past, oblivious that the ones they were pursuing were now behind them.*

*Eli pushed me against the wall, smiling against my lips. I nudged him away teasingly, shushing him through my laughter as more security walked by. He pinned me and told me he needed me, needed more than I had already told him I was willing to give. He got mad. More than he usually did when I told him no.*

*I got worried, and a little scared, so I reached for the door handle, but he grabbed my hand, and shoved me back against the wall. I cried out, calling for help, but he smacked me, stunning me enough to get me to be quiet. He took my shirt off. I told him I didn't want this. I tried to scream but every time I made a sound he hit me again. Eventually I gave up, and felt myself go numb. He hit me to the point of unconsciousness, to where I could do nothing, even cutting my shoulder with his pocketknife.*

*And the whole time, the lights overhead buzzed and flickered, spasming in time with ragged breathing, colors blooming behind my eyelids and ingraining the images for life.*

*Inside, my trust had been broken so deeply, and the boy I had loved was gone, replaced by this greedy perverted monster. I had no idea how I could get out of this, and hoped with all my being security would pass us by again, see what was happening and make him stop. But they didn't. And neither did he.*

*It wasn't until after Eli left me in that closet with the door open, that the security had found me, barely conscious in a small pool of blood from my shoulder, feeling so used.*

*I switched schools after that, telling Sean and Linc that I wasn't feeling safe at the school. To press charges they would need to know and I didn't want them to know. I felt ashamed. Even with distance between us, I could still hear his voice, rasping my name into my ear.*

"Corinne!" Someone is shaking me by the shoulders but I can't see through the tears. "Hey, listen to me! You're okay, breathe, hey, I'm here." I blink away the water clogging my vision and Rowan's face materializes.

"Why—what are you doing?" I pant, trying to get my breathing in check.

"I came to see if you were ready, but you were on the floor, sitting so still," he worries, looking shaken. "Are you okay? Are you hurt?"

"Um—nothing. I'm fine," I whisper, blocking the images attempting to worm their way back to the forefront of my mind.

"Okay, um, okay," he mutters to himself. "What do you need me to do?"

"Just—quiet."

I give myself thirty seconds, avoiding Rowan's gaze. Then nod to myself and stand up on shaking legs, collecting my bag and shuffling into the hallway. Rowan follows, unsure, picking up his backpack after me.

"What was the holdup?" asks River as we join them in the same room we came down the stairs to. I sense Rowan shake his head behind me and River instantly snaps his mouth shut. No one else asks anything, Victoria only purses her lips and Jax eyes me. Then he wordlessly escorts us up the stairs and into the pinkish orange light of the Drillwood. Jane doesn't see us off, which I find strange.

I'm shaking still, the sting of his cold knife fresh on my skin. I rub the spot where I still wear the scar on my left shoulder. The arm is still in the sling, nearly fully healed, and it throbs in time with my heart.

"Let's go I guess," sighs Jax, leading the way into the death trap of a forest. I watch a large, sleek jaguar lope off between the trees, and memory from a couple days ago strains at the surface of my consciousness; I push it away.

## Chapter 40

# Corinne

Eric's house looks no different than it did the last time we were there. Off-white walls and peeling paint. The back door is already unlocked. Now, though, there are countless plants everywhere. Window boxes blooming with daisies, vines creeping up the siding, and spider plants dangling from the eves and ceilings. Did Jane deliver them?

Eric sits at the kitchen counter just inside, sipping a glass of water, looking lost. He glances up when the door creaks open, a watering can hanging limply in one hand.

"Oh, you're here already," he says distantly. "Rooms are upstairs, make yourselves at home." He waves a hand in the general direction of the staircase and goes back to drinking his water. I climb the stairs two at a time and find myself in a creaking hallway, two bathrooms on one wall, three bedrooms on the opposite wall and Eric's room at the end. Breanna and Jax claim the closest room, Rowan and River take the far one, leaving me and Victoria the one in the middle. It's simple, with a collection of potted lilacs and roses scattered about. I have to look away, every splash of color reminding me of Selena.

Eric is in the same spot as when we entered, and I sit down on the stool next to him, the others still upstairs. He doesn't pay any mind to me, instead stares at the wall and runs his finger along the rim of his glass.

"When do we start?" I ask hesitantly, nervous to break into his thoughts. He looks up at me and studies my face for so long, I begin to squirm.

"Soon enough." Is his gruff reply before he turns away again. "Tell your friends to get down here." With a huge sigh, he stands up and puts his glass by the sink, propping the back door open before disappearing into a basement. I gather the others, who are quietly chatting in their rooms, and come back down to find Eric depositing a final crate out in the woods behind his house. He waves us over and my curiosity gets the better of me; I peer into the boxes. They're overflowing with dusty assorted weapons, from small knives to automated rifles.

"Are we learning to use all of those?" asks Breanna with a grimace on her face.

"You wanna back out?" barks Eric. Breanna jumps, shaking her head aggressively. "Then you, dark haired boy. Pair with the nosy one here. Crazy eyes and miss prissy, yes, you two together. And the green-eyed one, you're with the ginger. You'll start every day with warm up sparring, I will select your opponent every day. We will review basic use for multiple weapons, until you settle on your strongest, then you will practice with that every day. Training begins at seven sharp, breakfast at eight-thirty, and training until five when you'll eat dinner. Is that clear to you, rugrats?" Shocked by the amount of words just spoken, I nod dimly and he claps, setting us in motion.

"I'll go easy on you, yeah?" soothes River, crouching into a defensive position. It's all wrong though; his weight is distributed unevenly and his fists are too low, not by his chin where they should be protecting. I smile.

"You won't have to," I muse, lunging. Even if River had his

mind pulled together enough to move out of the way with his ability, I have the technical side, and even he's surprised when my fist connects with his jaw. The blow throws his balance off and he teeters precariously for a moment. I drop and sweep my leg beneath him. He topples without even a moment to retaliate and I have him pinned in the next two seconds. Even with a broken arm, I was lucky enough for it to be my left arm since my right is dominant.

"Hey, girl!" Eric draws my attention away from my victory and to where he's standing with Victoria panting beside him and Rowan looking over at us. "This one seems to have more of a brain, and so do you. Swap." I walk over to Rowan, throwing River one more smug glance over my shoulder. The movement and burning in my fist distracts me.

Breanna and Jax seem to be evenly paired, exchanging blows with solid repetition.

"This will be a quick match," sighs Rowan, smiling.

"What do you mean? Are you so confident?" I inquire.

"Quite the opposite. With your advanced skills and enhanced senses, I've got my work cut out for me," he laughs. I clear my mind with a single exhale. No thoughts allowed in a fight. "You ready?"

I swallow, trying hopelessly to slow my racing pulse.

Unlike his brother's stance, Rowan's is evenly balanced and his fists are up, one guarding his chin and the other out and poised for defense. I nod, and the fight begins. Rowan shoots forward, attempting a head on attack, but I easily sidestep. He's good about stopping to face me immediately, not letting his momentum get the better of him. I stay mainly on defense for the next few minutes, but Rowan's relentless attacks are successfully draining my energy. I have to keep my gaze sharp because his style, although modeled after mine, is wild and powerful, while mine stays with the traditionally tight, clean movements.

Finally, I notice him getting slower, longer pauses between attacks, and I make my move. I recreate the same move I did in Kaylee's arena, closing my fingers around Rowan's wrist with my right hand, turning one-eighty degrees, and pulling him over my shoulder as I drop to one knee. He lands on his back. I keep hold. Never let go of your opponent on the ground. I swing myself around and straddle his chest. Lock his hands above his head with my good wrist. Hold my knee against his throat.

"Surrender?" I ask breathlessly. My face is inches from his.

"Not yet," he growls, an evil grin peeking out from the corners of his lips. Sometimes, strength is the better attribute when being pinned. Because even with my tactics and him being just as exhausted as me, he executes a move I've never seen before: rotating his pinned hands under my grip and pressing his thumbs against the inside of my wrist, against my pulse. My hand spasms and I jerk it back.

He pushes my knee forcefully with both hands and knocks it out from under me. I lose balance as things are literally turned upside down. Before I know it I feel like I'm back at the arena, the Mimic snarling down at me. But this time, it's Rowan. Not with a hateful smile on his face, but a triumphant one.

He puts his mouth right next to my ear and murmurs, "Told you it would be a quick match." But I can't respond. I can barely breathe. Rowan has one hand against my throat, a touch with just enough pressure to make breathing a little difficult. The other is next to my head, left knee holding down my good arm. Tendrils of static coil down my spine and into my toes. His breath is warm against my ear, and he laughs softly. "Nothing to say?" He rolls off and gets to his feet, offering me a hand with a smile on his face. I take it, head spinning and pulse even faster than it was before the fight began.

"Both of you have excellent form," comments Eric, coming to join us from a now double-beaten River, who looks like his second fight lasted a grand total of five seconds. Breanna and Jax are still going. But Eric calls a draw on them and they stumble over, both exhausted. "Five minute break, then weapons training," he grumbles, stalking over to the crates. He seems to have taken his sadness and loss and hardened it into a shell of aggressiveness. The rest of the day passes by in an exhilarating blur of activity, and at the end, my energy is completely, but satisfyingly depleted.

I fall asleep as soon as my head hits the pillow, the smells of the blooming flowers providing a blissful, nightmare-free night. The following day, I spar again with Rowan, but this time I win.

I seek out Eric following dinner, sitting on his dusty couch. He's staring at a large cactus in the corner of his house. I want to see if he can figure out anything more about our necklaces. With his background in blacksmithing, I figure it's worth a shot.

"Hey Eric?" I ask, sliding onto the couch across from him. "Can I ask you something?"

"You seem to ask whether I give you permission or not," he mutters, meeting my gaze head on. "What is it?" I unclip my necklace and hand it to him.

"My sister, Rowan and River all have this same necklace, and we suspect it's more than just a decorative piece of jewelry." He examines it in his palm, and I locate a spark of life in his hollow eyes. He knows this.

But then his eyes go wide.

"Where the hell did you get this, girl?" he asks, suddenly panicked.

"I—it's a family heirloom. Does it mean something?" I clutch the pendant tightly in my fist.

"Your parents, who are they?"

"I don't know. Only that this necklace has always been with me and no one knows where it came from."

"And you really have no idea what this is?"

"No. My sister and I each have one. Rowan and River have them, too."

"Fucking Christ. These necklaces belonged to the four founders of the Lotus Protection Corporation. Whoever wears them bears complete control over the organization, no questions asked. Their whereabouts went unknown after the Phantom Order built itself up, and one of Jane's primary goals has been to find those necklaces for herself. Don't let her see those at any cost, girl, or she won't be so hospitable."

I stare, bewildered, at the gold chain around my neck, the simple lotus gleaming in the sunlight filtering through the windows. Were my great-great-grandparents the founders of Lotus? Or have these necklaces been passed around between generations and families for years following the war? And how the hell did we get a hold of them?

I leave Eric to his own troubled thoughts and hurry upstairs. Rowan is just coming down. I pull him into my room and shut the door, ignoring his confused protests.

"Rowan, you were right," I say. I turn to face him.

"About what?" he fumbles.

"About the necklaces. They're not a coincidence. They belonged to the founders of Lotus Protection."

He gapes at me, then says, "How do you know this?"

"Eric took one look at it and just about fell off his chair. He said that Jane has been looking for them for years now."

"Jesus, okay," he mutters, still trying to process the first piece of information no doubt. "Well, let's tell just River for now, and we can figure the rest out when we get Selena back, yeah?"

I nod in agreement just as Eric's voice echoes down the hallway.

"All of you get yer asses down here and help me light the forge! We're gonna make some toys."

*Chapter 41*

# Rowan

Eric finishes making the weapons by the afternoon two days later, the fastest I've ever known anyone to be able to create straight from the mind. He had us all tell him what we wanted the weapons to be able to do, and how portable or concealable we wanted then. And after dinner, he proudly shows us the finished products.

"For Jax," he starts, presenting the dark-haired boy with a small cylindrical key chain about four inches long. "Pull the bottom part off," Eric urges.

Holding the invention as far away from his body as possible, Jax pulls off the bottom half of the key chain. Instantly, a six-foot long rod springs out. He catches it on instinct. On either end is a pronged blade. In wonder, Jax snaps it in half, giving him two, three-foot long spears. He laughs shortly but rather psychotically, marveling at his new toy.

"For you, Breanna." He hands her multiple things.

First is a leather bracelet with long pointed spikes all around the circumference. She wraps it around her knuckles approvingly and throws a few punches in the air. Next is a lipstick tube concealing a retractable blade that can extend up to seven inches. Last is a decorative hair comb that splays out into a fan of spikes. She thanks Eric absentmindedly, ogling at her new, fashionable weapons.

"For Victoria." Eric smiles, handing her a fan. She lets it fall open, revealing a bladed edge and magnetic throwing knives as the supports. She tries flinging one at the wall and it sticks, before zipping back to its place among the others. Corinne is handed two slender revolvers with intricate details, a new, deadlier looking machete, and a custom belt to holster all three items. She takes the guns gracefully, but I don't miss her falter at the first feel of the metals.

My brother receives a set of wicked sharp knives of varying sizes, some single-edged, some double, others with curved blades and some serrated. He thanks Eric profusely.

"Finally for you, Rowan," he sighs, smiling as he hands over a thin, sleek rifle. I let out a breath. Just by looking at it I can tell this thing is on another level than any regular gun. Eric gives us all a small smile, but a proud one. I wonder how much we remind him of his own kids.

He sniffs, and wipes his eyes quickly. "Now go have fun with them, you're all making me soft," Eric says gruffly.

I look over to Corinne, and the butterflies in my stomach come to life, muddling my thoughts. She meets my eyes, leading me to drop her gaze again. She makes me infuriatingly nervous. I clear my throat and go outside with the others.

My mind flashes back to our first sparring session, when she first had me pinned. I had barely kept my head together, and then I had my hand around her neck and she was so close. I want to go back and tell myself to not get carried away. I had nearly lost control of myself. And what would have happened if I had gotten any closer?

*Get it together, Rowan.* My mind growls at me. I reach out to Corinne with our mental voices.

*Are you there?* I ask.

*Yeah, why?*

*I need something to do that isn't training.* There's a pause.

*I was thinking about going out to find some flowers for Eric since he likes them so much. Do you want to come with me?*

*That sounds great.* I wait for her by the edge of Eric's property.

She arrives shortly after, smiling and humming softly while forging ahead, eyes searching the ground. I want to say something as we wander along, but there's nothing *to* say. I can't read her, either. She's closed herself off from me at the start, but I want nothing more than to be the one she lets in.

Her hair falls around her shoulders in waves, and her smile is the most vibrant thing I've seen. That's when it hits me. If I were to have one weakness, it would be her. She's a poison I can't help but become addicted to. The thing that scares me the most, though, is that I'm not sure that I'm upset about it.

Suddenly, my eyes pick out the vibrant red petals of a flower. I stop, and so does Corinne, always noticing any movement.

"Hey, I found some," I say dumbly, making my way over to the flowers and leaning down to uproot them. They're beautiful, bright and inviting.

I pick from the ground, and the movement frees some of the pollen. It smells sweet. Too sweet. Immediately, fog consumes my brain. I feel giddy as Corinne appears in my vision, all blurred around the edges. I can barely make out her words.

"You're—very beautiful," I slur. She looks scared, but I don't know why, pulling back from me when I lean towards her. My mind is screaming at me to stop, but my body is broken, acting on its own ahead of my brain.

"Rowan? What's wrong?" Corinne asks. Her voice is distant, distorted. I want to sleep. Breathing feels difficult. But I'm not scared, quite the opposite actually, I feel happy, euphoric.

"Dammit, this was a terrible idea," she mutters. "How

stupid do I have to be to try and pick flowers in a forest designed to kill you?"

She says this to herself, and then to me she says, "Come on, we need to get you back to Eric's house." She slides under one arm to support me as I stumble along as if in a dream, my eyes never leaving her face. She really is pretty. I sigh and she glances at me worriedly until we come into view of the house, swimming in my vision. Two figures rush over, but my vision is so fuzzy at this point that I can't make them out. Corinne, however, is now crystal clear as she brings me inside and upstairs. I giggle hysterically as she lays me down on my bed, trying to pull her down with me.

"Rowan," she snaps sternly. "Pull yourself together." I know I should feel hurt, but I don't. Instead I mumble something incoherent before I'm gone, lost in swirling sleep plagued by invisible terrors.

*"Rowan," snarls my mother, sharpened teeth gnashing and black eyes staring tearfully. "It was all your fault." She stands angled to my right, half of her body burned away. Charred skin and clothes are all that remain. "Just ask your brother."*

*I turn around, and there he is, River, accusatory stare directed at me.*

*"I promise, I didn't mean to!" I beg, tears streaming down my face. I fall to my knees at my brother's feet, looking up at him in fear. "I didn't mean to! It was an accident!"*

*"It was all you. You did this," he says coldly. No emotion leaks through his cutting words. I sob, their faces swirling around me in a firestorm, a heat so intense I feel my body dissolve.*

"How are you feeling?"

I blink open my eyes to see my brother sitting on a chair next to me. Sunlight streams through the window, highlighting the air with gold. My brain still feels foggy, but at least I can piece together some of what happened. Thinking of Corinne, the details hit me out of nowhere like a brick to the face.

"Oh shit," I hiss, drawing the blanket up over my head in an attempt to block out the thoughts. River peels it back and looks me in the eye with a smirk tucked under the corner of his mouth.

"I have never seen that side of you," he snorts, hiding it behind a hand.

"Please don't remind me," I mumble, slowly trying to erase the memories. Maybe if I don't think about them, they'll go away.

"You couldn't stop staring." He falls on the floor laughing, and I muster enough strength to sit up and kick his arm. River almost never shows this much of himself, and it's only when he's with me. He wipes his tears and sits on the mattress next to me, patting me consolingly on the shoulder. "I'm sure she understands. You weren't in your right mind. I had to physically pull her from your side. She was hysterical." His face is serious now, and I don't doubt his words.

"Where is she now?" I ask meekly. Just imagining her face is enough to set my pulse galloping at the pace of a crazed racehorse.

"Out training. When I wouldn't let her in she gave me a murderous look and hasn't stopped. Please don't let her kill me. I'm too young to die," whimpers River. I have to hold back a smile at that before a thought strikes me.

"River? How long was I out?"

He contemplates that for a minute, then counts something on his fingers. "Couldn't have been longer than a day and a half. You woke up a few times and muttered something about mom before passing out again." I blow out a sigh of relief. Not too long then. I recall my dream and shiver; that was not a pleasant one. I can barely still hear my mother's anguished screams as she turned to smoke.

"Let's go downstairs. People are worried," sighs River, all cool and calm once more.

*Chapter 42*

# Corinne

Rowan and River emerge from the house at last, and I run over to greet them. River answers my questions while his brother looks at the dirt. He tugs at the hem of his shirt nervously. As soon as the former walks away, Rowan follows him without a backward glance, leaving me standing there feeling out of place.

"What the hell!" yelps Breanna from the edge of the field. River, Tori, and I all run over to her, Jax glancing over from his conversation with Rowan.

"What's all the screeching for?" I berate. Breanna is too spooked to return the sarcasm.

"There's a whole fucking jaguar skulking about over here," she shrieks, pointing to a spot in the trees. Two golden flowers shift and I realize they're not flowers at all, but eyes. A sleek jaguar slips between the tree trunks and over to me. Everyone takes a healthy three steps back, but I stand my ground. The jaguar I had been seeing throughout the Drillwood finally clicks into place. This is Jotaro, it has to be.

Ascertaining my assumption, the creature nears me and sits calmly staring, shortly followed by a flash of light and then Jotaro in his human form by my side. Everyone stares in poorly disguised confusion and surprise at our former rival-turned-companion. He takes my hand in both of his, sweeping into a bow and pressing a kiss to my knuckles.

"My lady." He grins. I sigh and give him a strained smile, retracting my hand as soon as he releases me.

"What are you doing here, Jotaro?" asks Rowan coldly. He, River, and Jax had wandered over after the flash from Jotaro's shifting, and the foremost of the three is glaring at the newcomer with murder in his eyes.

"Kaylee assigned me to follow you guys for a ways to make sure you reached your destination." Jotaro shrugs. "I lost you once the train took off, but waited at the edge of the Drillwood since that was where the trains would be passing through. Sure enough, you obnoxiously loud people tramped through looking thoroughly depressed and so I've been keeping an eye on you since. Especially you." He smiles in my direction, setting my skin crawling. I laugh nervously to brush it off, but Rowan bristles at the comment.

"If you've completed your job, why are you still here?" inquires River, attempting to smooth over the whole situation.

"What? I've come all this way making sure your sorry asses stayed alive to be so cruelly treated? I need to rest a few days, and then I'll be on my way," replies Jotaro. I don't know why he cares. It's strange that he's been hanging around for so long.

"I think that would be fine with Eric, as long as you don't touch his plants," Tori says. Breanna stares skeptically at Jotaro and Jax shrugs, him and River entirely unfazed by the whole thing. Our new companion nods vigorously, then heads inside with Tori to consult Eric with one last sly grin in my direction. I shiver, and eventually we all disperse back to our training.

Another two days go by, training, eating, more training. I practice with my gun.

Over those two days, Rowan does nothing but avoid

me, and Jotaro does nothing but seek me out, asking me questions, trying to get me alone. The former won't talk to me, won't answer me, and his unnecessary embarrassment is starting to piss me off.

River has no explanation, so I spar with Victoria and Jax for the most part. Everyone's improving greatly, and I now know several different ways to kill someone with a board of wood, none of which include hitting them repeatedly. I've also gotten better at fighting with one hand tied up, literally. Eric says my arm can be taken out of the cast and put to use tomorrow.

But I find myself spending more and more time practicing and avoiding Jotaro because something's off with the latter. Both leave me with less time spent sleeping, eating, and talking to the others. Selena, Jinx and Naomi blend together in my mind, pushing me farther, compelling me to excel in every way I can. They haunt my dreams while I'm laying in bed at night, trying to sleep. It doesn't help that Tori talks in her sleep, but the fact that I can hold an entire conversation with my roommate while she's unconscious can be quite amusing at times.

I finally get fed up with Rowan's drama since he'll barely even look at me, and make up my mind to explain a few things to him. The others are out training, but unlike me, he's been training *less* in an attempt to evade me, River said. His room is empty, but I hear the shower running in the bathroom. Grumbling in frustration, I go to take my own shower in the second bathroom downstairs; stripping, washing myself, and toweling dry before realizing that I left my clean clothes on the bed in my room.

Muttering to myself, I wrap a towel around my body and exit the steaming bathroom, trying to slink down the hallway and upstairs unnoticed, my personal cloud of irritation accompanying me the whole way.

I lock the door behind me once inside my room and sigh deeply. Turning around however, reveals Rowan staring at me in disbelief, another towel wrapped low on his waist.

Oh fuck. This is his room.

"Oh my god, I'm so sorry," I stammer, fumbling with the lock while my mind stages a battle between embarrassment and absolute fear. My resolve to give him a piece of my mind crumbles like a sandcastle being wiped away by the tide.

Rowan comes closer to help me since my hand is shaking so badly. His wrist brushes my collarbone as he reaches for the door handle and I falter, causing my hands to slip and my towel to slide low to my stomach. The air around me gets clogged in my throat, and Rowan's eyes flit down as he swallows hard. He's so close I would feel his skin against mine if I leaned forward just an inch. For a moment neither of us move, water from Rowan's sopping hair dripping onto my shoulder. Then he pulls himself together and whirls away, exhaling sharply. "Oh god, oh god, oh god," I moan. Finally the lock turns and I fling the door open, hiking my towel up and sprinting to my room.

I slam the door behind me, my breath hiccuping violently, then slide to the floor with my head leaning against the wood, letting the tears fall. Why can't *something* just go *right?* Eli's face swims in my vision, smiling and reaching out with lust.

Just then someone knocks almost desperately on the door. I shoot to my feet and rub my eyes, holding my towel tight before shoving open the door. It's Rowan; he's still in his towel.

"I'm sorry," he breathes, riveting his gaze on my face. "I'm really sorry."

"No, that was my fault." I laugh hysterically, folding my good arm around my chest. "I should've paid closer atten-tion to which room I was in."

"I mean, for not turning away—immediately," he says quietly, looking like a terrified kindergartner. My mouth goes dry and I press my hand to my forehead. "But also, I want to apologize for being such an asshole lately. It's not fair to you or me if I keep running away from this." He sidesteps into the room and shuts the door behind him. I back myself into a corner. Nothing good can come from this.

"It's fine, Rowan. Really," I whisper, feeling more than a little nauseous.

"No, it's not. I really don't know what happened the other day. What I said—it wasn't true." Words spill from his lips like a waterfall. The unforgiving cold in my stomach thaws into panic. He pauses, silence so thick you could cut it with a dull knife, then plows on. "I—well—you are beautiful, not that part, but whatever I did, whatever I tried to do was the flower acting, not me. I know you don't think of me in that way anyway, but I—yeah." He's looking me straight in the eyes as his words fizzle out. His restlessness and fear are plain on his face, but all I can do is stare with wide eyes back.

"It's fine—" I sputter, then cover my mouth and try to make a break for the door. I need to get out. But he drops his hands on my shoulders and turns me to face him while still keeping me at bay, desperation and relief and confusion warring for control of his features.

"What would you have done if the flowers had nothing to do with it?"

"I—um—I don't know—this is too much to think about right now. " I'm shaking now, breaking, drowning, dying. "Rowan—"

"What—why? What happened?" he asks, startled back to his mind. I close my eyes tight, trying to slow my breathing to keep myself from hyperventilating. He's too close. Way too close.

"Rowan," I stutter. "Your hands—shoulders." He backs away quickly, releasing me, and I release a trapped, painful breath.

"Did someone do something to you? Are you hurt?" he asks, all his previous emotions gone, leaving nothing but the bones of fear. He stands back up straight when I don't reply, shoulders tense, his chest rising and falling quickly. "Did—did I do something to you?"

I bark out a laugh, shivering uncontrollably. "No, no Rowan, you did nothing wrong. It was—something happened a while ago, that's it."

He clears his throat, looks at me with pained eyes. They're Eli's eyes, pine green and glinting, but then they get lighter, to the cornhusk color I much prefer. This is not Eli, this is Rowan.

"Do you—do you mind if I ask what happened?" he asks haltingly.

I mind. I don't want to tell him anything. He'll hate me, tell me that I'm overreacting. My lips don't move. The words are choking me, killing me.

*I'm here. Take your time.*

His words are inside my head, drowning my doubts and my insecurities. Before they fade, I pull the plug, letting the past spill forth for just a moment. And then the words are flowing, moving, rushing to be heard. I'll tell him. I *can* tell him. I trust him. And so I begin my story.

I talk briefly about what Eli was like, how he always seemed so caring and considerate, but looking back I can see all the little flags I missed. His episodes of anger when I said I needed space, the way he stared at me even in public places, his over-possessiveness when any other man came close.

I talk about that afternoon, how Eli's desire got the better of him, and how he took me alone in the closet. How he hit me, cut me, and never left my head after that. And how I couldn't do anything about it. How I was powerless to stop him, to make him go away. And I tell him about the dream I had that night at the tracks, with the Dream Reaper. About how I'm absolutely terrified that anyone I become too close with will just end up using me, whether it's the way Eli did or some other way.

When I'm done, Rowan asks if he can give me a hug. I nod, touched by his consideration.

I fold. Not crying necessarily, just shaking silently as he strokes my hair. He doesn't say anything, doesn't tell me it will be okay when we both know this isn't something that will just resolve itself. I feel safe with another person besides my sister for the first time in a year, and my mind shuts down.

If it's sleep or unconsciousness that takes me down, I don't care. But I leave reality feeling lighter than I have in a very long time.

***

I don't open my eyes again until morning, when the full weight of my overexertion and last night's events hits me like a cinder block to the face. My body feels like it's been run over by a concrete truck, and I grit my teeth as I drag myself out of bed to get dressed and go downstairs; I'm still in my towel from yesterday.

"How was your sleep last night?" asks Jotaro, materializing as soon as I leave my room.

"Fine," I say, breathing out sharply through my nose. This guy's excessive closeness is driving me insane with irritation. He grins, flicks a strand of my hair, then disappears. Revulsion poisons my thoughts, so instead I try to remember last night to the best of my ability.

During my fitful sleep last night, I had a strange dream, and strain to recall the order of what happened. I dreamed that we were back at the facility, I think. There are hazy images of Pierre in a lab, clean and white and cold. Researching? Experiments maybe? Either way I didn't like it. Had he made a new discovery regarding a cure, or was it something else?

*Chapter 43*

# Corinne

I spend the next couple days pouring over maps and old books from Eric's study, trying in vain to find *anything* about past experiments on removing mutations, or any leads on where the sister facility might be. The aged texts and torn maps yield nothing but dust and useless rabbit holes of random facts. I don't leave for anything, to eat, to sleep, to use the bathroom. I distantly notice when Victoria or Eric poke their heads in, telling me to come out, but I wave them off. Both Rowan and Jotaro check in frequently, too. But rather than saying anything, they just watch for a good minute or two, then leave again. I'm subconsciously aware of their movements, where they are, what they're doing, both for entirely different reasons.

Finally, Rowan fully enters the room, drawing eighty percent of my attention. The other twenty are still focused on my work.

"When's the last time you ate?" he asks. I rack my brain, but I don't have an answer for him. "Come on, you need to get something in your body." He sighs, marching over and closing the book I was studying about the flight patterns of the crows in Aeludora. It sends up a poof of dust and I sneeze violently.

"I don't want to," I protest stubbornly. "I'm close to something, I can feel it."

"Yeah, close to malnutrition," he scoffs, taking my hand gently and pulling me along. "You need food. You're not a snake that can go weeks without a meal."

"Humans can last up to a month with water alone," I mutter, so quiet only I can hear it.

"What's that?" he asks over his shoulder.

"I said you're an ass. I had almost found something." I grumble as he seats me at the counter and places a frozen dinner in the microwave. Dejectedly, I watch the plastic box rotate under the buzzing, yellow light before the machine dings and Rowan removes the steaming container.

"Where's everyone else?" I inquire, noticing the lack of movement.

"Asleep," he answers bluntly. "It's past midnight." Surprised, I look out the window to see that indeed, the sky is black as tar and a huge yellow moon hangs high above, only a few dull stars blinking through the coating of clouds. It's magical in a haunting, horror movie sort of way.

Neither of us speak as I pick at the steamed carrots and dry chicken in front of me. Rowan glares at me, arms folded, until I start eating. It's gross, but I have to admit it's warm and my stomach feels satisfied once I finish.

"Now, you're going to sleep," he orders, tossing the box and walking upstairs. I follow begrudgingly, but pause at my door as the exhaustion finally washes over me, sinking its claws deep in my brain and locking my legs. I lean on the frame for a minute before Rowan helps me stumble to my bed, and I collapse on it. I lay on my side but take Rowan's hand before he can leave.

"Thank you," I whisper through the fog of sleep. "For last night, and putting up with my drama."

He doesn't smile; if anything, he gets more serious. "Thank you for trusting me. You know you can talk to me about whatever you need to right?"

"Yes, I know. That's what friends are for, right?" I laugh, quiet and short. Rowan's features tighten, and he smiles a little sadly, giving my hand a squeeze before leaving and letting the door shut softly behind him.

***

*Jinx is still, asleep or unconscious I can't tell. Her head is in Naomi's lap, who's singing 'You Are My Sunshine' in a hushed whisper and absentmindedly playing with Jinx's hair. It seems to have a soothing effect on my sister, and eventually Naomi's light voice fades and her eyelids slide shut. My dream self sits in their cell with them for some time, noticing the bruises and dried blood along their arms and legs.*

*I place a translucent hand over Jinx's and talk to her, knowing she can't hear. I tell her about everything that's happened and what we're planning to do, because I need someone to talk to even if they can't hear me.*

*Eventually though, a security guard comes and unlocks the iron bars, holding out a taser should either of them attempt to run. Neither of them do, instead Naomi mimics Selena's movements, shrinking back against the wall and holding Jinx's still form protectively. She must be out cold then, if she hasn't woken up.*

*The guard reaches for Jinx, but Naomi kicks out her free foot and makes contact with his kneecap. I silently applaud her for her aim as the guard drops to one knee and grunts in pain. I want to strangle the life out of him, but I'm not even there, so all I can do is watch.*

*But I feel some sort of tug in my brain, and a silvery strand of light seems to link from the center of my forehead to the center of the guard's. I watch as the string tenses, and then the sensation of the air all around me takes me by surprise. I know the air is there the whole time, yet this is different. It's like I can literally physically feel the air, yet I touch nothing solid.*

*I concentrate on the string and give it a mental tug. The guard coughs and sputters, but then catches his breath again and looks around in confusion. Naomi is pressed against the wall, staring, holding Jinx protectively against her chest. This time, I pull the string taut, and don't let go. The man's hands go to his throat and he starts choking. He's clawing at a non-existent enemy, and I feel my confusion turn to curiosity, then to excitement.*

*The string is tight, and it shines brighter the longer he struggles. Then it snaps, and the guard drops like a stone, body still and eyes glazed over. The smile slides from my face and the sickening pleasure evaporates, leaving behind a shell of disgust at myself.*

*Naomi looks around the room in shock, and begins to cry. It's such a delicate, fragile sound and it breaks my heart. She drags the guard outside but doesn't try to run. Instead she locks herself and Jinx in, and hides the key behind a loose stone in the wall before returning to Jinx. Of course. She wasn't going to just leave her here. She's biding her time, waiting for the perfect opportunity.*

*Another person stomps down the stairs and discovers the body of the fallen guard. Naomi is still weeping silently, hiding her tears from the second guard as he tests the gate only to find it locked. I don't know what happens next because my vision is being obscured by tears of my own. I killed that man, and I enjoyed it. Just like the monster I always tried to avoid becoming.*

✳✳✳

My pillow is damp when I wake up, and I feel the tracks of the silent tears as they slide down my face. It's still dark out.

The guard's still face and glassy eyes are ironed into the back of my eyelids. I can't shake it no matter what. I must be too tired to fall back asleep, because despite my exhaustion, I can't. I stare at the popcorn ceiling for at least an hour, counting the little bumps until I lose track. I made it to six-thousand six-hundred and forty-three before I lost track of the ones I'd already counted.

Suddenly, there's a rapping on the window, and I sit bolt upright, the jaguar on the roof outside staring in expectantly. I stand slowly and approach the glass, resting a hand against the crystal. The animal paws at my hand and stares at me.

I crack the window slightly, watching the jaguar glow and slide into the form of a lean muscled boy. His eyes glitter like the sky in the dead of a winter storm.

Jotaro.

"What are you doing here?" I ask, taken aback.

"I've been trying to catch you alone—" He grins, sliding the window up and deftly hopping inside. "—but Rowan was always watching me like a hawk."

"What's so important that you need to visit me at two in the morning?" I hiss, starting to get irritated. "Just tell me tomorrow morning."

"Listen closely," he purrs, stepping closer. As he stops, merely a foot away, his coy expression drops, and his eyes only hold cold rage. "How did you kill the Mimic?" He takes another step in my direction. I stumble backwards, tripping over the area rug on the floor.

"I—I don't understand any more than you do." I try to keep my voice steady, but even I can hear the slight waver laced through my words. Apparently this wounds his pride, because he stops for a second, but quickly recovers. He prowls closer, ebony eyes shining with anger, and elongated canines glinting in the moonlight.

"That was my best friend," he murmurs, catching my wrist and yanking me towards him. I gasp, trying to twist free. But his other hand closes around my barely healed arm, sending sharp pain sparking through my nerves. My eyes water and I open my mouth to cry out but Jotaro puts a finger to my lips, staring at my face.

"Jotaro—I thought you were trying to, well—" I whisper, fear making my voice hoarse. I breathe and try again, with more force "Let go of me."

"What, that I had taken a liking to you? Quite the opposite, really. I merely conjured up an image of what you would look like with your neck broken and smiling was simple enough. Kaylee had no right sending you off like that after killing him. I'm taking you back, and you're going to take his place," he growls. I see the sparkle of metal at his belt and my gut twists into a knot. It's a knife, and he's more than willing to hurt me if I don't go along.

I steel my nerves and make my next words come out stern. "Let me go, now. If you leave without a fuss, I won't let anyone know. But if you don't, I won't hesitate to call out, or better yet, knock you out myself."

He stares at me for several long seconds, as if surprised. Then he says, "You don't get to walk off scot-free little lady. Scream and I cut out your tongue. We're going." He pulls me toward the window.

Accepting that I won't be getting out of this without a fight, I raise my good hand and slap Jotaro as hard as I can, sending him reeling back, a hand to his cheek. I'm breathing hard, my own eyes stinging with tears. I am so shamefully scared.

"You're strong," he observes, rubbing his cheek gingerly. "But I told you not to put up a fight." He drops his hand to his belt and frees his blade, smiling at the terror he can undoubtedly read in my eyes. He lunges then, and I cry out as the cold metal breaks skin, parallel to the cut on my shoulder from Eli.

I'm starting to hyperventilate, hot tears leaking from my eyes. But I made a promise, and I do not need someone to save me from a problem I can't face myself.

"And I told you to back the fuck off," I grit out, pushing past the pain in my shoulder to shove him away, dropping simultaneously to hook my foot around the back of his knees. His legs buckle on contact, dropping him like a broken tin man. I wrestle the knife from his hand. The movement provides an opening, and not in my favor.

Jotaro grabs my ankle and pulls me off balance, bringing me down with him. I hit the floor hard, head slamming into the wood with a sickening crack. Warm blood spills from the wound, slicking the floor as Jotaro tries to get a grip on me. He's successful in reclaiming the knife from my grasp. He's gasping from the effort, but raises it to my neck gleefully.

This has escalated more than I'd anticipated, and more than I can handle on three hours of sleep and one full trauma dump. Jotaro now wants to end my life.

*Rowan. I need help.*

I send the words through my mind, using the last of my mental strength to push the message through. Several seconds go by with no response. Did the words even get through at all? Jotaro grins, pressing the knife to my throat. I can feel the blade break through my skin, blood pushing its way to open air.

Then my door bursts off its hinges, slamming into the opposite wall.

I turn my head towards the door and through the haze of pain I see a figure wreathed in fire lunge at Jotaro, whose eyes are as big as sinkholes.

They wrestle on the ground, trading blows, streaks of burning green going in and out of sight. Finally Jotaro frees himself and springs away, shooting daggers at me with his eyes before disappearing again out the window. The silhouette slams the window shut and locks it before hissing something to multiple someone's just beyond the door frame. I hear someone answer, followed by the sound of footsteps retreating.

It's Rowan, his entire body coated in flickering orange fire. The burning green from before were his eyes, which are starting to fade now. His face is a mask of unfiltered, livid rage.

"What did he do to you?" he spits, looking at the wounds on my head and neck. The carpet beneath me is starting to turn red. I try to convey my thoughts to him mentally, but I just don't have the strength.

He closes his eyes and takes a deep, shaking breath before helping me sit up, one hand resting gingerly against my back. Then he treats the wounds, securing bandages around my head and neck, pressing gently on the bleeding to get it to stop.

"Do you want to sleep or stay awake?" he whispers hoarsely. "What can I do for you?" My thoughts eventually start to defrost, stirring from their stupor and chugging along slowly.

"Stay awake. But stay, please, I'm—scared he'll come back," I say, feeling nauseous.

I get unsteadily to my feet and sink into my mattress. I hear the bed creak and then there's a warm presence next to me. When I look over my shoulder I see Rowan leaning against the headboard, eyes glued to the window.

"I'm not leaving you alone after that. Not a chance," he growls. A hint of a smile tugs at the corners of my mouth, but not enough to actually form one. I wonder what I did to deserve someone as kind, as genuine as this.

"Thank you," I whisper, settling back against my pillow. He's my anchor at this moment, sitting next to me solely because I asked, close but not possessive.

His presence doesn't scare me, rather, gives me the slightest glimmer of hope.

"What was he trying to do?" he mutters, gaze consistent.

"He was, um, friends with the Mimic. He was upset and he tried to bring me back to the haven to take his place," I tell him. Rowan says nothing, but a muscle feathers in his jaw. He's so incredibly tense.

"Hey," I whisper. I lift my hand to his face, resting it on the side of his face so that he has to look at me. "I'm alright now. I'm alright."

"Are you sure?" he murmurs. His pale eyes soften as they reach mine, shoulders dropping and tension draining. I nod. Rowan takes my hand from his face and brings it to his lips, pressing soft kisses against my knuckles. My breath catches, but I lean into his touch with confidence and wrap my arms around his waist in a tight embrace. He brushes the hair from my face and tucks it behind my ears. The quiet is comfortable. I feel safe.

***

Thin, foggy sunlight highlights just the very edges of the furniture in the room. Rowan is asleep next to me, still breathing slowly.

I have no hope of getting any more sleep, so instead I get up and creep into the hallway, making sure not to wake Rowan as I tiptoe my way down the stairs. The digital clock in the living room reads 5:36, meaning I only got maybe two-and-a-half more hours of sleep. Doesn't matter, since I can't feel the exhaustion yet. I walk outside barefoot, the dew on the grass cool and soothing against the soles of my feet.

I make sure not to go out too far into the woods, just far enough to lose sight of the house around the trunk of a wide tree. The woods are peaceful, serene, although I know the dangers that it conceals. I steer clear of a fallen tree shot through with holes about three fourths of an inch wide. That's where the Drillworms would be hiding, lying in wait for some gullible creature to venture too close to their homes.

I have to think over last night, fully process what happened.

I sit down against a tree, my perspective taking me back to my room last night, with Jotaro's form blocking the moonlight, silhouetting his body.

The one time I could have actually used my freakish ability, I was absolutely powerless. For god's sake, I enrolled in a self-defense program for this exact purpose.

I gnaw at my nails, trying to reign in my scattered thoughts.

I walk for another half hour or so before looping back, barely even noticing the scratches and bruises on my feet from traipsing through the underbrush without shoes.

I return to Eric's home and slip in the back door. Mostly everyone is up already, minus of course Breanna, who is sleeping late as always. River eyes my torn-up feet and my new bandages as I limp in, and slides a plate of bacon and eggs in front of me.

"What were you doing out there? Making friends with the rocks again?" Jax snorts, lifting a forkful of scrambled eggs to his mouth. I find myself ignoring them; they're never going to drop that.

"But, Corinne, I have to ask, what happened last night? We heard some commotion and then Rowan lit up in flames and rammed your door down," comments River. "Those bandages are new, too."

I freeze. I should have been fully aware that they were going to ask me this. I need to explain.

"Jotaro stopped by around two in the morning," I say through gritted teeth, minutes replaying themselves like some infernal movie in my head. His image flickers behind my eyelids. "He wanted revenge for the death of the Mimic by taking me back to the haven as a replacement. I said no, and he tried to kill me." I sugar coat it as much as possible without full-on lying, because if I say too much, I might shut down.

The kitchen is dead quiet for too long, then Tori pushes River off his stool and sits next to me.

"You, me, and Breanna should have a girl's night tonight," she states, looking at me earnestly. I can only stare back because I have no idea what she's talking about. "You know, where you hang out and gossip and talk about boys and just be girls without anyone judging?"

Tori seems genuine about it, and knowing Breanna, it will end in something entertaining at least. I nod slowly and she smiles, relieved and timid, very different from the Tori who robbed us back in Westol. Then she gives me a tight hug, promising to find some snacks. Jax gives me a side-hug, too, and River makes me another serving of food. He's a rather astonishing cook.

Suddenly I realize who's missing, aside from Breanna.

"Where's Eric?" I ask.

"He said he was going out to collect some dry wood before the next storm," shrugs River.

"Although come to think of it, he's been gone for a while," says Jax hesitantly. He sets down his silverware and peeks out the door. His different colored eyes reflect the light. His look resembles that of a cat searching for a mouse.

"I guess if he's not back by lunch we should go look for him," suggests Rowan, who just wandered down from upstairs. I agree with him; wait a little longer, and then search.

His eyes linger on me, the bandages painfully obvious, then flick up to my face, trying to read into my expression.

I feel vulnerable with his penetrating gaze on me for so long. I feel like he really can see my thoughts.

The hours to lunch pass much too slow and Breanna still sleeps late into the day. She's still asleep in fact, by the time we're heading out the door to look for Eric. Jax checked on her, and reported back that she is indeed dead to the world with drool all over her pillow.

I zip up my boots and throw on my jacket, bracing myself against the biting gale that slices through my layers immediately. The sky is out of character, with howling winds and a gray, sky overcast with low hanging clouds the color of smoke. I shiver uncontrollably, adding body temperature regulation to a mental list of skills I want to learn. It's actually the first and only item on the list, but I'm sure it will grow.

"Dream Reapers," mumbles Tori to herself. "It has to be. Just don't fall asleep, no matter how tired you may get. If there are some hanging around, they can make you very sleepy."

Leaves swirl through the air, blasting me with a tornado of crumbling foliage and dirt kicked up from the ground where we practice sparring. They dance around and lower the visibility by half at least. Just yesterday, the sky was sunny and pink and only a few leaves had been knocked from their perches. A lazy breeze had sifted through the trees high above. Now, the pale trunks stand barren and empty, and a foreboding feeling settles in my stomach.

"Corinne!" Jax calls. "Come with me and Tori!" The wind should distort his voice, making him sound much farther away than he actually is, but my ability helps me to understand his words. I stumble over to them, the fierce draft of air tripping me off balance every time I lift my feet. Tori takes my hand as we delve into the trees, wind relenting just a bit with the forest shielding us. Now we can speak closer to normal and I can hear myself think.

"Alright," Tori begins. "I don't think we should split up, but we can fan out just a bit, maybe a dozen yards in each direction and check in every half hour or so." I nod; it's a sound plan. We part ways: I head left, Tori goes right and Jax heads off in a straight line between our two directions. Through some of the trees to my left I catch Rowan's golden-brown hair and take comfort in knowing where he is.

We comb the nearby area for an hour and a half, meeting up every thirty minutes. On the third time, we're all worn out. We go out once more as a trio, and bump into Rowan and River, also paired up. River is calm, never showing his concern or any other emotions. He keeps those locked away tight. Rowan is pale and won't meet my gaze.

"Anything?" pants Tori. Everyone shakes their heads. A look flashes across her face for about a nanosecond. "I don't know. Maybe he's back at the house and we've just been stressing over nothing." She doesn't sound sure at all.

We begin to turn back, but then a branch snaps behind us. I whirl, everyone else assuming a defensive position, just like Eric taught us.

"Whoa there!" laughs Eric, slipping out of the bushes with his hands raised in a sloppy gesture of surrender. Rowan trips, leading me to again notice the lack of color in his face.

*What's wrong?* I ask.

*Don't worry about it,* is all he says. I glance up at him but his eyes are firmly glued to Eric's face. Tori looks absolutely sick, as if she's going to throw up, or cry.

"Eric?" Jax asks in disbelief. "Where've you been?" River's eyes narrow almost imperceptibly.

"Out—looking for Drillworm teeth," he says slowly. "They're a great source of—calcium." He shifts his weight from one foot to the other. I have plenty of experience reading people, and he's not giving us the whole truth. I look him dead in the eyes, making him shift again.

"Why would you risk your life for those?" responds River, looking him up and down, examining every movement he makes, just like we all are. Eric pauses for a moment.

"Fine, you got me," he says, deflating. I tense, and Rowan can feel it. "I was off at HQ talking to the head of operations; I was asking for permission to keep you here a little longer. I wanted you to stay; it's nice having kids around."

My body unfreezes. It has to be hard without his wife and kids around. It's true he must miss them terribly, but River isn't so easily persuaded.

"You mean Jane?" he interrogates, his expression a mask of stone.

Eric starts, hesitating before he answers. "Yes, Jane, right." None of us respond, and he claps his hands to get her to break the silence. "Uh, let's get going then, I'm starved." He starts off in the direction of the house and Jax and follows suit. River does too after one more long look at the back of Eric's head. I start to follow as well, but Rowan takes my hand and pulls me back.

"What's up?" I ask. But his eyes aren't on me, they're roaming the woods, darting back and forth between trees. "Rowan, what's going on?"

"Nothing, never mind. Just go back with the others," he breathes, disappearing into the pale trunks. I wait a moment, but I'm curious as to what he's doing, so of course I follow, careful to keep as silent as possible behind him. He stops at the edge of a small clearing, muttering to himself and getting more unsettled by the second. The space beyond the tree line couldn't be bigger than a backyard patio. I push past the foliage and come into view. Rowan spots me immediately.

"Corinne, stay there," he warns, stepping in front of my path.

"What's in the clearing?" I protest as he tries to turn me around.

"Nothing," Rowan lies. "Stay away from it. You need to rest after last night."

I struggle in his grip before dropping straight down, catching him by surprise and dodging around him. I burst into the open space just as Rowan yells my name. The sight in front of me stops me dead in my tracks.

A body lies on the ground, nestled in the leaves. All noise is abolished. The corpse is peppered with holes, small ones, like the ones I steer clear of in the trees because I know what's where the Drillworms are. The sockets in the head are empty, but that's impossible, because I just stared down those ice blue eyes not even minutes ago. Blood is dried around each little hole, some still newer than others. The blond hair is falling out in tufts and a pale pink something is slowly oozing from the holes in the skull.

I put a hand to my mouth, but in the end I have to turn away and retch into the trees, collapsing to my knees and bracing one hand on a trunk. Rowan's there in an instant, holding back my hair and then helping me get back to my feet on unstable legs.

"Who—" I take a shuddering breath. "Who did we send back with the others?"

*Chapter 44*

# Breanna

I was awake when Jax came to my room, but I didn't feel like joining them for the search. I knew Eric was missing, and I tried not to care. I'm worried though. They've been gone for hours, and the sun is *just* starting its slow descent to the western horizon.

As soon as I heard the door shut behind them, I looked out the window and watched them disappear into the woods. I also knew something was wrong immediately, because the usually vibrant forest looked dead, and the sky was dark, the wind whistling through the empty creaking branches. Once they were out of sight, I padded downstairs and explored the house a bit, rummaging through Eric's study and heating up a cup of ramen. I slurp up the hot noodles now while I wait for the telltale slam of the screen door.

Finally, I hear them come in, and Eric's voice among them. Inwardly, I sigh to myself in relief. I don't want to become attached to him, but I'm glad he's okay. They round the corner into the kitchen where I am. I look over, preparing my resting bitch face to greet them, my mask of nonchalance. But when they come into view, the cup of ramen slips from my hand and splatters all over the floor.

"Jesus, Bre," mutters Jax. "What's wrong with you?"

But I barely hear him because I'm staring at Eric standing

next to them all, my face no doubt a sheet of horror. The thing beside my brother shivers slightly, the mirage disappearing in front of my eyes like a second skin peeling away. Of course, I'm the only one who sees it. The grossly enlarged vulture blinks at me with round human eyes, each the size of my fist. It ruffles its greasy feathers while cocking a skeleton head to the right. Rotting skin is visible where patches of feathers have sloughed off, and the stench is overpowering. I breathe through my mouth, but it only helps a little.

It's not Eric at all; it's a Rotling, and it's staring at me with a hungry gaze. I swallow hard, forcing my face into a look of apologetic relief as I imperceptibly move my shaking hand to the knife block.

"S—sorry." I laugh quietly. Rotlings are one of the most dangerous creatures I know of, second only to the Dream Reapers my mom manufactures. She creates them in her own special lab, similar to Pierre. I'm the only one who can see through its disguise, and my money's on the fact that I inherited the Sight from my grandparents.

"Well, we found Eric," sighs River. But I know he sees straight through my facade, and he's itching to figure out what's wrong.

"Yep," I say, another high shaking laugh slipping past my lips. It's very quiet, and I slowly wrap my fingers around the hilt of the serrated bread knife. The block is directly behind me, blocking the movement from their sight. They turn away to go their separate ways.

All hell breaks loose.

The door slams open again. I chuck the knife across the room.

Corinne screams, ducking as it sails overhead. It alerts the Rotling, which sidles out of the way. Corinne and Rowan just tumbled through the doorway and into the wall, their forward momentum too strong for the small space.

"Dammit Corinne!" I yell. "I almost had it!" Everyone else starts yelling too, but I ignore them, launching off my stool with my spiked bracelets already wrapped around my fists. The Rotling screeches, flapping its enormous wings and opening its skeletal beak wide in excitement.

"Breanna, what is that thing?" shouts Corinne. She probably sees the Rotling as Eric, too, but must know that it's not actually him somehow. River grabs my arm before I can get close enough to make contact with the monster, but it takes both him and Jax to stop me from moving.

"Bre, what's gotten into you?" my brother yells, his two different colored eyes flashing. "It's Eric!"

"No, it's not!" contradicts Corinne. "Eric's body is in the woods, shot through with Drillworms!"

Silence falls, a breath of a warning. The Rotling makes its move. It shoots towards us and we all dive to either side, taking shelter behind the counter. Victoria is knocked aside by its wing, head connecting with the corner of the table. She's out cold, and the Rotling shuffles over to her, opening its beak again to sever her neck in half.

Suddenly River's not next to me, but whisking Tori out of the creature's reach. It shrieks in frustration, skinless head whipping from side to side, looking for a target. Everything is quiet, no one says a word. I barely even breathe.

Rotlings have poor vision, but they aren't blind. They rely primarily on noise created by their prey to make successful kills.

After a minute or two, I slowly raise my head above the counter, searching for it. Maybe, just maybe, it gave up and left. The kitchen appears empty.

Victoria groans, slowly coming back to consciousness. There's a flap of black feathers and the huge head of the Rotling pops up from the other side of the counter. For a moment, I stare into its glittering eyes. It snaps at me and

I drop, screaming as it jumps on top of the counter. An ear-splitting screech ensues, drowning out my cries. River grabs onto my and Jax's arms, Victoria over his shoulder, and zips us out of the way.

It swipes at us with a blackened talon, and Jax yelps in surprise. We're now in the corner of the kitchen with no way out. The Rotling knows this, and cackles throatily, stalking towards us and lashing out.

Rowan leaps out from who knows where with the knife I threw, driving it into the creature's side. Thick black blood spatters the wall and floor, and it shrieks in pain, whirling on him as he scrambles away, knocked to the ground. It caws again, flapping its wings angrily as it runs towards him. He's cornered.

Then it just…stops.

It's so quiet in the room you could hear a pin drop. That is until the bird starts choking. It flails around on the floor, strangled by an invisible force.

Corinne is in the kitchen doorway, the veins in her temples straining against the skin there. She's hanging a few inches off the floor, hair floating around her head as if she were underwater. What scares me the most though, are her eyes. They glow pure silver, like liquid mercury, getting brighter and more intense by the second.

A malicious grin slides onto her face and she twitches, manic. She jerks her head to the side just a fraction and the Rotling goes utterly still. The silver glow fades immediately, and Corinne's eyes roll back in her head. She drops from the air and hits the ground hard. The whole thing lasted only seconds, but the moments after seem to go on infinitely.

No one moves. I'm panting heavily, my heart racing much too fast and pumping pure adrenaline through my veins. Next are the tears. They prick my eyes and slide down my face uncontrollably, until I'm just a shaking heap against the wall.

"Ow," mutters Jax. I look up and see red blood dripping between his fingers where he's gripping his forearm.

"Jax!" I cry, scrambling to his side just as his head lolls back. "Did it scratch you?" He doesn't answer, instead his hand slips from his arm and reveals a small gash along the inside of his wrist. Already the bleeding is slowing, replaced by veins of green and black swirling under his skin. Mold edges the wound, and is spreading quickly.

"What's happening to him?" pants River.

"Get me hydrogen peroxide, a syringe, and see if there's anything in the medicine cabinets labeled alderase mensoline or gemcine adorax," I snap. River and Rowan scramble to look in both bathrooms. I have no doubt Eric has all of it stashed away somewhere. Jax starts to thrash around, trying to roll away. I hold his arms to keep him from tearing at the wound. Not more than thirty seconds later, they both return.

"I have the syringe," gasps Rowan. River holds up the hydrogen peroxide and a small bottle of alderase mensoline.

"Fill the syringe with four milliliters of the mensoline," I manage, struggling to keep Jax still. Rowan hands me the needle and I push the air out of it before jabbing it into Jax's arm. He howls in pain and I need both the boys' help to keep him from injuring himself. But the tendrils of rot begin to recede, and in another minute the only thing dripping from the cut is blood. I let out a breath as my cousin's breathing returns to normal and he quiets down, a sheen of sweat along his brow.

I rest my head on his chest and breath deeply, telling myself that he's fine, he's okay now. The Rotling is dead, not Jax. In, and out. In, and out. Three times more. Then I pull myself together and sit up.

Tori and Corinne are still out, but the former is beginning to stir. River and Rowan are laying on the ground, eyes closed and trying to process what the hell just happened.

And then there's the Rotling, already beginning to disintegrate in a pool of its own poisonous blood, which fans around it like hot tar.

It took all of us to kill a single Rotling. What have the past few weeks of training done for us, really?

Tori is sitting up now, and River is talking to her quietly. Rowan is barely coherent, shock or exhaustion or both wearing him thin. And Corinne is still a crumpled pile on the floor. I'm surprised Rowan didn't sprint to her aid immediately after she collapsed, but I guess he's just that done right now.

So we wait, trying to get ourselves back together so we can decide what happens next.

## Chapter 45

# Corinne

The pictures I see are too blurry for me to make any sense out of them, so I patiently await the moment when I'll wake back up. It arrives in the next few minutes, hours, I don't know which, but it can't have been too long because I'm still on the floor where I fell after killing the Eric-monster. It was hard killing Eric, even if it wasn't actually him. He still had the same sad blue eyes, begging for help, but soon enough my emotions were overridden with the all too familiar glee of having absolute power over someone.

I lay on the floor for a few more moments before dragging myself up to my knees, rubbing my eyes aggressively and muttering to myself.

"That was quite a spectacle," muses Breanna, Jax's head in her lap and the other three conked out on the couches. The Eric-Monster is just a pile of dust and gooey black blood in the middle of the kitchen now.

"I hated that," I grumble, pulling back the details of what happened.

"You certainly looked like you enjoyed it," she says coolly.

"Yeah, well, that's just a side effect," I huff, leaning against the doorframe.

"Either way, um, I just want to say, you know—" She

struggles to form words, then spits them out quickly as if they taste bitter in her mouth. "Thank you."

A smile, a genuine smile, grows on my face.

"Was that so hard for you?" She nods sourly, her face contorting.

"Yes. I still don't like you very much," she retorts.

"It's progress," I sigh, settling on the floor. We stay there for a good five minutes before I push myself up, fighting off the memory of Eric's body in the woods, and go upstairs. I want to shower, but I have no energy. Every time I use that ability it leaves me feeling like I haven't slept in days and as if I could go eat a whole roast by myself. I barely make it to my bed before my body gives out, and the nightmares return.

***

I wake up in a cold sweat, alone in my room. My breath is shallow and I'm shaking like a leaf stuck in a gale. Taking a deep breath in, I fall into a coughing fit. My throat is raw, as if I've been yelling. Or screaming.

This time I dreamed of Selena being beaten with a baton, her torturer's grin revealing just how excited he is about his newest subject. Her silent pleas are still ringing in my ears now in the minutes I'm awake. And I can't fall back asleep, so instead I get up and pace around my room, impatiently waiting for the day to arrive.

Before long—maybe it was a long time, I can't tell—the sun is shining through the window as if everything is alright. I bury the grief and anger spawning from Eric's death deep inside of me, along with all the other complicated things I don't want to deal with. Then I quickly change out of my clothes from yesterday, swapping them out for clean ones, and tiptoe downstairs. It's quiet, and outside the leaves are already growing back from the freak windstorm.

A slim breakfast of an apple from the fruit bowl on Eric's kitchen table and I'm getting my shoes on and heading out the door. I feel too exposed, paranoia gnawing at my gut, jumping at every shadow, thinking it's Jotaro back for revenge.

I start at a jog then speed up until I'm full out sprinting, racing over the loamy ground and darting around trees. I deliberately steer clear of the break in the trees housing Eric's corpse, and keep going until I break through the tree line.

I look out over the fields of tall grass before us, closing my eyes and breathing deeply, slowly. The crisp breeze stirs the stalks of the long grass and shadows dance over my eyelids in the setting sun. I take another long, deep breath, smelling the fresh air, the scents of grass and the forest just barely laced through.

I let the wind carry my senses away to another world, where the Phantom Order doesn't exist, where Selena and I are back in Kleka, making our escape, where we don't have to watch every shadow in fear.

No matter what my friends say, I know Pierre and the Order have something to do with Eric's death, and I won't stop until I figure it out. Fortunately, both my sister and answers reside back at his sick facility.

With Jinx, Naomi, and Selena in mind, I pray that the wind will deliver my words to them, to let them know I'm on my way.

"I'll see you soon."

Sigma's Bookshelf (www.SigmasBookshelf.com) is an independent book publishing company that exclusively publishes the work of teenage authors, who are between the ages of 13 and 19. The company was founded in 2016 by Minnesota teenager Justin M. Anderson, whose first book, *Saving Stripes: A Kitty's Story*, was published when he was 14, and has since sold hundreds of copies.

"I know there are a lot of other teenagers out there who are good writers and deserve to have their work published, but don't have access to the kinds of resources I do. I wanted to help them," he said.

*Sigma's Bookshelf is a sponsored project of Springboard for the Arts, a nonprofit arts service organization. Contributions on behalf of Sigma's Bookshelf may be made payable to Springboard for the Arts and are tax deductible to the extent permitted by law. Donations can be made online at www.SigmasBookshelf.com/donate.*